There was a loud knock at the door. Please, not Pam, she was thinking, as she opened the inner door . . .

She saw a huge bouquet of flowers, an Armani trenchcoat, and Brutini shoes.

"Who is it?" She asked. Impossible . . .

"Hey, girl, ain't no mystery . . ." Lawrence lowered the roses to reveal his face.

Chaney fumbled with the latch of the screen door, barely managing to get it unlocked before he threw it open. He dropped the flowers on the ground and grabbed her so tightly she was hardly able to breathe. She was laughing and crying and she heard Ronnie and Nicole screaming "Daddy" over and over.

She expected to wake up, but he was still there when he released her. He kissed the children, then the three of them fell on the ground, the children giggling as he tickled them.

"Time out," he finally said, turning toward his wife. "Hi."

"Hi." She smiled.

He looked at the children. "I need some time with your mother. Can you guys give me ten minutes?"

They both went into Nicole's room. As soon as the door was closed, Lawrence came toward Chaney again, taking her face in his hands to kiss her. "This is just what I needed. You are beautiful."

Chaney suddenly realized she was crying. Her body went limp and he held her, just held her, until the tears stopped.

"I missed you," he said softly. "My beautiful wife. My beautiful Chaney."

"I need you," she said imploringly, gazing into his eyes.

"I'm all yours."

* * *

"Maria Corley is a new strong voice in women's fiction. Watch and be dazzled!"

—*Laura Parker, author of* Risque

SENSUAL AND HEARTWARMING
ARABESQUE ROMANCES FEATURE
AFRICAN-AMERICAN CHARACTERS!

BEGUILED (0046, $4.99)
by Eboni Snoe

After Raquel agrees to impersonate a missing heiress for just one night, a daring abduction makes her the captive of seductive Nate Bowman. Across the exotic Caribbean seas to the perilous wilds of Central America . . . and into the savage heart of desire, Nate and Raquel play a dangerous game. But soon the masquerade will be over. And will they then lose the one thing that matters most . . . their love?

WHISPERS OF LOVE (0055, $4.99)
by Shirley Hailstock

Robyn Richards had to fake her own death, change her identity, and forever forsake her husband, Grant, after testifying against a crime syndicate. But, five years later, the daughter born after her disappearance is in need of help only Grant can give. Can Robyn maintain her disguise from the ever present threat of the syndicate—and can she keep herself from falling in love all over again?

HAPPILY EVER AFTER (0064, $4.99)
by Rochelle Alers

In a week's time, Lauren Taylor fell madly in love with famed author Cal Samuels and impulsively agreed to be his wife. But when she abruptly left him, it was for reasons she dared not express. Five years later, Cal is back, and the flames of desire are as hot as ever, but, can they start over again and make it work this time?

Available wherever paperbacks are sold, or order direct from the Publisher. Send cover price plus 50¢ per copy for mailing and handling to Penguin USA, P.O. Box 999, c/o Dept. 17109, Bergenfield, NJ 07621. Residents of New York and Tennessee must include sales tax. DO NOT SEND CASH.

MARIA CORLEY

Choices

PINNACLE BOOKS
KENSINGTON PUBLISHING CORP.

PINNACLE BOOKS are published by

Kensington Publishing Corp.
850 Third Avenue
New York, NY 10022

First Printing: March, 1996

Printed in the United States of America

10 9 8 7 6 5 4 3 2 1

Acknowledgments

I would like to thank Sandy Grimes for her indispensable assistance in my quest for publication; my agent, Marlene, for introducing me to Arabesque; my editor, Monica, who made me feel right at home in the Kensington family by being not only professional, but also warm; Sandra Kitt, for her generous support and advice, and Laura Parker, for agreeing to read the work of a perfect stranger despite impending deadlines.

I would also like to express heartfelt thanks to my family for their wholehearted support of what seemed like a fantasy—to my parents, who have always instilled in me the desire to succeed, and the belief that I not only could, but should do so; to my siblings, for all the life experience they provided me (smile); and especially to my husband, who is not only my toughest (constructive) critic but also my best friend.

About the Author

Maria Thompson Corley was born and raised in Alberta, Canada. She graduated with a Doctor of Musical Arts degree from Julliard School, majoring in piano. A newlywed, she lives with her husband in Tallahassee, Florida.

Look for these upcoming Arabesque titles:

May 1996
BETWEEN THE LINES by Angela Benson
MOONRISE by Roberta Gayle
A MOTHER'S LOVE, A Mother's Day romance collection
with Francine Craft, Bette Ford, and Mildred Riley.

June 1996
SUDDENLY by Sandra Kitt
HOME SWEET HOME by Rochelle Alers
AFTER HOURS by Anna Larence

July 1996
DECEPTION by Donna Hill
INDISCRETION by Margie Walker
AFFAIR OF THE HEART by Janice Sims

Prologue

Chaney woke with a start. It was the dream again, the same nightmare she had been having off and on for months. She would always be walking through her house. There was usually a fire in the fireplace, and for a while she would feel secure. Then something would always happen; things would change. The fire would be too hot, suddenly on the verge of burning uncontrollably. Ordinary objects would grow larger, menacing; the African sculptures or the prints on the wall would come alive—frozen in place, but living and breathing, somehow, ready to spring at her at any time. The wall unit would threaten to collapse, crushing her. Any number of things, or nothing specific, would make her stumble into the hall, where she would inexplicably be on a large ship. Then she would wander from room to room, with a growing sense of dread . . . there was no one on board but her. Every door she opened had the same contents—a bed, a nightstand; standard cabin furnishings. She wanted to call for help, but she couldn't get to the radio; it was in the engine room, which she could never find. I'm doomed, she realized; there's no one to help me, I'm doomed . . .

Slowly and carefully she settled back against her pillow. Her husband's breathing was undisturbed. She gazed over at him and relaxed a bit. She was glad he was here this time. It was always easier to get back to sleep when he was here, especially when he didn't wake, which was usually the case—Lawrence was a very sound sleeper. The rare times when he woke up, she had to try to explain why she had screamed or started thrashing around, and the dream always sounded ridiculous, far too silly to have upset her so much. So she started telling him it was nothing—go back to sleep. And since he was more than half asleep anyway, he always did.

But tonight he didn't stir. She looked at him again. He was so peaceful. *Why can't I do that?* she thought. It took longer to get back to sleep each time she had this stupid dream. It was understandable when she was alone, but he was here this time, which was supposed to make a difference. She sighed, staring at the ceiling. *What's the matter with me? Maybe it's that he's leaving again tomorrow.* She wanted to be well rested, because then her energy level would be higher, and that always made the whole experience easier for all of them, especially the children. Well, no such luck this time. *It's okay,* she thought. *This unsettled feeling isn't exactly a novelty anymore . . .*

One

October 16

"Nicole, put your hand back inside the car!"

Chaney Rivers glanced over her shoulder, watched her eight-year-old obey her, and turned back toward the road, sighing. Another goodbye. There was a time when she had thought it would get easier, but it never had. There was a time when the anticipation of his return had made all but the first week almost exciting, like counting down to Christmas when she was a child. But maybe he was gone longer now, or maybe the absences, like Christmas, had become too familiar, had lost their magic. One thing was certain—the empty feeling never became routine, and the resignation to another month or two of loneliness was anything but calm.

"Ronnie, sit still." Her six-year-old son was standing on the backseat and leaning over the front passenger seat. "What do you think you're doing?"

"Mommy, that station's boring," he whined.

"And so you took it upon yourself to change it without asking first? Uh-uh, something is *definitely* wrong with this picture. You'd better sit your little butt back down before something happens to it you won't really like."

Nicole snickered, and Ronnie slapped her.

"Mommy, Nicole's laughing," he complained.

"He hit me!" Nicole exclaimed, ending the sentence by returning the favor.

"Look, I'm not in the mood for this!" Chaney snapped, in a voice much louder than she'd planned.

The children stopped in surprise. Chaney sighed again. She didn't yell like that often, although lately, that tone of voice had been happening more and more. Sometimes her voice surprised her—she sounded like a woman with frayed nerves, like she was getting closer and closer to losing control.

"Can you two just sit still until we get home?" she asked, almost pleading.

"Yes, Mommy," came in unison from the backseat.

"Thanks." She glanced back again and smiled a bit, then changed the radio to an R & B station and watched the children start moving in time to the beat. *It's not their fault he'll be on a stage in Milan while I'm stuck in the Bronx,* she thought, resolving to remember that.

This time, he was going to miss their anniversary. It would be nine years in two days. He had promised never to miss another anniversary after last year, but his agent had called. So they'd had their anniversary dinner early and, *You understand, baby, don't you? Yes, baby, you go ahead and* chirp *for those people. La Scala—I'm so proud, Lawrence.* She'd watched his face light up. *It ain't nothin' if you're not proud,* he'd said, which was almost the truth, and she'd hugged him and kissed him and said, *This is the best anniversary present yet,* which was almost a lie.

She remembered the first time she'd laid eyes on him. He was tall and broad-shouldered and had a face as angularly handsome as her first love's had been pretty: high cheekbones, square jaw, full lips, and large doe eyes surrounding a nose that was wide enough that his blackness would have been unmistakable even if his skin hadn't been brown. Lawrence had a face like an African mask—it was dramatic and beautiful in a way that had nothing to do with Europe.

Chaney hadn't seen how handsome Lawrence was, though—

not at first. She'd just heard a voice so amazing that she'd stared, almost unblinking, unable to believe that she was witnessing a performance like that for free. It was Christmas Eve, he was singing a solo in her church, and she had to meet him. It would serve Taurique right, she thought to herself, for having the nerve to find someone new at his college out in California, and to write her nonchalantly, so by-the-way and matter-of-factly, that instead of coming home for the holidays, he was spending it with "Christine," who turned out to be two things Chaney would never be—white, and blond. The letter arrived in November, turning Thanksgiving into some other, unnamed holiday that had nothing to do with joy or praise. Chaney wallowed in self-pity, even though she and Taurique had agreed long before he'd left that since he was going to be clear across the country, they wouldn't make any promises. The problem was, he wasn't supposed to *replace* her, especially not in three months, especially not with a blond valley girl (not that Chaney knew anything about where Christine was from), not when they were supposed to be each other's one and only, not after he had been her first kiss, first commitment, first sexual experience, not when they had learned all about love together, from scratch. But he had done it, met someone new in no time flat, and decided she meant enough to him that he didn't even need to see Chaney at Christmas.

But Lawrence, singing up there, made her forget for a moment. Who says Taurique isn't replaceable, too? she thought. And who says I have to spend the holiday missing him and feeling depressed, and besides, he has somebody else; why shouldn't I? And it would be too embarrassing if he came back and found her still waiting, like she couldn't get over him, or something. By the end of the song, Chaney had resolved to meet Lawrence, and when the service ended, she walked up to him, vowing to go through with her plan, even though her bravado had mostly disappeared.

"I really enjoyed your singing," she said, her heart pounding.

"Thanks," Lawrence replied, and Chaney saw, for the first time, the smile that could light up not just a room, but a whole neighborhood. It was then that she realized how physically attractive he was, and despite having basically lost her nerve, she decided he was going to get her phone number somehow.

"You plan to sing professionally," she said.

"Is that a question or a statement?" he asked, an amused tone in his voice.

"Well, you do, don't you? It would be a shame if you didn't."

Lawrence smiled again and looked down.

"I want to," he said. Looking up, he added, "I already do, actually. In places like this."

"You're taking lessons?"

"Yeah."

"With who?"

"With whom?"

"Whatever," Chaney said, and she was already comfortable, because he hadn't even annoyed her by correcting her grammar.

"Do you study voice?"

"No."

"Would you know who the person was if I told you?"

"No."

They both laughed.

"I actually just changed teachers, anyway," Lawrence said, and from the look in his eyes, Chaney knew there was something else to be added, but he was trying to be modest.

"Why's that?" she asked.

"I'm going to Juilliard now, so I started studying with someone who's on the faculty there."

"Juilliard?" Chaney responded. "I'm impressed."

"Don't be too impressed," Lawrence said. "It's really not as big a deal as all that, trust me. A lot of people are there who aren't going to have lucrative performing careers."

"And then there's you," Chaney said, as he grinned at her.

"Nothing's guaranteed," he replied.

"But you've got something special, believe me."

"Are you free right now? Maybe we could have coffee, or something."

"It's Christmas Eve. I really should go home."

"Oh, yeah," said Lawrence, embarrassed. "By the way, thanks. For the compliment, I mean."

"You're welcome."

Chaney glimpsed, out of the corner of her eye, her father, waiting with unusual patience for the conversation to end. Of course, she thought, he's been waiting for over a month now for me to become a human being again. What's a few extra minutes?

"I guess I'd better go. My dad's waiting for me."

Lawrence looked across the room. "Who's your dad?" he asked, and Chaney pointed him out. "He looks like he thinks I'm trying to ask you out," Lawrence remarked, without looking at Chaney, who smiled, but wasn't quite sure how to take his comment.

"I am," he added, "but if it can't be tonight, I need a little more information, like your phone number." He glanced at Chaney and they both smiled.

"Do you have a pen?" she asked.

"No," he said, "but I can have a great memory when it's important."

"Okay . . ." She told him the number, and he called her later, on Christmas day, found out where she lived, and somehow sent her flowers on the day after Christmas. The more they talked, the more comfortable she felt with him. Soon she began to think that even if Taurique came back she would stay with Lawrence, though she compared everything he did with what Taurique did and still stared, involuntarily, at every guy who, even for a split second, looked like Taurique.

Nine months later, she and Lawrence were married, and four months after that Nicole was born, and Lawrence kissed Juilliard goodbye and Chaney kissed college goodbye. It seemed like they would end up living like Chaney had decided she would never live, with a baby and a husband whose career was uncertain in a dusty old building with graffiti on the walls and the smell of urine, marijuana, or both in the stairwells. But Lawrence's voice was too beautiful, and everyone who heard it was too impressed by his sound and his rock-solid technique. So after only 5 years, when Lawrence was 26 and Chaney was 24, he went to Europe and he was a sensation.

To Chaney, it seemed that one day they were living in a tenement and the next they were pricing houses in Riverdale. The one they decided on had three bedrooms upstairs, a working fireplace in the living room, a separate dining room, and a Eurokitchen with a built-in microwave and dishwasher, plus a yard that, although not really huge, seemed the size of Central Park, compared with what they were used to.

Lawrence gave her free rein to decorate, so Chaney took the credit cards and went crazy. There were mirrors of varying sizes interspersed with framed photographs of Chaney, Lawrence, and the children in the entranceway. In the living room, which had an off-white carpet, there was a sectional sofa the color of champagne with leopard-print throw pillows and a glass-topped coffee table supported by ivory-toned elephants. A mirrored wall unit contained a large-screen TV, a stereo, and a collection of records, CDs, and tapes, as well as a bar. There was a baby grand piano in one corner and there were large ceramic vases full of curly willow branches in the others. Potted plants, lamps of hammered bronze, African sculptures, and prints of works by black artists provided the finishing touches.

The kitchen was beige and pale peach, the latter Chaney's favorite color and the dominant shade in the master bedroom. She found a bedroom set in an antique shop and had it refinished—finally, furniture to complement the iron canopy bed that had belonged to her parents. She bought a peach satin quilt and some printed pillows in a warmer shade. Then she bought a French phone to put beside the bed and some gilt-edged frames for the faded photographs of her and Lawrence's grandparents that she placed on the walls.

She papered the bathroom in bronze, hung ferns from the ceiling, and decorated with reproductions of ancient Egyptian art. For Nicole's room, she deliberately avoided pink (having overdosed on it as a child), choosing instead a wallpaper depicting shoots of bamboo with light green leaves. The furniture was white, the bedspread had cartoons of animals on it, and tossed on the bed were a combination of black dolls and stuffed toys. Ronnie's walls were white, but he had posters of expensive sports cars on them. There was a bright blue, yellow, and red quilt on his bed, and the overall effect was sunny and cheerful.

The dining room was one of her favorite rooms in the house. One wall was gradually being covered with decorative plates from all over the world, wherever Lawrence had performed. The table was made of teak, and a matching buffet and hutch held the linens and the good china. The centerpiece, though, was a modern chandelier of dangling glass balls of various sizes and curving spirals of brass.

Once Lawrence got over the initial shock of receiving the bills, he agreed that it was money well spent, not only because they had such a beautiful home, but also because furnishing it made her happy.

The chance to decorate extravagantly wasn't the only satisfying thing about being married to Lawrence; having money was an unexpected bonus. Actually, Chaney didn't take for granted that their married life would be happy at all. When Lawrence proposed to her, she tried to convince herself, after she said yes, that everything *was* going to be okay, that her life wasn't ruined by her having become a wife and mother so young.

She loved Lawrence. She loved him before she found out she was pregnant. She hadn't been ready, in her mind, to seriously consider getting married at the age of 19, though. It was the old cliché—she wasn't sure she had found out all about herself yet. Besides, she *knew* she hadn't fully dealt with Taurique, because she had avoided the whole issue, and suddenly here she was, saying, "Till death do us part."

A year later, Chaney was quite sure she'd done the right thing. Over and over, Lawrence proved himself to be the kind of man she could rely on. He went back to the job he'd left when he'd decided to go to Juilliard—the hotel was glad they had a front desk position available, because even though Lawrence felt very unfulfilled spending so much time on something that wasn't related to singing, he was a great worker who got along with everyone, and his supervisor had always felt that he had great management potential. Lawrence also got a church job and did weddings here and there to make ends meet. They didn't have a lot of money, but Lawrence never complained, even though he was raised attending private schools, growing up in a house out in Queens. Somehow, being in one of those neighborhoods where the sounds of sirens and gunshots were normal and the streets were never clean and there were always people hanging around on the corner wasn't so bad, after a while, even though Chaney didn't want to raise her baby anywhere near the inner city. They were managing.

It wasn't just his ability to provide that made Chaney glad to be with him, though. Life with Lawrence meant flowers at least once a week—when he couldn't afford a dozen roses anymore, he bought one perfect bloom, always peach, because it was Chaney's favorite color—and little cards (unsigned, usually) left taped to the bathroom mirror or propped up on the kitchen table; Godiva chocolates in tissue paper tied with ribbon, placed on the bed as she showered, for her to find after he left for work, or free samples of the latest perfume, gathered by repeated strategically timed trips to the cosmetics department at Saks, or two beads of fragrant bath oil on the bathroom counter. It meant impromptu love serenades and candlelight dinners, which might have consisted of pizza when they were really struggling but wanted to treat themselves to eating out.

Lawrence didn't always verbalize what was on his mind, but he had a lot of little ways to say, "I love you."

Or, "I'm sorry." I'm sorry, because, like most true artists, he could be obsessive and difficult, succumbing to blue moods that could last for days after a bad voice lesson or an unsatisfactory performance, and because, as the only son of Ronald Rivers, CPA, the eldest grandchild of William P. Rivers, attorney-at-law and civil rights activist, and the great-grandson and namesake of Lawrence Rivers, a successful businessman in an era where being black made you legally less than human, he lived with the constant awareness that he was turning out to be the first failure in a long line of overachievers. A Rivers male was expected to be financially successful and respected in the black community, with a lovely, capable wife and brilliant children (or at least, brilliant sons): the only part he was living up to was the part about the wife and child.

Sometimes the shame and frustration were too much and he had to direct it somewhere, and Chaney ended up being the target. On top of that, Lawrence tended to be moody, and there were times when he had no patience, when Chaney's problems with the children seemed trivial and her need for physical affection a pressure he had no energy left to deal with. But at least he always said, "I'm sorry," one way or another, and tried to make it up to her.

As his career took off, the dark moods became rarer and rarer. So did the serenades, the candlelight meals, and the gifts. The last development was kind of natural, since he usually picked up gifts on the way home from work, and he did that only every few weeks now. Besides, the gifts were so much more expensive these days; it would be shameful to complain. At least he still remembered to indulge her sometimes. Funny, how those material things didn't make her smile like they used to anymore . . .

Two

October 17

"Nicole, stop playing with your food," Chaney said, and Nicole stopped rearranging her breakfast, looking at her mother innocently.

"I'm not *playing* with it," Nicole protested. "I'm making *designs* with it."

"You're supposed to be *eating* it," Chaney said, taking the fork out of her daughter's hands. "Do I have to feed you?"

Nicole turned her head.

"Mommy . . ." she complained, as Chaney raised the food to Nicole's lips.

"*Okay.* Then don't make me feed you. Hurry up, you'll be late for school."

Nicole rolled her eyes and began to eat with lightning speed.

"You can chew it, Nicole. I never said you couldn't *chew* it."

Nicole grinned, slowing down a bit. Chaney smiled at her—she was going to be a knockout, her little daughter. She had been blessed with Lawrence's high cheekbones but not his square jaw, and she had Chaney's almond-shaped eyes and Lawrence's full lips. She was bright, too, this one—she *will* go to college, Chaney vowed again, kissing Nicole on the forehead as her little girl rose to go to the bathroom and brush her teeth.

"Ronnie?" Chaney called out.

"Yes, Mommy?"

"What are you doing?"

"Getting dressed."

"For the last half hour?"

"Uh-huh."

"Come down here right now and get your breakfast."

No answer. What a shame to be so vain, thought Chaney, at such an early age. And so disobedient.

"Did you hear me?"

"Yes, Mommy." Footsteps sounded upstairs. Chaney was always amazed how much noise one small child with an attitude could make. She put two pieces of whole wheat bread in the toaster and was pouring a glass of milk when he appeared.

"Your eggs are cold, Ronnie."

"Yecch—why'd you have to make them so early?"

"I told you I was making breakfast, didn't I?"

"Uh-huh. It's okay, I'll just put it in the microwave."

Chaney shook her head. "You look nice," she remarked—he was only 6, but already he could put together an outfit. "You'd look nicer if you'd eat your breakfast when I make it."

"That doesn't make sense," Ronnie said.

"You're right. Eat. I'm not taking anybody to school late."

"Cool," said Ronnie.

"And any children I leave at home will be *so* sorry, they'll wish they were in school."

"Uncool." Ronnie began to eat faster. The toast popped up just as the phone rang.

"Take care of your own toast, honey; don't touch the toaster, 'cause it's hot," Chaney said, as she rose to answer the phone.

"Hi, baby."

She smiled. His voice was like velvet, so warm and rich you could almost feel it, and for a moment she pictured touching his face. Then she realized how far away he was and her smile faded.

"Good morning, Lawrence," she said. "How are you?"

" 'Good morning, Lawrence, how are you?' " he imitated her. "Why so formal?"

"Trying to set an example for you-know-who," Chaney explained, the smile returning to her lips. His impressions of her always amused her, because she had a high, disarmingly girlish voice that many men found beguiling, and despite the natural timbre of Lawrence's speech, he was always able to nail it.

"You're such a good mother," Lawrence said.

"Of course. I've had years of practice."

He chuckled. "You're such a good lover," he said. " 'Of course, I've had years of practice,' " he imitated her again.

"I miss you," she said, and she wasn't smiling anymore.

"Can I say hi to Daddy?" Ronnie exclaimed. "Nicole, Daddy's on the phone!"

The other line clicked as Nicole picked it up.

"Hi, Daddy, did you sing yet?"

"Next week, honey."

"Here's Ronnie," said Nicole, and she was gone.

"Break a leg, Daddy."

Lawrence laughed. "Thanks, Ron, I'll try."

"I love you, Daddy."

"I love you, too. Now—are you kids ready for school? I think you'd better get off the phone and get ready. Give your sister a kiss for me."

"No way!" Ronnie squealed.

"Then tell her goodbye for me, okay?"

"Okay. 'Bye, Daddy." He hung up.

"I'd better go, too," Chaney said, glancing at the clock and wishing he had called earlier—today she needed to listen to his voice for a while longer.

"No way! I call halfway around the world to tell my gorgeous wife I adore her, and she's gonna cut me off before I get that far?" He was almost kidding, but not quite. *He misses me, too,* thought Chaney, and somehow she felt a bit better.

"No," she replied with a little smile, "I've always got time for that."

"Good. Are you sitting down?"

"Yes."

"Good." Lawrence's voice took on a tender tone. "I miss you, sweetheart, and I wish you were here, and I can't wait to see you again, and I only wish I could hold you right now."

Chaney caught her breath. This time, it hurt to hear the words she usually waited for. She was trying her best to keep smiling, but somehow it felt superficial, like a thin layer that was almost worn through in places.

"Baby, I miss you so much," she managed.

"It won't be like this forever, Chaney, I promise."

"I know." He'd been saying that for four years; it didn't mean anything to her anymore. "Listen, I have to take the kids to school."

"Okay. I love you."

"I love you, too." She hung up slowly. I know he loves me, she thought. He loves the children. He's so damn perfect, that's why I feel like a single parent.

She swallowed the emotion rising within her, determined not to let Nicole and Ronnie see that she was upset.

"Are you kids ready?" she called out, her voice almost convincingly cheerful.

"Yes," in unison.

"Let's go." She picked up her purse, waited for the children to come down the stairs, then opened the door, locking it behind them.

I need something new, Chaney thought, working her way downtown. She smiled to herself. This is definitely depression, she thought. I have all the classic signs, right down to a need to shop. She wondered if Perry was free for lunch today, although her brother didn't always make her feel better these days. His advice always seemed to be, "You deserve better, Chaney." As if it were that simple. Maybe I'd better just shop, she thought.

She still got a rush of excitement realizing that she could walk into any store and buy things now, instead of just window-shopping and dreaming. She still felt vaguely guilty about buying really expensive things, though, spending more than it cost to feed her family for a few weeks on a suit or dress she would only wear twice all year.

Maybe I'll get a facial instead, she thought, Elizabeth Arden is close by. And then maybe I'll go to Saks, if I still need a fix. She pulled into a parking garage, feeling a bit better.

When Chaney walked out of the salon, she felt fabulous. She usually felt that way after a day at the salon, because she spent less and less time on her hair and makeup these days, and it was always pleasant to be reminded how glamorous she could look. Actually, she had been told she was beautiful for long enough that she basically took it for granted—it was like her voice, a given that bought her instant goodwill from men. She had clear milk-chocolate skin, long chestnut hair with natural tawny highlights, and a long-limbed, lithe body that she worked hard to keep toned. Her narrow, almond-shaped eyes were framed by relatively thick but perfectly arched brows, and beneath her button nose was a wide, sensuous mouth—Lawrence always compared it to a ripe plum—full of even white teeth. She didn't have to do much of anything to turn *somebody's* head, but it was still gratifying when the reaction she got on the street confirmed her suspicion that she was *the* finest woman in New York. At least this afternoon.

"Lord have mercy . . . damn, baby, you just made my day."

She glanced at a twentyish boy in jeans and a tank top who was smiling at her and checking her out.

"Thank you," he called after her as she continued on her way, and she had to smile a little. Baby, you just made my day? It doesn't take much. Some people like the simple things in life, she thought.

"Chaney."

She stopped. The clear baritone voice was familiar, but . . . she spun around and felt her eyes and mouth widening involuntarily.

"I don't believe it," she said. It was like being in a dream. Suddenly there was nobody else on the whole sidewalk, somehow, even though a steady stream of pedestrian traffic was swirling by in both directions.

"*I* don't believe it. You are *gorgeous.*" His awe seemed so genuine that Chaney felt herself blushing.

"I don't *believe* it!" she repeated. How mindless, she thought, temporarily unable to come up with something better—how many times had she imagined what she would say to him in this situation? And now it was happening, and they were staring at each other, speechless.

"Have lunch with me," he finally said.

"I don't know, Taurique . . ." It was unsettling, seeing that face again. She had almost gotten to the point where she couldn't conjure it up if she wanted to, but here he was. Mahogany skin still flawlessly smooth, hair a little wavy and perfectly cut, even teeth, a little mustache, his Native American grandmother's straight nose, and those slightly downturned, lavishly lashed eyes that were always his greatest weapon. He had aged some, but he was still the kind of man women stopped dead to look at. Chaney was frozen; she wasn't sure if she wanted to hug him or beat him senseless, but she knew she was unable to take her eyes off him.

"Please?"

"I'm not sure it's a good idea . . ." Snap out of it, she commanded herself and she was relieved to find that she was finally able to look away.

"You're married, I know, I know." He took her hand and began to lead her in his direction. "Obviously, matrimony agrees with you."

"Taurique." Her palms were getting sweaty, and she pulled her hand away from his.

"Don't say no, please? Or are you busy?"

"No . . ."

"Please?"

He was acting as if he'd never been gone, as if they'd stayed friends or something, and Chaney was completely off balance. *What's the matter with me? It happened too long ago for me to feel this way,* she told herself. And besides, part of her always wondered what he was doing. She took a deep breath, relaxing.

"Okay," she said, scrutinizing him. "Are *you* married?"

"No." He gave a crooked grin. "Divorced."

"I'm sorry."

"Why? She wasn't a woman I could spend my life with. I don't see how it's so tragic."

He was looking directly into her eyes, smiling in the same sexy way that used to make her want to kiss him all over, just because he was able to radiate that much sensuality unintentionally. She glanced down. *Some things never change,* she thought.

"So—what would you like to eat?" he was asking.

"What were you going to eat?"

"Doesn't matter, it's a special occasion now."

Chaney looked at him—sincerity again, not a line; she could see it in his eyes and hear it in his boyish inflection. He was always irresistible when he was being boyish, and it was heightened now because at a glance he was anything but— sleekly handsome in his elegant suit, wearing a cologne that really should have been a controlled substance, whatever it was, and giving off the aura of a quiet awareness of his own physical charms. And yet here he was, with the same open, wide-eyed expression Chaney saw sometimes on Ronnie. No, she wasn't going anywhere with him, not today, when she looked like her femme fatale fantasy of herself and was in the mood to play the part . . .

"I can't, Taurique," she said, staring at her hands.

"Why not?" He looked disappointed.

"I—I was kind of in a hurry," she lied.

"Oh." He smiled slowly. "Guess what? So was I. I was about to make myself late, though."

"You mean, you didn't even have time for lunch, but you were going to go somewhere with me anyway?" Chaney tried not to look as flattered as she felt.

"No, I mean I had time, but only for a hot dog or something."

"I wouldn't mind a hot dog."

"Really?" He raised his eyebrows.

"Really."

"Okay." He put his hand gently on the small of her back and they began to walk again. Any excuse, thought Chaney, as usual. Then again, this was Taurique's personality—he hugged everybody, male and female, and he was always touching people. He probably doesn't know he's doing it, she decided.

"I'm surprised you eat hot dogs," Taurique was saying.

"Why?"

"Because they're not nutritious. I bet Lawrence has you eating nutritious food, right?" He looked her up and down. "You're looking very . . . healthy."

"Taurique . . ." He'd meant it as a compliment, but the once-over annoyed her. Why did I smile when that boy did it? Chaney wondered. Well, at least he still thinks I'm attractive . . .

"I know, I know, you're married, I can't even look anymore," Taurique said. "That's fair."

"You married that—what's-her-name?" Her tone was convincingly disinterested. Good, she thought.

"No. Married a sweet little girl from the islands."

"Which ones?"

"Jamaica. Oh, that's only one island, right?" He had stopped in front of a street vendor. "How many do you want, one or two?"

Chaney smiled. "Two." God, he's gorgeous, she thought,

unable to resist looking at his body as he turned away. Hypocrite, she thought. Well, at least I'm discreet . . .

"Five hot dogs with everything, two Sprites," he was saying.

Something occurred to Chaney. "How did you know my husband's name?"

Taurique rolled his eyes. "Hold these," he said, handing her two hot dogs. "Actually, do you have a box or something, so I can carry all this stuff myself?" he asked the street vendor.

The man produced a cardboard tray, and Taurique put everything in it.

"Thanks, keep the change." Taurique grinned at the man.

"Thanks, Mr. Williams," he said.

"You eat this stuff all the time?" Chaney asked.

"I don't have a woman to look after me, you know." He smiled mischievously. "No, I eat properly, Chaney. Anyway, Perry."

Chaney looked at him, and he laughed. "If I could package that look. You think I'm crazy, I know. Your husband's name. Perry told me everything."

"You *are* crazy," she said, and she was beginning to enjoy herself now. "And what do you mean, Perry told you? You're still friends with Perry?"

"Sure. Hey, you got a minute to see my car?" He took a big bite of his hot dog. "And did I tell you I'm selling real estate?"

"What is it?"

"It's this business where you sell people land, houses, stuff like that."

Chaney laughed. "Taurique," she scolded him gently.

"No, I mean, that's really what I do."

"You *know* I mean your car."

He chewed and swallowed. "It won't be a surprise," he said playfully, "if I tell you."

She rolled her eyes, considering his invitation. Harmless, she thought.

"Okay," she replied.

"Eat your lunch, it'll get cold."

He stopped walking, holding out the box as she took a hot dog and her drink and rearranged the remaining contents so everything didn't tip over.

"I can't believe Perry never mentioned you were friends again," Chaney remarked, as they began to walk again.

"I can't, either," Taurique replied. He took another mouthful of food, chewing slowly. "Maybe," he said after a while, "it was because he knows you hate me."

Chaney stopped, taken aback. "What are you talking about?" she said, blushing.

"You hate me. Or you did. Right?"

He looked so vulnerable that Chaney had to look away.

"You did, right?" he asked softly, and she gazed at him. She nodded.

"Do you still hate me?"

He was looking directly into her eyes again, trying unsuccessfully to be nonchalant.

Chaney hadn't thought about him in a long time, not enough to deal with this question. Then again, hate was such an active emotion, the fact that she hadn't really thought about the whole thing much lately was an answer in itself.

"Why would I?" she replied, shrugging for emphasis.

He copied her movement, and began to move forward again, looking embarrassed.

"My car's really close," he said, and he began to walk faster, trying to regain his composure.

"Check *this* out," he said, stopping in front of a champagne colored Jaguar, back to himself.

Chaney smiled. "You're doing well," she remarked, and noted how it was one of her favorite colors.

"Was there ever any doubt?"

"I knew you'd make it somehow."

"You just didn't know it would be legal. I know, I know. Listen, I was a rogue, I admit it, but I never did anything *really* bad—well, not for long, anyway."

"How did you pay for UCLA?"

"My rich aunt." He smiled slightly, put the box on the car hood, and opened the passenger door. "Can you take that inside the car, please? Thanks."

He walked around to the other side and got in. "You want to go for a ride?" he asked suddenly.

"No, that's okay," Chaney responded, sitting in the passenger seat but not closing the door.

"Why not? I don't bite—well, not you, not anymore—you're blushing, Chaney. After all these years, I can still make you blush. Anyway, what then? Oh, of course. What color's yours?"

"Maroon." Chaney felt the annoyance she'd experienced earlier, coming back.

"You didn't do badly, either," he said.

"I didn't do anything. Lawrence was the one who started winning competitions and singing all over the world. It's his money," she replied, ready for the conversation to be over now, before he made another sexual innuendo and she really got angry.

"Baby, you're married to him. What's his is yours. That's how it works in divorce court, anyway."

Chaney unintentionally laughed. "You'll never change," she said, and although the comment was meant to sound good-natured, she heard an edge in her voice she hadn't expected.

"Did you?"

There was something about the way he said it that was a bit too personal, somehow, and Chaney stopped chuckling. Taurique looked away.

"I'm sorry," he said, and he looked at her again. "No more deep questions."

"Don't you have somewhere to go?" Chaney asked, in a tone that wasn't completely friendly.

"Why? Is my company that bad?" He looked almost hurt. Maybe he didn't mean anything by that question, Chaney thought; he doesn't adopt that expression lightly.

"No," she said. "I figured that to support this car, you must have some kind of work you do regularly."

He brightened. "I call it real estate."

"Right." She rolled her eyes.

"Yes, I do, that's why you have to hurry and eat—so I can get rid of you."

"Thanks, and you have two hot dogs left yourself."

"You're right." He took a big bite of one of them.

They sat in silence for a while, eating. Suddenly, Taurique turned toward her. "It's really good to see you again, Chaney," he said very seriously. "I'm glad you're taking such good care of yourself"

"Same here, Taurique."

"We still have a lot of catching up to do. Maybe we could have lunch—I mean really have lunch—sometime."

Chaney hesitated. I was never able to understand or control the chemistry between me and this man, she thought. I didn't feel anything I couldn't handle, but . . . best to leave it as a diverting, one-time change of pace.

"Not a great idea," she finally said.

Taurique nodded. "I understand," he said.

"Thanks for the hot dogs."

"You're welcome."

"Take care, Taurique." She climbed out of his car, closed the door behind her, and watched as he started the engine, slipped on his sunglasses, and pulled out of his parking space, almost in one motion. She smiled, and the words came back to her . . . *Baby, you just made my day* . . .

"Thank you," she said softly, watching him disappear down the street.

The phone was ringing as Chaney stepped out of the shower. She wrapped a robe around her dripping body and rushed into her bedroom to turn on the answering machine. The message ended, then came a beep and then a voice. She sighed and walked back into the bathroom to dry off. Pam from next door—she couldn't be bothered today. Lawrence always tried to make her feel guilty about not having time for Pam. After all, the woman was so friendly, and Chaney did spend a lot of time without adult companionship when Lawrence was away. What he didn't understand was that Chaney was never comfortable with Pam; she never felt she could be herself around her. She'd never really had very close girlfriends, actually; she was always more comfortable with boys, and as a result of Zac, Perry, and Jimmy's athletic endeavors, she had always known almost everyone on most of the boys' teams. Twice girls had used her to get closer to her brothers, twice Chaney had been rudely disillusioned, and twice she'd decided she didn't need girlfriends. The second time, she'd stuck to it.

"Just because your mother left when you were four," Lawrence often said, "doesn't mean you can never trust another woman."

Actually, at least half the time it was the other way around—women didn't trust *her*. They sized her up competitively and looked at her with contempt, and she learned not to care enough to try to prove herself to them. She wouldn't take their men. She'd never done it in her life, she didn't even know how, but enough boys had fallen in love with her that she was a threat. She didn't understand it. She was pretty, but so were other girls; she was smart, but so were other girls; and she was athletic, but so were other girls. Maybe it was the combination. Or maybe it was her shyness that men liked so much. If so, it was ironic, because her shyness was really due to insecurity. Once she realized that people could be fake, or that they would like or dislike you just because of how you looked and what people said about you, she was afraid to let anybody get too close to her. Maybe it made her seem like a cold-hearted witch, but it was too risky, being different. Anyone, male or female, who made the effort could find out who she really was. It just turned out that people who wanted to know her tended to be male.

Lawrence wasn't really wrong about the effect Chaney's

mother had had on her, though—Chaney hated his amateur psychology, but she had to admit he was at least a little bit right. Because of her mother, Chaney believed all women were capable of any betrayal. After all, if one seemingly normal person could turn her back on a husband and four young children, well, couldn't anybody? Couldn't she? Maybe not. She had devoted her life to raising her kids and being a good wife, determined never to inflict on anyone what her mother had done to *her* husband and children, and most of the time she was happy. At least, until recently . . .

The frightening thing was, Chaney had no idea why her mother had done what she had. If her brothers knew, they would never tell her—the whereabouts of Sylvia Rivers had been a taboo subject for years, and any secrets Chaney's father knew had gone with him to the grave. And as much as Chaney had always wondered what had happened, she wasn't prepared to hire somebody to solve the mystery. The wound was too deep; she didn't want to deal with the consequences of knowing where her mother was anymore. It hurt her too much to think her mother could be out there somewhere, living her life without even trying to make contact with her children.

How many times had Chaney wished she could talk to her mother, or even a big sister or an aunt? She had gotten to know a few of Perry's girlfriends, but not well enough to really get close to them. By the time his relationships had lasted long enough for her to start bonding with them, Chaney was already married and it was too late to be mothered that way; she had to be a mother herself.

It was okay now. Chaney had learned, over the years, not to need a lot of people. Along with Perry, her boyfriend was always her best friend, so getting married meant that she had a live-in friend for life.

Not that she had a lot of actual boyfriends. Several of her brothers' friends fell in love with her, but she went out with only one of them—Taurique. That had lasted almost three years, and then she'd married Lawrence. She'd met Taurique through Perry. They were both on the track and football teams, and for a long time Perry and Taurique were best friends. The friendship had lasted until Christine. All of Chaney's brothers were mad at Taurique at least for a while, but Perry felt personally responsible, because he had engineered the whole relationship. Zac was the first to forgive. He was the one who sat down with Chaney and told her, yeah, it's rough, but you agreed to the no-commitments thing, didn't you? And besides, your life isn't exactly over, is it? Chaney tried to be reasonable and logical, and it didn't work, so after Zac was through playing oldest and wisest, she ran to Perry and James for sympathy and took pleasure in plotting revenge.

But that was over when Lawrence appeared, and suddenly it didn't matter anymore, at least for a while.

James liked Lawrence instantly. They were both artistic—James had played bass guitar and a little jazz piano before deciding to study chemical engineering. Zac was just glad Lawrence was man enough to face up to his responsibilities and marry Chaney. And Perry tried to talk her out of it, because she was rebounding and pregnancy was a rotten reason to get married, even if the groom seemed to be a nice guy.

Chaney wondered how long Perry and Taurique had been friends again. She also wondered how long Taurique had been back in New York. Not that she had never thought about him after marrying Lawrence; she just decided not to even try to keep track of him. She figured that the best way to forget about him was to ignore the fact that he existed.

Maybe I was ready to see him again, she thought. *It was a shock, and of course he's still attractive, but I feel almost nothing now, compared to before. Besides, chemistry has a lot to do with friendship, too—don't my brothers have good friends who used to be girlfriends?* Chaney almost regretted not agreeing to have lunch with Taurique. His life couldn't have been boring all these years, that much was guaranteed. Not that he had a long history of hard-core criminal activity or anything, but she was almost sure that the rumors about him dealing drugs to put himself through the university were true. A rich aunt had put him through school, he'd said—she shook her head at his nonchalance and wondered if dealing was the only illegal thing he'd done since he'd left. That was Taurique—he did what he felt he had to to get ahead, and somehow he was almost able to justify his actions, no matter how blatantly questionable or downright inexcusable they were. This was a quality that Chaney admired initially, knowing she could never be that way. She later became uncomfortable with it, but his air of self-assurance at least as much as his good looks had hooked her thirteen years ago, and when she'd found out that most of his cool persona was an act, it had only made him more attractive, because it had meant that there was a side to him reserved for her eyes only, and that made her feel special.

Chaney finished smoothing lotion over her skin and slipped on her nightgown. It's only 9:30, she thought, and I'm already all set for bed. I must be getting old. She decided to have some hot chocolate before she went into her bedroom. Actually, there were times when she enjoyed her solitude, with the kids in bed, feeling warm and fresh, her just-washed skin caressed by silk, sitting alone with her thoughts and her hot chocolate. She smiled to herself. I can still shake off the blues, she thought, and as long as I can do that, I'll always be all right.

She poured some milk into a small saucepan. The phone rang again. Chaney let it ring—the machine would get it. She strolled back into her bedroom, heard her brother's voice, and picked up the receiver.

"Perry!" she said.

"Hey, she's home. I wondered where you'd be at this hour."

"Let me go to the kitchen phone."

She ran to the kitchen, then back to her bedroom to hang up that phone, then back to the kitchen.

"You're out of breath," Perry remarked.

"Temporarily, very temporarily. What's up? How's Valerie?"

"She's doing fine. How was your day?" He sounded almost

too casual, and Chaney grinned, deciding to play with him a bit.

"Same old, same old," she replied innocently.

"For real?" He was losing already—he sounded shocked.

"I took the kids to school—oh, actually, something *did* happen."

"What?" His voice was full of anticipation.

"I went to the salon." Chaney was smiling wickedly now.

"That's it?" He sounded conversational again. He's on to me, she thought, deciding to end the game.

"Perry, you talked to Taurique, I know you did, because he told me you two still speak. Why don't you just be direct?"

"Okay, you got me. You had lunch, he told me."

"He bought me hot dogs."

"He said you were looking really hot."

"Just stepped out of the salon."

"Told me you turned down having lunch with him."

Chaney stirred the milk, turned off the heat, and poured the warm liquid into a cup. "That's right," she said. "Hang on, okay?"

She reached up into the cupboard, took down a jar of Ovaltine, and placed three spoonfuls in the cup, stirring. She sat at the kitchen table, and picked up the receiver again.

"So what, Perry?"

"Nothing. Don't you think you could have had lunch with him?"

"Why?"

"Because you have absolutely no fun, that's why."

"I resent that."

"Listen, Chaney, you go on and on about how you have nothing to do when your husband's away, which is practically all the time. You love Lawrence, right?"

"Of course I love him."

"So why is it a big deal to have lunch with Taurique?"

Chaney sipped her Ovaltine. "Can I ask you something?" she said.

"Sure."

"What's it to you?"

"It wouldn't be anything to me if you had some friends, but you don't, and I worry about you."

"I'm fine."

"You think so? Have you noticed that you're depressed all the time?"

"I am not," she protested.

"Yes, you are," Perry said firmly. "Or at least, too much. It started when Ronnie went to kindergarten, and it's getting worse, now that he's in school."

She sipped more chocolate, her face suddenly hot. "What does Taurique have to do with that?" she demanded.

"Nothing, if you had more friends. Look, you guys were always tight. Why don't you just have lunch with him? Some of my best friends are ex-girlfriends."

"I don't know, Perry."

"Be honest with me, Chaney. What's the problem? Are you still mad at him? Because you shouldn't be, not after all this time. I mean, what was he? He was a childhood sweetheart who let you down. That's it."

It was much more than that, thought Chaney, surprised that Perry was downplaying the intensity of the relationship so much just because she had been young at the time.

"Why hold a grudge for years and years?" Perry continued. "It's petty, after all this time. I mean . . ."

"Why didn't you tell me you were talking to him again?" Chaney interrupted irritably, just to change the subject.

"I didn't want to seem disloyal. I mean, you hated him, after all."

"That's what Taurique said!" she exclaimed in disbelief. "Who told you I hated him?"

"You. That was the last thing you said about him, and it's stupid. I think he could be the best friend you've ever had now. He's really grown up in a lot of ways. I mean, we all have, but . . ."

"He could be the best friend I ever had," Chaney repeated slowly, emphasizing each word. "That's a hell of a statement, Perry."

"And I stand by it."

"Explain." She was amused now.

"Two people can't love each other like that and not like each other later."

"That's the stupidest statement you've ever made, Perry," Chaney said, laughing.

"No it isn't," he replied with mock indignation. "Look at Donald and Ivana."

"They're in one Domino's Pizza commercial, and that makes them best friends?"

They were both laughing now.

"So how are Ronnie and Nicole?" Perry asked good-naturedly.

"Oh, just great, Perry. Nicki's just as into getting the best grades in her class as ever, and you know how much Ronnie likes little girls; he's having a great time, too."

"Takes after his Uncle Perry."

"Mr. Atomic Dog. But don't worry, I'll straighten him out."

Perry laughed. "You think so?" he said. "It's genetic, baby. You have to chase the cat, at least for a while, until you meet the right girl, or you get tired."

"Uh-huh. Well, no son of *mine* is gonna treat women like you did," Chaney retorted.

"What did I do? I was no worse than a lot of guys."

"You just *think* you weren't, because of who your friends were."

"For real, Chaney," Perry protested, "who wants to be tied down at seventeen? Or eighteen, or nineteen, or twenty-two? I mean, you've got to find out a *little* something about yourself before you know who you want to be with, and in the meantime, you have to find out some other things about pleasing women, or else they don't want you."

Chaney rolled her eyes. "You mean it takes all that time to

learn what restaurants to go to and what flowers to buy?" she said sarcastically.

"Don't even try it, Chaney. *You* know how you women are. You want a man who knows his way around in the bedroom, and the only way a man learns that stuff is by experience. And don't say you could learn about it together, because most women won't put up with an amateur, not unless they're one of those older women who likes to educate adolescent boys."

Chaney smiled. "So *that's* what all that sleeping around was about. Trying to be a good husband for Valerie."

Perry laughed. "Exactly," he said.

Chaney took a long drink, thinking. "Is Taurique seeing somebody?" she asked casually.

"Yes. Why?"

"Just curious."

"Why?"

"Because I was wondering if he was still a dog or not."

Perry chuckled. "You should listen to yourself," he said. "You *are* still mad at him. And you know what? He didn't dog you, not really. I mean, that girl in California happened when you two had decided not to be so committed, remember?"

"You sound like Zac," Chaney remarked disdainfully.

"Maybe Zac was right. Look, we don't *have* to talk about Taurique. We haven't talked about him in years, and we both did okay. Let's just drop it. I mean, if you don't want to deal with him, fine. I was just making a suggestion."

Chaney considered it, imagining the Taurique who loved to go dancing, or out to eat, or to the zoo, or to the playground to swing really high on the swings and slide down the slide and climb the monkey bars; the Taurique who loved old classic films but would also go to the really dumb comedies Chaney would have enjoyed from time to time if Lawrence would only have agreed to watch them; the Taurique who could talk intelligently about almost anything; the Taurique who would try almost anything once. The Taurique who was an interesting way to pass the time . . .

"Okay," she said.

"Okay what?"

"Okay, if he still wants to go to lunch, you can give him my number."

"What happened?" Perry asked, surprised.

"Nothing. Look, maybe you have a point," Chaney replied in a grudging voice.

"*Maybe* I have a point," Perry repeated. "Like I don't always have a point, like I haven't looked out for you since you were a baby."

Chaney smiled, thinking of all the times Perry had taken her side against Zac or her father, the times he had cursed out girls who had spread rumors about her, the way he was always there to listen when she and Lawrence had a fight or a problem or when she was feeling down. And he's right, she thought, I *am* depressed a lot these days.

"You have," she said. "Look, thanks for calling. Say hi to Val and give Kenny and Calvin a kiss for me."

"Goodnight, Chaney."

"Goodnight, Perry."

She smiled as she hung up. I love that guy, she thought. She loved Zac and Jimmy, too, but they lived in Atlanta, and like her, they were writers, not talkers, which meant their contact was a lot less frequent. On top of that, Perry was less than two years older than Chaney, and he had always been her closest companion, even when the four of them had lived at home. Her closest companion, and the one member of her family who didn't try to force her to adhere to a rigid moral code. Not that she rebelled against the moral code much, or at least, not openly, which made it a huge deal when she and Lawrence had gone to her father to explain that Chaney was pregnant. Chaney would never forget the expression on her father's face—suddenly he'd looked old. A light went out behind his eyes and his whole body seemed to sag, and Chaney felt tears rolling down her cheeks, tears she couldn't control. She was rarely able to control when she cried and when she didn't, but she had really hoped to keep her cool this time, because the experience was traumatic enough without her adding to the drama. Yet here were the useless tears, flowing down her cheeks, making her unable to speak.

Lawrence saw her weeping and put his arm around her, pulling her so close that her tears fell on his shoulder as he explained to her father that he would never abandon his wife and his child, that he had a job lined up that would allow him to support his new family, and that he loved Chaney with all his heart, all said in the manliest of voices, even though he was shaking the whole time.

Chaney's father listened quietly, and then he spoke.

"I suppose I don't really have much to say about this, do I?" he began, his voice trembling just slightly. "I didn't raise you to behave this way, Chaney, or at least, I *thought* I didn't raise you to be so loose. I wanted . . . well, you're taking responsibility for your actions, at least. But I'm very, very disappointed. That's all."

Chaney looked up, and for one horrible moment her eyes met her father's. She saw how completely defeated he was. A knot formed in her throat, a knot she couldn't swallow, so she coughed and buried her face in Lawrence's chest, sobbing. Sobbing, because each time she'd made love to Taurique, she had a secret wish that they would somehow make a baby, that the condom would burst, or something. Something to create a moment just like this, a moment when her father and her brother Zac would have to see her not as their precious, pampered flower, but as a woman, with sexual appetites they could neither imagine nor condone. How she had longed to shatter their image of a perfect little lady somehow—not by using drugs; that had never appealed to her, really; not by compromising her intelligence with low grades . . . actually, she really didn't have the guts, deep down, to do anything in particular, but imagine what Daddy would think if he knew what an expert his little girl was at the fine art of love-making. Well, here she was, face to face with her father, and whatever illusions about her virginity he had kept alive during her long relationship with Taurique were irrevocably destroyed. Here was her chance to stand up and assert her right to make her own decisions, and what was she doing? Sobbing in Lawrence's arms, so ashamed she was unable even to open her eyes, never mind look at her father again, wishing she could disappear.

Lawrence had stopped shaking. Chaney looked at him and saw that his square jaw was set resolutely, and her despair turned to dread, because she could feel his anger building. Not now, she thought. Not with my father. Please.

"Your daughter is not loose, Mr. Davis," said Lawrence, his voice as cold and hard as steel.

Chaney's father's shoulders stiffened. "Really? Did you *rape* her?" he replied evenly, and Chaney could see a gleam in his eyes again, one of pure fury.

"No, I didn't," Lawrence shot back, unintimidated. "I made love to her, just like we'll make love the rest of our lives."

Chaney held her breath. Did he have to bring up the image of the two of them in bed? She wished she could faint; then, at least, she wouldn't have to watch what happened next.

"Make love?" Mr. Davis thundered. "I believe it's called fornication when it happens outside marriage. You've heard of the Bible, haven't you?"

Chaney closed her eyes, amazed that as bad as things had just been, they had somehow reached a new low.

"Don't even go there, Dad."

She looked up. It was Perry, and he had raised his voice. Not that he hadn't done that before, but he didn't do it often, not with his father.

"Stay out of this, man," Lawrence warned.

"Look, it's fornication for her and it's education for us," Perry went on, ignoring him. "That's completely unfair. You know it is."

"This is not your business, Perry," said Mr. Davis, but his tone had relaxed slightly.

"You made it my business when you said my sister was loose." Perry's gaze was unflinching; if he was intimidated at all, it was impossible to tell.

Chaney's father stared at Perry for a while, as if daring him to continue. Finally, Lawrence spoke again, and Chaney could feel the tension in his body as he tried to restrain his response.

"Mr. Davis," he said very carefully, "I understand why you're upset. I think I would be, too. But I'm telling you that I love Chaney and I'm going to spend the rest of my life with her, and I hope the two of us can be friends."

Chaney's father studied his face, scowling. Finally he nodded. "I can't change what's happened," he said bitterly, "can I?"

Then he turned and left the room.

"He'll come around when he sees the baby," said Perry, flopping onto the couch.

"Thanks," said Chaney, sniffling. She still couldn't believe he had taken on her father like that. She glanced at Lawrence, who was glaring at her brother.

"Yeah," he said pointedly. "The thing is, I didn't need your help."

Perry raised his eyebrows. "You didn't?" he snapped. "Fine, never again. Listen, I wasn't helping you. I don't even *know* you, really. And even when I do, what's best for Chaney will come first. Understand?"

"Stop it, both of you," Chaney interjected, before Lawrence could respond. She had seen him clenching his fists, and she was not prepared to sit back and watch another confrontation. "Just stop all the macho bull, okay?"

Perry and Lawrence stared at her in amazement. She never shouted, and she was suddenly embarrassed.

"Yes, ma'am," said Perry, rising. "Look, I'm glad you're both so sure about this." He looked each of them in the eye, then left the room.

Later, he tried to talk Chaney out of it for over an hour.

You're rebounding, he said. You, of all people, should know that children can't keep a marriage together. We'll help you raise the baby; you don't have to marry him to do that. I know you want to get out of Dad's house, but this isn't the way. This is your whole life you're talking about, and if you're not thinking about it that way, you have a big problem. You're a teenager, Chaney. How do you know if this is really the one? What about school? How will you go to school if he's working all the time? Who's going to look after your baby? He asked her questions till she felt like her head would explode.

"I'm not rebounding," she'd said. "Taurique was a long time ago. I'm not having a baby to save my marriage, or to get married at all. I *want* to raise a baby with two parents, not one parent, one grandparent, and a bunch of uncles. I know I can leave this house in other ways. I plan to make this last a lifetime. How is anyone *ever* sure they have the right person? I'm willing to sacrifice whatever it takes so my baby knows I'll always be there, and if that means not going to college, fine." The more she answered, the more terrified she became, so she ended the conversation by saying she had made up her mind, and he had had his say, and she didn't want to hear any more from him unless she brought it up first.

And Perry sighed and agreed. That was one thing about him—he would tell you exactly what he thought about you and what you were doing wrong for as long as you'd let him, but when you said stop, he'd stop and let you make your own decision.

This time, Chaney thought, he might be right. And if he isn't, at least seeing Taurique again would be a welcome change in my routine.

She finished her drink, rinsed the cup, put it in the dishwasher, and went to bed.

Three

October 18

When Lawrence called, at 6 A.M., Chaney was having the same bizarre dream about the ship. She woke up, sweating, when the phone rang.

"Lawrence?" she said in a tiny voice.

"It's me. Sorry to call so early."

"That's okay."

"Are you all right, baby?" he asked, concerned.

Chaney sat up, yawning. "Uh-huh," she responded, trying to sound calm.

"You don't sound okay."

"I was dreaming."

"Bad dream?"

"Uh-huh." *I sound like Nicki or Ronnie,* she thought, disgusted.

"I'm sorry I can't hold you and kiss you and make it better," Lawrence said softly.

She sighed. "I wish you could, baby," she replied wistfully.

"How are the kids?"

"Fine."

"Good. I was just killing time before I have to go rehearse."

"What is it you're singing, again?"

"The Count in *Figaro.*"

"That's a good role for you."

"I try."

"All I want is a live performance."

"That's what I want, too—you in the role you do so well—'*between the sheets.*' "

Chaney smiled at his Ronnie Isley impression.

"What did you do yesterday?" Lawrence asked.

"Nothing much. Got my hair and nails done, a facial, the works."

"Feeling down, huh?" he asked quietly.

"Uh-huh."

"I bet you looked especially beautiful."

"Some kid told me I made his day," she said, grinning.

Lawrence laughed. "I bet you did," he remarked.

Chaney debated telling him about Taurique. Lawrence was rarely jealous, but this was probably different . . .

"I wish I could see you right now," Lawrence went on. "What are you wearing?"

"A nightgown."

"The peach silk? Not the peach silk."

"Uh-huh."

"With the straps that always slide down over your shoulders? That one?"

Chaney smiled. "Yes."

"And me thousands of miles away."

"And you thousands of miles away." She sighed. All at once, she missed his touch so much that she felt a twinge in her stomach. There was an uncomfortable silence.

"Did you get a package yesterday?" he said after a while. He was trying to sound cheerful, but his voice was tinged with regret.

"No."

"Damn, I guess I'm not as famous as I thought. Can't pull strings like I want to."

Chaney laughed, relaxing a bit. "What are you talking about?" she asked.

"Your present."

She smiled. "I thought maybe . . ."

"No, of course not, don't you even say it. Just 'cause I'm not there. I thought *you* forgot."

"Touché."

"Happy anniversary, Chaney."

"Happy anniversary, Lawrence."

"I adore you, baby."

"I adore *you*, baby. Your present is here, waiting for you."

"I know. It's wrapped in peach silk, and I can hardly wait to get my hands on what's inside."

"Mmm. Don't do this to me."

"Close your eyes."

She did, smiling.

"I just walked in the room. You were still asleep, so I bent over you and gently kissed your lips. You stirred, but you didn't wake up, and I started to caress your shoulders, sliding the straps down . . ."

"Lawrence, please stop, my heart can't take this." It was the truth. She had never gotten used to not being touched by him for weeks on end, and her resistance was very low right now. She realized she had begun to stroke her inner thigh with her free hand, and she stopped herself.

"I love you, Chaney, and I'll make up for this, for being away, I promise." He was whispering. "I'm sorry."

"Don't apologize," she replied, and suddenly she wanted to cry.

"I wish I didn't have to."

"Lawrence, your career is as important to me as it is to you." She had said it so often, it had almost become automatic.

"Baby, just promise me something," he implored her.

"Anything."

"Don't sit at home. Please? I can't stand the thought of you sitting at home alone on our anniversary."

"I promised to spend the evening with the kids," she said, her voice wavering.

"Go to Perry's. You can take them with you."

"I only want to be with you," Chaney said, realizing that she sounded like a frightened child.

"I'll be home soon," said Lawrence, in a voice that pleaded with her not to make him feel any guiltier than he already did.

Chaney took a deep breath and closed her eyes. Don't make it any worse, she thought; it's not his fault he's getting the chance to do the one thing in life that makes him want to get up in the morning. It's not his fault that he's so good that he's becoming a star in one of the toughest careers known to man. It's not his fault. And besides, she thought, he's explained this business a thousand times, even if I sometimes have trouble accepting what he tells me: until you're firmly established, you can't really turn things down, and that means you have to sing wherever they want to hear you, whether it's Paris or Malaysia. He's on the verge of being famous enough to be at home more. Can't you just hang on a bit longer?

"I know," she said. "Take care of yourself, honey."

"I love you."

"Goodbye, sweetheart."

She hung up the phone slowly and wished they had moved to Europe. Then, at least, she would be closer to him. But when Lawrence suggested it, she was afraid to take such a big step, afraid to uproot herself and her children and move somewhere where everyone and everything was unfamiliar. Besides, she had no way of knowing just how much time Lawrence would end up spending there. One thing she had to say for the Europeans—they seemed to cast their operas on talent. They listened to Lawrence's voice and didn't care that he was black. So many years since Marian Anderson, and Americans were still wary. A zillion Porgys were okay, but Rigoletto was harder, and God forbid a black man should have a tenor voice, because then he might have a leading role and kiss some white woman on the lips, or something.

Not that Chaney wanted to see a black man lusting after a white woman on stage herself, but if it meant that a talent would go to waste because of the bigotry of the powers that be, she could put her own prejudices aside. Well, things seemed to be changing a bit, at least in drama. Maybe one day some of that would be reflected in opera.

She hadn't had to put anything aside, really, because Lawrence was a bass-baritone, and the critics were calling him the new Simon Estes, or rather, the newcomer Lawrence Rivers. He had sung all over Europe and was starting to get more engagements in the United States and was on the roster at the Metropolitan Opera for this season, singing Leporello—a buffoonish part, but a major role nonetheless. Chaney couldn't wait. Finally, he would be performing in a place where he could come home to her every night. Until then, she would just take care of her children and her house. The time will go sooner than I think, she told herself again, pulling the covers back over her shoulders and drifting back to sleep.

Lawrence's uncle was gay. No one really talked about it much, but he was one of those liberated, out-of-the-closet types, so that if you met him even once, you couldn't help but know. He was very comfortable with himself and completely unselfconscious, and Lawrence's father hated him. Actually, he didn't really hate him, but he tried to keep his brother away from Lawrence. When Uncle Willie refused to be shut out of his nephew's life, Lawrence's father began to lecture, ad nauseam, about what a man was and was not. A man was responsible; he could have his fun, but not too much. A man was a provider with a solid career. A man owned his own home and had the final say in his household. A man stayed in control of his emotions. A man wasn't given to excesses—he dressed conservatively, wearing no jewelry besides a watch, or maybe an inconspicuous chain. Most of all, a man never looked at other men, no matter what. Mr. Rivers made it clear that Uncle Willie was family, but he was no example of a man. Lawrence listened carefully, deciding that even if his uncle's occasional finger-popping flamboyance, pierced ear, and flashy clothes made him something other than a man, it didn't make him any less of a friend.

The day Chaney found out she was pregnant, Uncle Willie was at the house. Chaney got the test results at a clinic. She was afraid to go to the family doctor—he knew her father too well, and she wasn't completely sure he wouldn't tell him everything. She was alone, but so were most of the girls in the waiting room. A few were there with their mothers or female friends; very rarely, a girl was there with a male who seemed to be her boyfriend.

In the waiting room, Chaney tried to ignore two girls with doorknocker earrings, and fuschia-colored extensions who were talking "that bitch" this and that. She glanced at them, afraid to stare. They were the kind who would take that as a challenge, and Chaney was not up to it.

She was trying not to listen to them; she was trying to come to terms with her own terror. She had not had a period in over two months, and only when she began to have bouts of nausea had she started to acknowledge the terrible possibility that there was a reason, a very good reason, for the changes her body was going through. She told no one, and she rode the train for over an hour to get to a clinic far from her home. She tried to pretend that everything was okay, then she wallowed in guilt, for being sexually active and unmarried, and besides, for just plain enjoying it so much. She was getting punished, that was it . . .

And I deserve it, she thought. Please, God, please let me not be pregnant. But He didn't have to listen to sinners like her, and besides, He didn't always respond favorably to the prayers of far better people than her. After all, what excuse did she have for her fornication? It wasn't like she hadn't grown up going to church; it wasn't like she didn't know it was wrong.

So she sat in utter misery, waiting, and the two girls kept practically screaming at each other. She really wanted to knock their heads together, they were so uncouth . . .

Then, just when she was feeling superior to them, she realized they were all probably in the clinic for the same reason. We were all equally stupid, she thought.

Chaney had a good idea when she had conceived—or potentially conceived; she still held the slimmest of hopes that there was some other reason she had stopped menstruating. Any disease would be better than pregnancy. At least she could explain a disease; diseases weren't her fault.

She'd skipped two days in a row taking her pills; that had probably been it. She had no good excuse; she'd just forgotten. Early Saturday morning she went to the Catskills with Lawrence and his family, leaving the pills in the nightstand by her bed. She stayed in the mountains for the weekend, and on the first night Lawrence and Chaney sneaked out, very late, to listen to the crickets.

The night wasn't still—actually, it roared. The crickets were very loud. She and Lawrence walked through the pitch blackness and the world was vast and limitless and the sky was huge and she was very happy. She reached for his hand and he squeezed hers and there were stars, a million of them, and Chaney and Lawrence gazed up and tried to find the Big Dipper and Sirius and Andromeda, and she was still gazing up when she realized that he was looking at her, and she stared into his eyes and there was an expression in them she had never seen before.

He kissed her, gently at first, then more insistently, then he was holding her a bit too tight, and she was holding on for dear life, and she was being swept along by his passion; she was unable to think. He began to kiss her neck—a vulnerable spot, that had always been a vulnerable spot—and then he whispered in her ear, "I love you," and it was the first time he had said it.

He paused then to look at her, a smile on his face, a vague hint of smile, like the Mona Lisa's, and his eyes were very bright. Chaney's heart was beating very fast. "I love you, too," she said. She wasn't quite sure it was true at that moment, but she wanted him very badly, she wanted to do all kinds of things to him, because she hadn't been with him before and she hadn't been with anyone else since Taurique had left eight and a half months ago, and the self-control she had been practicing was about used up. She had known it wouldn't last forever, which was why, when she'd met Lawrence, she'd gone on the pill. She'd never told him this. In fact, she'd never let him touch her below the waist, because she was determined that he wasn't going to leave her, not because he had had his way with her and she was no longer mysterious, or whatever the reason was that led men to dump women the minute they slept together and to go off and find somebody else. Basically, she wanted to find out how serious he was. She was not about to allow him to play games with her, to use her and discard her, just another conquest. Not that Taurique did that, but he could have, she was so trusting, and she'd overheard enough of her brothers' conversations that she didn't want to put herself in the position of having to be lucky, again, that her boyfriend really cared about her.

So now, after all this time, Lawrence's touch was driving her absolutely crazy. And if she loved him, then it was making love, because he loved her, he had just said it, so it wasn't just cheap sex, then. He loved her—he was kissing her face again, he had her face in his hands, and he was kissing her all over her forehead, her cheeks, her lips, and then he stopped and just hugged her, rubbing his hand up and down her back.

"You love me?" he asked.

"Yes." She did, after all. She cared about him, she loved being around him, she respected him, and just because he wasn't Taurique didn't mean she wasn't in love with him . . .

She smiled at him then, fondly. "You love me?" she asked him.

"Oh, yeah." He squeezed her again. "I was waiting until I was sure to tell you. I've never loved anybody before, not really. Not like this."

He pulled away, looking into her eyes. "Chaney . . ." he said, and his face was very serious.

It was a very warm night, for the altitude and considering it was May. Lawrence buried his face in her hair and took her hand, putting it against his chest. She could feel his heart pounding against her palm. He was nibbling on her ear as he moved her hand down, gently, to touch his stomach, and then down—he was very hard, and he rubbed her hand up and down, then released it, stroking her hair. She didn't take her hand away but continued to caress him; then she found his fly and unbuttoned the waist of his jeans, and she heard his breath start coming in gasps, and she would have knelt in the grass and taken him in her mouth, but she was afraid to show him just how experienced she was, so she kept doing just what she was doing, all the while kissing him.

The crickets were very loud—maybe they were treefrogs. Were there treefrogs in the Catskills? Lawrence was unbuttoning her sweater, then he was kissing her, kissing her throat, between her breasts, then he was kissing her breasts, and she arched her back—he had kissed her there before, but this time was different, because she knew she wasn't going to stop him.

They sank down, slowly, into the grass, and he was very quiet. All she heard was him breathing heavily, gasping for air, and he still wasn't touching her below the waist.

"Chaney," he was sighing.

"Uh-huh?" she managed, in a barely intelligible squeak.

"I need you."

She got a chill. It was a line. It was a line men used. He had waited four and a half months, and now he would have his conquest. He stopped.

"What's the matter?" he asked, his voice very deep. His voice was always very deep, but it was deeper somehow, very quiet, and as sultry as a summer day in the tropics.

"Nothing."

"I'm sorry." He gazed at her. "I'm sorry."

He held her, again a bit too tight, like it was all he could do not to crush her, to forcibly make her a part of himself. He was barely able to hold himself back; he was frightening her because he was very strong, much stronger and bigger than Chaney, and she could feel a passion so powerful, struggling to be free, that she wasn't sure it wouldn't destroy her.

"We'll go back inside," he said, smiling at her, a slightly pained smile, and he fastened the button on his jeans, was about to fasten his fly, when Chaney stopped him. He looked at her, surprised. There was a slight breeze.

"No," she said. She believed in him. He wasn't using her; she felt that deep in her heart. She kissed him, and they looked at the sky, and she was sitting in the grass and he sat behind her, one leg on either side, and held her, pulled her into his arms, and she leaned her head against his shoulder and he began to rub her arms.

"Are you cold?" he asked, in that deep voice.

"No."

"Chaney, I love you, but I know you've been hurt before and all, so . . . I'm just saying . . . I love you enough to wait."

"I know. But . . ."

"Yes?"

"I don't think I can wait anymore."

His face changed. His expression was still solemn, but there was a light behind his eyes. He looked down again.

"There's another thing—I wasn't really planning this." He looked embarrassed.

"I wasn't, either, but I went on the pill, just in case."

They looked at each other. The grass was cold and slightly damp, and it wasn't very soft, but Chaney didn't notice for long, because Lawrence made love to her with an intensity that consumed all of her senses, and she would have screamed loudly enough to wake up the whole house, to wake up all of nature, actually, if Lawrence hadn't placed his hand over her mouth. She was surprised. Taurique had never done that. They made love as loudly as they wanted to, and Taurique was at least as loud as she was, and besides, they talked to each other a lot . . . but Lawrence was quiet, and he wanted her to be quiet. He was quiet until he couldn't stand it anymore, and then he called her name over and over again, and his excitement was infectious. She gazed into his face, as she had done a million times with Taurique, who always told her to look, begged her to see what she was doing to him, to read it in his eyes. But Lawrence's eyes were closed until after it was over, and then he held her in his arms, looking at her as if he'd never seen her before.

"I do love you," he said.

I know, she thought. I know, because as much as you wanted to take me, you held back until you thought I was satisfied. Even though you've been with me all this time and you've never made love to me, you held back. He's not using me, she thought.

"Lawrence," she said, and she felt tears in her eyes.

"Yes?"

"I'm so glad—I'm so glad I met you." And she'd grabbed him and held him too tight, crying.

I wish I could hold him now, she thought, sitting in the waiting room. Finally, one of the doorknocker girls was called away, and the other one fell silent. Chaney glanced at her again. She looked scared. She's just the same as I am . . .

"Chaney Davis."

She swallowed and followed the nurse to a consultation room.

When she emerged into daylight, her life was over. She walked out onto the street, not really seeing anything, and stumbled as she went down the stairs to the train, catching herself against the railing. Pull yourself together, idiot, she said to herself, the drama is not necessary. She glanced around—no one was staring at her. They have no idea what's going on, why should they stare? No one knows, no one cares, really. Even if I had fallen, she thought, they wouldn't notice. For some reason, this made her feel better. She reached into her wallet for a token and went through the turnstile.

There was a train coming already. Chaney wasn't sure if this was a good thing or a bad thing, because she wasn't sure where she was going. Should I go home? Or should I go to Lawrence's? Should I tell him at all?

A wave of fear shot through her. What am I going to do? Have a baby? Have an abortion? I can't. I can't have an abortion. I can't have a baby . . .

The train came and Chaney sat in a nearly empty car. Lawrence will leave me. He wouldn't do that. He'll take care of the baby. He won't be ready to—he's a *student.* His father won't help. I could go home. I could tell Perry. He would tell me to have an abortion. I don't want one. But if I do have one, everyone else won't need to know I was pregnant. But suppose I'm aborting someone special? A future musical genius? Then again, suppose I'm not ready to raise a baby and I end up with a neurotic? Or a psycho?

I can't have an abortion. I would regret it forever, I would always wonder who that person would have been. But if I have a baby, I have to raise it for the next twenty years or so. What am I going to do? *What am I going to do?*

Her head hurt. You have to tell Lawrence, and you have to tell him first. Then, if he really doesn't want anything to do with you . . .

But he says he loves me. Then again, so did Taurique. But Lawrence is not like Taurique, he's not wild, he won't run away.

Chaney felt tears fighting to escape from her eyes, and she blinked very fast and tried to take her mind away by reading the ads above her head. It didn't work. Half of them seemed to be advertising gynecological services.

The train was moving at lightning speed. She was sweating—her shirt was sticking to her back, and her feet were very hot in her sneakers. She glanced around. A tear had trickled down her cheek. She brushed it away and took a deep breath, trying to find some calm somewhere. It didn't work. Her stomach felt like she had swallowed a lump of clay. I can't get away, she thought, and so she decided to rehearse what she would tell Lawrence.

It took forever to get to his house, but she still didn't know what she was going to say when she got there. The speech changed every time she tried to go over it. By the time she reached his door, she wasn't sure she could ring the bell. She didn't have to—Uncle Willie was there, and he had seen her coming and thrown open the door.

"Get in here, girl," he said. "How you been, Chaney? I ain't seen you in—too long. Give me a kiss." He hugged her and kissed her cheek, then inspected her. "I swear, you're almost enough to make me change my ways . . ."

He always said that. Chaney couldn't manage a smile, and he put his hand under her chin, forcing her to look at him.

"What's the matter, baby?"

She tried to find a voice and knew that if she spoke, she'd lose her composure. She shook her head.

He hugged her again. "Did somebody hurt you?"

She shook her head.

"You need to talk to Lawrence."

"Uh-huh."

"Okay, you come with me." He took her hand and led her down the stairs to Lawrence's room. "Everything's gonna be okay, sweetheart, don't worry."

He knocked on the door. "Lawrence, you got a visitor," he yelled.

"Who is it?"

"Your girlfriend."

A moment later, he opened the door. "Why didn't you just tell her to come in . . . Chaney?"

She was trembling.

"Honey, what's the matter?" He held her, and his uncle went upstairs, closing the door behind him.

"Can I sit?" she managed, and they sat on his bed.

"You're scaring me," he said. "What is it?"

She searched his face. I had a speech . . .

"Talk to me," he said, a bit impatiently.

She cleared her throat. "Lawrence . . ." Her voice was wavering, but she was able to hold onto it, it didn't break. This was encouraging, and she felt a bit stronger.

"Lawrence, I went . . . I went to the doctor."

"Why? What's wrong?" He took her hand, his eyes very wide.

"Nothing—well—I . . ."

"What's the matter with you? *Tell* me!"

She stared at him and then she couldn't keep her composure anymore. She burst into tears.

"I'm pregnant."

The words hung in the air. Lawrence's hand felt suddenly cold and lifeless, so Chaney took her hand away and wiped her eyes with it, feeling uncomfortable. Now here it comes, he'll offer to pay for the abortion . . .

She watched him stand up. He walked very slowly to his desk and got her some tissues, which he handed to her without looking at her or sitting down again.

When she had finished blowing her nose, he asked, "How many months?" in a voice that sounded completely unfamiliar—it was much higher than she had ever heard it, and although he had spoken quietly, there was so much underlying tension in his speech that Chaney was slightly afraid.

"About three." she replied reluctantly.

"Three!"

Chaney swallowed hard. "Three," she repeated.

He turned away, shaking his head and biting his lip. "How?" he demanded incredulously. "I thought you were on the pill."

She stared at her hands. "I guess . . ." she cleared her throat. "I guess I forgot to take them when we went to the Catskills."

He swore silently and began pacing, his hands on his hips. "What should we do?" he said, his voice barely controlled.

"I don't know."

He started to laugh then and he sat at his desk, still laughing,

"Life is funny, isn't it, Chaney?" he managed. "It's pretty damn hilarious sometimes, huh?"

When he was finally able to collect himself, Chaney took a deep breath and said, in a voice so tiny she could barely hear herself, "You don't have to worry, I'll take care of everything . . ."

She jumped, for he had slammed his hand down so hard on the desk that everything on it had lifted into the air. She was surprised he hadn't put a hole in it.

"Is that what you think of me?" he demanded, jumping to his feet and glaring at her with such unvarnished hostility that she had to look away. She was trembling again. I shouldn't have told him, she was thinking, why did I tell him? I should have taken care of this myself . . .

"Don't look at me that way," she blurted out, glancing up at him miserably.

He sighed. "What way?" he replied, and for the first time in a while he sounded almost like himself.

"Like you hate me."

Lawrence took a deep breath. "I'm sorry," he said flatly, running his hand over the top of his hair. There was a long silence, and then he asked, "How long have you known?" in a colorless voice.

"I found out today."

Chaney waited for him to speak again, wiping her eyes with the already soaked Kleenex. He looked like he was two million miles away; he was staring at the wall just to the left of her, seemingly unaware that she was still there, and suddenly she felt so terribly alone that she couldn't stop herself from sobbing.

"Don't," Lawrence said quietly, focusing on her again. "Come on . . ." He came back toward her then, taking her in his arms a bit stiffly. He was like a coiled spring. Finally, he spoke again. "I'll take care of you, Chaney. It bothers me that you thought I wouldn't. We did this together. I wish you had . . . but that . . . it's not . . . your fault, it was me, too.

And . . ." He sighed. "You're keeping our baby, right?" He was still holding her, so that she was staring over his shoulder at the wall.

"I don't know."

He pulled away slightly. "You don't know?" He sounded surprised.

"I'm not sure. I'm too young to . . . I don't know."

"You're too young to be somebody's mother?"

The idea was suddenly chilling. "Yes."

"I see." He looked down, still trying, unsuccessfully, to relax, and she could sense him becoming distant again—there was somehow nothing comforting about his touch.

There was another silence. "You want . . ." she began, nervously. She couldn't say it.

"What? Chaney, finish a sentence."

His tone was impatient. She swallowed. He really hates me, she thought.

"You don't want a baby," she said. "And you don't want me, not anymore, right?"

He gazed straight up, then down again. "What are you talking about?" He looked like he was about to explode. "Did I say that?" he asked, seething. "I wasn't planning to be a father just yet, that's all. Look, I told you I love you. How many times have I told you that? Do I always lie to you, or something, so you can't believe me?"

"No." She felt like she had been punched. There was nothing loving in his voice. She watched him jump to his feet and cross the room, and tried not to start sobbing again.

"Then where the hell do you get off telling me what I want and don't want?" he continued, his voice rising in pitch and volume with every word. "You don't know a damn thing about me, obviously. Why do I even bother? I try to show you I care about you, and when the chips are down, you come to me telling me I don't want you? This is *hard* for me. I have no idea what the hell to do. Can't you understand that?"

Lawrence was breathing very heavily, pacing and glaring at

her, his gaze almost as hard as it had been before, when all at once he stopped and closed his eyes, calming himself. When he finally looked at her again, his face was softer and his shoulders sagged slightly.

"I love you," he said, in a caressing voice. "I'm sorry. I'm sorry." He said it over and over. "I just need some time. I'm sorry. I shouldn't have screamed at you. I just—I wasn't ready for this, you know? I wasn't expecting it . . . my God, my father will kill me . . . well, you know my father has a lot of plans for me, and . . ." He took a deep breath. "We're both responsible for this situation, I know that, Chaney. I just—I wasn't ready for this . . . well, that doesn't matter, does it, because it's happening. I'll just have to change—change my plans a bit, that's all."

He took a step toward her, then hesitated. "Can I hold you?" he asked.

She didn't move. "Okay," she said after a while, and he came over to her and collected her in his arms and kissed her and kissed her, and then he just squeezed her. His heart was still beating faster than normal. Suddenly, he looked at her.

"Tell me you'll keep our baby, Chaney, I promise I'll make it okay. Will you keep our baby, Chaney?"

She sighed heavily. "Are you sure you want a baby?" she asked, searching his face.

"Yes," he said firmly, his voice very intense. "I've known for a while that I wanted you to be the mother of my children—I've never felt that way about anybody. I just wanted it to happen after we were married for a while, and I planned to finish school before that happened. But if this is the way it's going to be, then I'll just have to deal with it. I'm not gonna lie to you and say it's not scary, but I know we can make it work, if you want it to. Do you believe that?"

She gazed at him, mesmerized. She wasn't as sure as he seemed to be, but Lawrence was nothing if not determined, and if he was going to work at this the way he worked at his voice, it would come out okay. It had to . . .

She nodded.

"Okay." He sighed, and rocked her back and forth for what seemed like forever. All at once he pulled away.

"Uncle Willie!" he yelled. "Uncle Willie!" He opened the door. "Uncle Willie!"

The sound of quick footsteps came from upstairs.

"What's the matter with you, boy?" he uncle demanded, appearing in the doorway.

Lawrence smiled at him. "I'm gonna be a daddy," he said.

Four

October 19

Just three more sit-ups, Chaney thought. Her stomach muscles were aching. Don't hate me because I'm beautiful, she thought to herself, you're probably having a lot more fun than I am.

There was a loud knock at the door. Saved by the bell, she thought, rising to her feet. Please, not Pam, she was thinking, as she opened the inner door . . .

She saw a huge bouquet of flowers, an Armani trenchcoat, and Brutini shoes.

"Who is it?" she asked. Impossible . . .

"Hey, girl, ain't no mystery . . ." Lawrence lowered the roses to reveal his face.

Chaney fumbled with the latch of the screen door, barely managing to get it unlocked before he threw it open. He dropped the flowers on the ground and grabbed her so tightly she was hardly able to breathe. She was laughing and crying, and she heard Ronnie and Nicole start screaming "Daddy" over and over.

She expected to wake up, but he was still there when he released her. He kissed the children, then the three of them fell on the ground, the children giggling as he tickled them.

"Time out, time out," he finally said. He turned toward his wife, smiling. "Hi," he said.

"Hi." He had never done anything like this in his life, as far as she knew.

"I bet you're surprised," he went on. Ronnie was bouncing up and down on his left leg, and Nicole was nestled against his right side. They both looked blissfully happy.

"Just a bit." She retrieved the roses, placing them on the table in the living room.

"Happy anniversary, darling. Sorry I'm late."

"How long are you staying, Dad?" Nicole asked.

"A few hours, Nicki."

"And then you have to go back?"

"Then I have to go back. But I'll be here again before you know it. Now, I need some time with your mother. Can you guys give me ten minutes? I won't be too long, I promise to come and get you when I'm done. Deal?"

He stood and shook hands with each of them, and they both went into Nicole's room. As soon as the door was closed, Lawrence came toward Chaney again, taking her face in his hands to kiss her. He pulled away, gazing at her.

"This is just what I needed," he said, smiling. "You are beautiful."

"I'm a mess. I'm sweaty, and . . ."

"I love you sweaty."

She laughed. "I could get sweatier, with a little help," she said.

"Let's go," he said, and he took her hand, leading her up the stairs into their bedroom. He locked the door behind him.

"How did you arrange this?" she asked, laughing as he began to undress her.

"Lots of money. You know how much it costs to fly from Milan to New York on less than a day's notice?" She was lying on the bed in her underwear.

"I don't want to know."

"You got that right." He was kissing her neck, unfastening her bra. "Thank God for frequent-flyer miles."

"Don't you have a rehearsal?"

"I told them I was sick." He had slipped off her panties and was caressing her thighs.

"Was that a good idea?" she whispered, trembling.

"Best idea I've ever had. Now, hush." He kissed her mouth, still stroking her, and all at once she couldn't restrain herself. She was attacking him, kissing him all over his face and neck, scratching him, biting him, completely out of control.

He stopped her, squeezing her so tightly that she couldn't move and rubbing her back, and she suddenly realized she was crying.

"I'm sorry," he whispered. "Don't cry, baby, I'm here. I'm here, and we don't have to rush, we can take our time. I'm here now, sweetheart."

Her body went limp and he held her, just held her, until the tears stopped. Then he lay beside her, stroking her cheek, smoothing her eyebrows, tracing her lips.

"I missed you," he said softly. "My beautiful wife. My beautiful Chaney."

He kissed her lips slowly, then he kissed them again, more urgently, then he kissed her neck and the tops of her breasts, and then his tongue found her nipples and she let out a little scream.

"Shh," he said, smiling and gesturing, with his head, toward the door.

"Okay," she gasped, reaching between his legs and feeling the hardness there and stroking him gently. "I need you," she said imploringly, gazing into his eyes.

"I'm all yours," he replied seriously, and he kissed her stomach, lingering on her navel for a moment before he began to explore her with his tongue.

She covered her mouth to stifle her cries as he brought her to orgasm, and when it was over she clung to him, but only for a moment to catch her breath.

"Your turn," she said, narrowing her eyes and playfully pushing him onto his back and straddling him. She took his throbbing penis in her hand and gently placed it just inside her, teasing him until he couldn't stand it before allowing him all the way in, then rocking him and squeezing him rhythmically, slow and hard, then faster and faster, her head thrown back, lost in the delicious friction of their bodies and the sound of his breathing, which was now almost as high-pitched as hers . . .

When it was over, she just lay in his arms, afraid to move, afraid to break the spell.

"We have to get the kids," he said finally.

"In a minute."

"Okay." He embraced her. "You know, I get into this mindset where I'm trying to be the world's greatest singer, and that starts to take over sometimes."

"I understand."

"I promised not to miss another anniversary, Chaney, but I did anyway, and I'm sorry. You sounded so alone that I had to come home, just for a little while."

"You didn't have to do that."

"Yes, I did. You're my wife, and I love you." He kissed her, and she smiled.

"What if they find out you're here?"

"Forget them."

"So you can just do this whenever?" It was meant to be a joke, but she ended up sounding hopeful.

He looked at her, then shook his head. "Not if I want to keep getting hired. But this is a special occasion, don't you think so?"

She smiled. "You're a wonderful man," she said.

"Thanks."

"I needed this, I really did."

"Then it was worth every penny."

Please don't leave me again, she thought, blinking back tears that had formed instantly in her eyes. Please.

There was a knock at the door.

"Daddy!" Ronnie was yelling, "it's been more than ten minutes."

"Coming." Lawrence sat up. "I guess I'd better get dressed," he said.

"And I like you so much just the way you are," said Chaney, clearing her throat, back in control.

He laughed. "I *love* you just the way you are."

There was more banging. "I *know* you didn't just knock on that door again," Lawrence called out sternly, winking at Chaney. Ronnie was quiet.

"I'm surprised they waited this long," Chaney remarked.

"Well, I'd better not keep them waiting anymore, they might put a hole in the door, and that would clash with the decor." He finished the sentence with a British accent, tucking his white silk shirt into his jeans. "On your feet, wife," he said, and she glared and threw a pillow at him, which he dodged, grinning.

"Okay, okay," she said, pulling the covers back and looking for her bra.

The children were asleep, finally. It took forever to get them settled, they were so excited by Lawrence's cameo appearance. Chaney closed her eyes. The bed was empty again—Lawrence had almost been like a ghost, or a mirage. She could still barely believe that he had spent ten hours on a plane only to turn around a couple of hours later and go back.

She gazed at the peach roses. He loved her gift—she had bought him an ornate pocket watch. He also loved the Valentino suit he had given her—she put it on to wear to the airport, so he could get a chance to see her in it before he came back. I still didn't get to remove your peach silk gown, he reminded her in a whisper as they embraced at the airport; that was the present I was *really* waiting for. But I'll be back. Then he kissed her passionately on the lips and gave each of the children a peck goodbye and boarded the plane, looking tired.

What a guy, she thought. How many husbands would fly all that way just to take their family out to lunch? Then again, how many husbands would have to?

You're impossible, she thought. He had done all that just to make up for missing their anniversary, and instead of making her feel better, it just left her wanting more.

Five

October 21

Taurique caught Chaney on Monday morning as she was rushing Nicole and Ronnie out the door.

"Are you free today for lunch?" he asked.

"Okay."

"Le Cirque, 12:30."

"Le Cirque? Is that necessary?"

"Okay, McDonald's."

Chaney smiled. "I'd really prefer Chinese," she said.

"Okay, there's this little place in the Village—or you remember that place on the Upper West Side we used to go to?"

"The West Side sounds great."

"Good. See you later."

She hung up.

"Who's that, Mommy?" Ronnie asked.

"An old friend of Mommy's, honey. Do you have your bag?"

"Yes, Mommy."

"Nicole, look at you. Go wipe around your mouth, you have toothpaste all over your face."

She ran upstairs, returning thirty seconds later with her face clean.

"Good. Okay, let's go."

Chaney paused for a moment, checking her hair and makeup in the hall mirror. Who cares, she thought, I'm not trying to *impress* the man, or anything. She smiled to herself—such *lies!* She wanted him to eat his heart out; she couldn't deny that. Oh, well, he always loved her in jeans anyway. She hurried the children out the door and locked it. If nothing else, this was going to be interesting.

Taurique was late—Chaney had forgotten about that part of his personality. She had been sitting near the entrance of the restaurant for nearly fifteen minutes when he came in with a guilty grin on his face.

"I got held up. I'm sorry," Taurique said.

"You'll never change," Chaney remarked, shaking her head and glancing at her watch.

He shrugged. "In some ways, maybe not, but I'm trying," he said. "How are you feeling?"

"Great. You?"

"Okay. I'm glad you agreed to have lunch with me."

"Perry talked me into it."

"He did?" Taurique looked surprised.

"In a way. Look, I wouldn't be here if I didn't want to be."

He smiled and approached the hostess, requesting a table for two in nonsmoking. She picked up two menus and found them a spot by the window.

"You must have had an anniversary lately," Taurique said, as they sat down.

"Nine years, three days ago."

He let out a low whistle. "Damn, Chaney, time flies, doesn't it?" he remarked.

"Uh-huh."

"I can't believe I'm almost thirty."

"I can't, either."

Taurique gazed around. "This is a great place, isn't it? I mean the food. It's almost as good as that Japanese restaurant. But then again, you never liked sushi, did you?"

He glanced at her mischievously and she remembered her

one ill-fated attempt at eating sushi. Taurique went on and on about how good it was, finally taking her to an expensive Japanese restaurant and ordering five different kinds for her, which she ate, politely excusing herself five minutes after her last bite so she could throw up.

"Why did you finish it if you hated it that much?" Taurique had asked.

"It seemed to mean so much to you," she replied.

"You've changed since then," Taurique was saying.

"How do you know?"

"You turned me down for lunch, and when you changed your mind about that, you turned down Le Cirque. But I guess kids teach you how to say no, huh?"

Chaney looked at him—she had been gazing around the room, but now he had her full attention.

"Are you saying I never knew how to say no?" she asked, as casually as possible, instantly beginning to fume.

"Yes."

"Thanks a lot."

"Oh, c'mon, Chaney," Taurique went on. "You have your assertive moments, but basically, you're a pushover. That's okay, you were about the sweetest girl I ever knew, but you never disagreed with me about anything important, or if you did, you almost always backed down. I bet you're still like that most of the time."

"Oh, really?" Chaney asked sarcastically.

"Yes, really. Especially with Perry. I mean, Perry can talk you into almost anything and make you think it was your idea. You know I'm right."

"Do I?" Chaney could feel the anger rising in her stomach, creeping into her chest.

"Name one time you didn't do just exactly what Perry told you to."

"When . . ." She considered it, trying to remember everything Perry had ever suggested all at once and feeling momentarily overwhelmed. It was important now; she had to prove Taurique wrong . . .

Suddenly, she felt triumphant. "When I got married," she announced.

Taurique grinned, shaking his head. "When you got married," he repeated, and Chaney realized her mistake. "I thought Lawrence was such a great guy."

"He is. It's just, Perry didn't know him that well and he thought I was getting married because . . ."

"You were upset."

"No, because I was pregnant."

"You were?" Taurique said, startled. "It never occurred to me. I thought you were just mad at me."

Chaney laughed derisively—maybe she hadn't made a mistake after all.

"Are you serious?" she said. You arrogant jerk . . . "Actually, I married him because I loved him."

"That's a good reason." Taurique was unnerved. Chaney was surprised—she would have expected Perry to fill Taurique in on all the details of her marriage, not just her husband's name.

The waitress arrived and took their order. There was an awkward silence. Chaney wondered what Taurique was thinking. Maybe he *has* changed, he's not even trying to pretend to be cool about this. Maybe the thought of her making passionate love to somebody else had suddenly become a reality to him. Or maybe he had this insecure need to feel like her whole life, even her decision to marry somebody else, somehow revolved around him. Whatever it was, seeing him like this reminded her of the day Perry had introduced them. She walked into the kitchen and there he was, glistening with sweat, holding a glass of water. She stared. She had met her brother's athletic friends before, but none of them had a face that actually almost outdid his sculpted body.

"Hi," Taurique said, smiling.

Chaney blushed and looked down and a bit sideways.

"Hi," she said. "I was getting some water . . ."

"My sister," Perry said, "is a little shy, so I'll handle the introductions. Taurique, this is my sister Chaney, the pride and joy of the Davis family, the sweetest, prettiest, most innocent girl in Brooklyn—hell, in the world. And she has three of the craziest bodyguards around, who also happen to be her brothers."

Chaney rolled her eyes, laughing, stealing a glance at Taurique and finding that he was still just as good-looking as she thought he was before.

"And Chaney, meet my man Taurique," Perry went on. "Best wide receiver on the East Coast, already a star, soon to be legend, as humble as he is talented, smart as a whip and saving himself until marriage."

Taurique's expression was now one of shock. He held out his hand, and he was somehow more attractive, now that he had temporarily lost all pretense of cool, than he'd been before. Chaney hoped her palms weren't sweaty . . . then she looked into his eyes and experienced, for the first time, the undeniable jolt of mutual electricity that would happen all through their relationship. He took her right hand, caressing her palm with his fingers as he released it, never taking his eyes off her, and she felt an uncomfortable blast of heat between her legs. She hoped he'd be different from her brother's other friends, because she knew being Taurique's adopted little sister would not be enough for her.

The waitress arrived with glasses of water and plates for the dumplings. Taurique sipped his drink.

"Tell me about your kids," he said, regaining his composure.

"Well, Nicole's eight and Ronnie's six. They're both beautiful and they're both smart and they've brought me more joy than I could have imagined."

"That's great, Chaney." He smiled. "So they're both in school now."

"Yes."

"You must have a lot of time on your hands. What do you do?"

Chaney forced a smile. "Relax," she replied, gazing at her hands.

"That's it?" Taurique shook his head. "Man, what a life. Nothing to do all day but . . . relax."

Chaney looked up. "I didn't say that was all I did," she retorted. "I have to make breakfast for the kids, take them to school, bring them home, help them with homework, spend time with them just having fun, make dinner, keep the house clean . . ."

"You're a housewife. Or is it domestic engineer?"

"Whatever." She was embarrassed—why? She had never been embarrassed about devoting her life to her children before. Of course, she'd never felt she was missing something before. She hoped he didn't keep asking about what she was doing with her time, because she wanted him to think her life was perfect, and it didn't feel that way right now. Damn him for catching me at a low point, she thought, and bringing up the main problem. Then again, he could always see right through me . . .

"You mean, you don't go to the gym?" Taurique continued. "It sure looks that way. Not that you haven't always had a great body naturally, or anything, but two kids? That's amazing."

Chaney smiled and tried not to be too flattered. It's just the usual Taurique charm thing, don't pay attention, she thought . . .

"Okay, I also work out, but at home, not at the gym."

"Figures."

"Why?"

"More private. A gym isn't really you."

"Something wrong with that?"

"Look, who am I to criticize anything that keeps you looking that good?" He grinned disarmingly, and Chaney had to smile back. I have to look away now, she realized, I'm looking into his eyes, and he might get the wrong idea, or something . . .

Mercifully, just then the tea and the dumplings arrived. Taurique took a dumpling, placed one on Chaney's plate, and poured both of them tea.

"Are you happy?" he asked nonchalantly.

Chaney was momentarily taken aback.

"Yes," she replied.

"You don't have to say that, you know."

"I live in a beautiful house with two very special kids, and my husband is gorgeous and successful and loves me to death. Shouldn't I be happy?" I sound defensive, she thought, and it made her grin.

Taurique smiled slightly, looking away.

"Nah," he said. "Just kidding." He picked up his chopsticks, looked at them, then looked at Chaney, who couldn't help but laugh, his brow furrowed as if he were pondering a deep problem. He put down the chopsticks, picked up his fork, and cut his dumpling in half.

"Eat," he urged her, and she obeyed him.

"What about you?" she asked. "Do you have any children?"

Taurique shook his head. "None I know about, anyway," he said with a wicked grin.

"You'll never change."

"Sure won't," he remarked. "Why mess with perfection?"

Chaney smiled. "Your marriage been over long?"

"Two years. It lasted three."

"What happened? If you don't mind."

He looked down. "I screwed it up," he said softly. He looked embarrassed.

"What did you do?"

"Acted like the immature jackass I keep trying to bury."

"Meaning?"

"I cheated."

"You *cheated?*" Chaney rolled her eyes.

"I'm not proud of it, or anything," he protested, putting another dumpling in his mouth. "I had lots of chances before it happened, believe me. It was one time, and things had been pretty bad for a while."

"Did you ever have a relationship where you didn't cheat?" Chaney asked, disgusted.

Taurique gazed at her steadily. "Yes," he said.

"Who was she?"

"You."

Chaney stared coldly. "Maybe my memory is a little messed up. I think you *did* cheat on me. And I don't mean in California. I admit we weren't really together then."

"Once."

"That doesn't count, though, because it rounds off to zero, right?"

Taurique laughed. "No. What I mean is, I always cared about you. I really felt bad about it. Besides, I was a baby—I mean, I was seventeen, I was crazy about you, my friends kept telling me I was too young to be so serious—except Perry, of course. Anyway, I was at a house party. I was a little high, but that's no excuse. This absolutely gorgeous older woman—I mean, at the time she seemed so mature, she was at least twenty-five—was coming on to me all night long. I should have said no, but I didn't." He took a bite of another dumpling. "Young and foolish. And ordinarily I would have just kept going, I wouldn't have told my girlfriend about it, but I felt so guilty that time." He looked into her eyes. "I guess it was because I was very much in love with you, Chaney."

His gaze made her uncomfortable. "Perry tells me you're seeing someone," she said.

"He's right. It's been—oh, about three months."

"Have you cheated on her?"

Taurique shrugged. "How can you cheat when there's no commitment?" he asked.

Chaney shook her head. "Have you heard about AIDS?" she asked pointedly.

"Of course. I'm careful; you should know that." He sipped his tea. "Besides, I'm not nearly so promiscuous as you seem to think. There was you, there was Christine, there was my ex, and now there's Charmaine. Plus, no more than twenty other women before and after."

"And in between," Chaney interrupted.

Taurique smiled. "You really don't like me anymore, do you?" he asked.

"I'm trying to decide," she responded, narrowing her eyes.

"That's fair." He shook his head. "I really screwed up with you, didn't I? You know what, Chaney? You may never believe this, but I'm sorry. I was a messed-up kid when we were together, but as mixed up as I was, I knew from the day I met you that you were something special, and it scared the hell out of me, because I knew I didn't deserve someone like you."

"Taurique . . ." His voice was wistful, and she felt awful.

"It's true." He took a deep breath, then picked up another dumpling. "These are delicious, and you've only had one," he said, trying to sound conversational. "Eat, or I'll have all of them."

"Okay." Chaney took another, trying to think of something to say.

"You know what my problem is?" he went on after a while, gazing at her. "I look for a lot of things in a woman. I really want to meet a woman who'll be all those things to me, but it's hard—I mean, the best ones are already married." He glanced at her with a little smile, and she grinned back, blushing. "So I meet one who has most of it, then I find myself drawn to someone else who has the missing piece of the puzzle. It's immature, I know, but I can't be completely committed to someone who doesn't satisfy me. Elaine—that's my ex—was my attempt to compromise on some things, but after two years I got tired, and I guess I didn't love her enough, deep down, to keep working on the problems." He sipped more tea. "You were my longest real commitment. And I was so committed, Chaney, in spite of what I did." His voice had gotten softer, and it was tinged with enough regret to make Chaney feel uncomfortable. But why am I feeling bad about this? she asked herself. I didn't do anything to *him*.

"But I wasn't enough, either," she shot back, "or you wouldn't have taken up with blondie at UCLA."

Taurique's face hardened. "Her name is Christine," he said. "Excuse me."

"Look, obviously there's no point in discussing that relationship with you."

"I'm curious, though."

"Some other time, when you can get that sarcastic tone out of your voice and I won't feel like I'm on trial, okay?" He glanced around. "Where the hell is that food?" he demanded.

Chaney finished her dumpling, feeling that she should apologize without feeling bad to her core about her attitude. The waitress came with the meals, clearing away the empty plates.

"I'm sorry, Taurique," Chaney said, with as much sincerity as she could muster, thinking of an approach she could pull off.

"Really?" he asked her, unconvinced.

"This has been really pleasant. I didn't mean to spoil it." That I meant, she thought.

Taurique looked down. "You didn't," he finally said, then he focused on her face and smiled a bit. She smiled back, and then picked up her fork and began to eat.

"Tell me about Lawrence," he said, after a while.

"Lawrence?"

"Your husband. You know, nine years of marriage? Oh— what did he give you for your anniversary?"

"A Valentino suit and matching shoes."

"Wow."

"It fits, too. He can always tell without me being there what's going to fit me perfectly." He's had *lots* of practice picking out clothes without me there, she thought.

"Even the shoes?"

"I'm a perfect size eight. I don't usually have trouble with shoes, as long as they're made by the right manufacturer."

"That's right, I remember now. Anyway, what else about him?"

"He's very talented."

"Of course."

"He loves me very much."

"Of course."

"He's sweet and kind and he loves taking care of me."

"Of course."

"What's with this 'of course' stuff? What does that mean?"

Taurique swallowed. "Any man who likes to take care of a woman would *love* taking care of you. You make a man feel like he's needed, like you're depending on him."

"Is that good or bad?"

Taurique shrugged. "You decide," he said. "Go on."

Chaney scrutinized him, chewing. "That's all," she said.

"Really? No bad points?"

"None."

"Amazing. I must meet this man."

"Maybe." Chaney concentrated on her meal.

"What did I say?" Taurique asked, after a while.

"Nothing."

"Then why the silence?"

"This food is very good."

"Oh."

He sighed. Let him feel frustrated, Chaney thought. She didn't feel like having her life analyzed, she didn't feel like having her husband analyzed, and she didn't feel like having her marriage analyzed, not by anyone, and especially not by Taurique Williams. The whole encounter was beginning to feel like an interrogation, even if it was a subtle one. And what was the point, anyway? Was he hoping that everything hadn't quite turned out for her without him, just as things hadn't quite turned out for him without her? Too bad, she thought, the breakup wasn't *my* idea. Then again, maybe he did me a favor.

I'm married to a wonderful man, and he's still looking for Miss Perfect, and he'll never find her. I feel a little sorry for him.

She glanced at him—he was making short work of his meal.

"Are you happy?" she found herself asking him.

Taurique swallowed. "I'm happier than I've been, Chaney," he replied, gazing at her. "You may not believe this, but I've come a long way, and it wasn't an easy trip. You knew me when I was still confused. I'm not saying I've got everything figured out, or anything, but I'm a whole lot more together than I was. You know the deal—I spent a lot of time pretending to be a player, but it was all an act. As I told you, I haven't been with nearly as many women as you think."

She believed most of it, but she still found this last statement hard to accept.

"So why the nickname 'Technique'?" she asked skeptically.

He smiled enigmatically, shrugging. "You'd have to ask the person who came up with it," he replied.

Actually, Chaney thought, I know the answer to that one from personal experience. She looked away—she had caught herself falling under the spell of his eyes, remembering how soft his unusually long lashes used to feel brushing against her skin . . .

"Anyway," he went on, "I spent a lot of time pretending I thought I was all that when deep down I felt like a nobody. I just knew I wasn't going to amount to anything, like my sister Yvonne or my father the drunk or my brothers, who were on welfare or hustling when they weren't in jail." He looked up with a sad smile. "I didn't end up like them, but I screwed up in a lot of other ways."

Chaney swallowed hard, remembering how reluctant he'd been to introduce her to his family, his complete humiliation the first time she'd seen his father intoxicated, the times he'd literally cried on her shoulder because of something that had happened at home. His revelations were making her start to feel close to him again, and she wished he would stop.

"After I got divorced, I decided to figure out what my problem was, why I was always messing up my relationships. You know what I found out?"

Chaney shook her head, hesitantly allowing herself to gaze into his eyes again and finding that she couldn't look away.

"I'm a lot like other children of alcoholics," he said. "I have a lot of problems, and I'm still working on some of them. But you know what? I have to thank you for putting up with me when we were together."

"Taurique . . ." She felt warm all over now.

"Really," he continued, smiling. "You made me want to try to do better. If it wasn't for you, I don't know who I'd be right now. And you know what else? I have to thank Perry for introducing us, because he knew an awful lot about me, but he believed in me anyway."

Chaney was so touched she was on the verge of crying . . . no. No inappropriate tears this time. She blinked furiously and took a deep breath.

"I'm glad I helped you somehow," she managed.

"I owe you," he replied softly, taking her hand and squeezing it for a moment.

The rest of the meal went by in silence, more or less. The waitress cleared the dishes and brought the bill and two fortune cookies.

"Yours first," Taurique urged, picking up a cookie.

"You're such a kid," Chaney said, smiling and breaking hers open. She unfolded the paper inside and read, "Good friends are like rare jewels."

Taurique grinned. "That's nice," he said. "Dull, but nice. Okay . . ." He broke his cookie in two and extracted the paper. "Greatest happiness comes from helping others." He reached into his wallet, pulling out money for the bill and the tip. He left it on the table and stood up. "I think I'll go help some people part with their money. That always makes me happy."

Chaney laughed and rose, following him out of the restaurant. "Thanks for lunch," she said sincerely.

"No problem," Taurique replied.

They walked to Chaney's car without saying much. She thanked him again and was about to get in when he stopped her.

"Here," he said, pressing a piece of paper into her hand.

"What's this?" she asked.

"My number. If you ever get really bored and just want to talk, or if you want to have lunch again, give me a call."

"Maybe when Lawrence gets back, the three of us and Charmaine can go somewhere."

"I'd like that. When's he back?"

"About six more weeks."

"Six weeks!" Taurique whistled. "That's a long time."

"Well, he's singing in Italy and France and doing a recording for Philips. He's also shooting a commercial—they really love him over there."

"You must be proud of him."

"I am." She smiled. "He's doing very well."

"I'm glad you're so happy, Chaney," said Taurique, putting his hand on her shoulder and gazing into her eyes. "I mean that."

"Thank you."

"Call me sometime, okay?"

"Okay." He released her, and she opened her car door and climbed in, watching him walk away. Maybe Perry was right, she thought; maybe we can be friends now. She had suggested him getting together with Lawrence just to see how he'd react, and he'd passed that test with flying colors. Maybe it was safe to let him back into her life. And it felt great, better than she'd expected, to talk to him again.

She put her key in the ignition and found herself wondering who this Charmaine was. Charmaine the undemanding—maybe she was perfect for Taurique. He surprised her. She'd expected him to have settled down by now, or at least committed to somebody. She wondered if his failed marriage had left him gun-shy, as afraid of love as he'd been all those years ago.

When Chaney had met Taurique, he was almost 17, but his nickname was already "Technique." Perry later told Chaney he was really reluctant to introduce his pretty-boy friend to his little sister, but Taurique begged him so much that he did anyway, after threatening to break every bone in his friend's body if he messed things up.

Twenty women outside of his "committed" relationships? Somehow the number seemed a bit small. Maybe "Technique" had gotten his nickname by being a fast learner. Or maybe it was because he was a perfectionist who made love to each woman until he knew exactly how to satisfy her. One thing about Taurique—he was very observant. And when he wasn't sure, he asked. For a split second, Chaney wondered what he would be like now, after all those years of practice . . . but it doesn't matter, she thought, because Lawrence is a great lover, no need even to think about it, and he's my husband and I made a promise to him in front of a lot of people, who might not know the difference, and God, who knows *everything*.

You weren't thinking about what it would be like to make love to Taurique again, she told herself, pulling out into the street. She didn't even know what made her think about his "Technique" days again, but she felt guilty about it, because Lawrence deserved better. Next time he calls, she thought, I'll tell him all about having lunch with Taurique, so I can't even *look* guilty, much less feel that way. She smiled and wished she could call Lawrence right that second and tell him she loved him.

The first time Lawrence and Chaney went out together, the wind was howling. It was one of those late-December days when the temperature was misleading—the humidity was very high, and there was no room for vanity—the best that could be hoped for was to survive without getting frostbite.

Lawrence arrived wearing one of those furry hats with ear-flaps that Chaney had always associated with hunting and trapping, or possibly ice fishing. He came inside, closing the door behind him. He glanced at her.

"What?" he asked, in a mock challenging tone.

"Nothing." Chaney looked down.

"You were going to laugh, right? Okay, laugh."

"I wasn't." She was giggling now.

"You're not laughing, is that what you're telling me?"

She looked up at him and lost it.

"Go ahead," Lawrence went on. "Here, let me help you . . ."

He started tickling her. Chaney shrieked, and he stopped.

"Shhh!" he said, putting a finger to his lips, and she focused on his mouth, really focused on it, for the first time. She stared for a moment, then looked away.

"Chaney, is that you?"

"Yes," she yelled back.

"Your dad?" Lawrence asked, looking a bit nervous.

"My brother Zac. In two seconds, you'll meet him," and she had barely finished speaking when he appeared.

"What's happening? Who's this?" Zac said, looking Lawrence up and down, but not sounding particularly unfriendly.

"Lawrence Rivers." Lawrence extended his hand.

"Zac Davis."

"I'm sorry. I was tickling your sister and she screamed."

He looked very serious, then he slowly smiled, glancing at Chaney. He's beautiful, she thought. Even in that stupid hat.

"Oh, is *that* all?" said Zac. "I should have recognized that scream."

"Yeah, my brother's very mean to me," said Chaney with mock petulance.

"You gotta keep these kids in line," Zac said.

"I bet you do," Lawrence agreed, glancing at Chaney.

"Well, *I* keep her in line, anyway." He was nonchalant, but he held Lawrence's eyes for a moment. "You guys going out in this weather?"

"That was the plan. It's pretty damn cold out there, though."

"I figured there had to be a reason for that hat," Chaney said, and she started laughing again.

"You see how she got herself in trouble?" Lawrence responded. "Do you mind?" He glanced at Zac, then caught Chaney as she started to run and tickled her again. She broke free and grabbed a cushion off the couch.

"One more step . . ." she warned.

"And?"

"And—Zac will kick your butt. Right, Zac?"

"I don't think so," said Zac. "I'll see you two later." He turned to go.

"Zac!" Chaney exclaimed.

"Nice meeting you, Rivers." He left the room.

"Nice guy," Lawrence remarked.

"He can be," she said, holding tightly to the cushion.

"You can put down your weapon. See? I'm unarmed." He held up his hands.

He sounded sincere. Taurique would have waited until she'd put down the cushion, then grabbed her. But that was T. This was somebody new. She dropped the cushion.

Lawrence took off his hat. "Hi," he said.

"Hi," she said, smiling.

"I was thinking of dinner, or a movie, or whatever. Or you could come over to my house and watch videos, and I could pop some popcorn, and you could meet my family. Or maybe I should save that one."

He must have a normal family, she was thinking. It might be nice to go out with someone with a normal family for a change.

"What do you want to do?" she asked.

"It's your night, baby. Your wish is my command." He bowed.

Chaney considered. "Dinner?" she suggested.

"If you want."

"Or we don't have to, if you're not hungry."

He smiled again. "You're hungry?"

She nodded.

"You are really, really pretty, you know that?" he said, still smiling. "Don't blush—my God, you are so cute. I can't believe there are girls like you left in Brooklyn."

"Girls like what?"

"Like you. Shy. Sweet. And beautiful."

She was completely embarrassed.

"I'm sorry, Chaney. I'm not trying to make you uncomfortable. Look, I take it back. I mean, you came up to me first, that's not shy. You just dissed me about my hat. That's not sweet. I don't think I can do anything about taking back the last one, but I'll try not to stare."

She smiled.

"So we're going to dinner, then?" Lawrence asked.

"Yes."

"Good. What kind of food do you like?"

"Something hot."

He laughed. "I'm with you on that one."

"I don't know. Whatever you want."

"Italian?"

"Okay."

"You're easy to please."

"I guess so."

"I know so. You're sure no guy's gonna come looking for me if I take you out?"

"Yes." She looked down.

"What did I say?" he asked.

"Nothing."

"You *don't* have a boyfriend, right? You told me that, didn't you?"

"Yes."

"Then what? You just broke up with somebody?"

She hesitated. She really didn't want to talk about it. "Kind of," she replied.

"Talk to me, Chaney. What's the matter?"

"Nothing."

He sighed. "I know you don't know me very well. I understand why you don't want to talk to me yet. I hope you learn to trust me, though."

She looked at him, not knowing what to say. He seemed a little bit hurt. He smiled, though.

"You should put on your coat if we're going," he said.

"We're going."

"Great." He put his hat back on. "And I bet once you get out there, you won't find what I'm wearing so funny."

She smiled.

"I can see why you'd be upset," Lawrence was saying, finishing his dessert.

"I've kind of accepted it," Chaney said quietly.

"Are you sure?"

She nodded, but couldn't look at him just then.

"If you say so."

There was a silence.

"What about you?" Chaney asked suddenly.

"What *about* me?"

"Have you ever been in love?"

He smiled a bit, that barest hint of a smile that Chaney always found irresistibly sexy.

"No," he said.

"You've never had a serious relationship?"

"Well, I have, in a way, but I don't really think I've ever been in *love,* or anything."

"Oh."

"How does it feel?"

Chaney grinned. "I don't know," she replied, blushing.

"I mean, is it all that music-in-the-air and floating-off-the-ground stuff?"

She thought. "Some of it," she said, and something in the sincerity of his curiosity made her feel closer to him, somehow.

"It was the best of times, it was the worst of times," Lawrence said.

She smiled. "What's that from? I've heard it before."

"*A Tale of Two Cities*. Dickens."

"Oh." An embarrassed flush crossed her face. "I remember."

"Anyway, is it like that?"

"It can be."

"I wish I knew. Do you think I'll ever really know what it's like?"

"I'm sure you will," she said, remembering . . .

"I hope so." He smiled at her, then glanced at his watch.

I can't, she was thinking. I can't do this, I can't pretend there's no Taurique. Even though he never had a problem forgetting about me . . .

I have to give this guy a chance. T. is gone. He doesn't love me anymore. He doesn't love me anymore. He doesn't . . .

"Chaney?"

"Yes?"

"You were thinking about him, that guy?"

She hesitated.

"You can tell me the truth. Look, I'm 20 years old, I've been involved before. I know it's not easy to end relationships and start new ones, even if you're not really in love. So don't worry, I'm in no hurry to have a girlfriend, or anything. I think you're special, but that doesn't mean you have to feel the same way about me, or anything."

"I like you, Lawrence."

He smiled. "I'm glad."

"It's just . . ."

He put a finger to his lips. "I understand," he said. "We can be friends, if you want. This guy was your first love; I can't expect to compete with that. Not yet, anyway." He glanced at her slyly.

"You get what you want usually, don't you?" Chaney remarked.

"Sometimes." He looked down.

"I bet you're your parents' pride and joy."

He started playing with his fork, twirling it between his fingers. He smiled enigmatically.

"In a way," he said. "They love to hear me sing."

"But . . ."

"But nothing."

"Oh."

She didn't find out until two months later that his father didn't really want him to be a singer, but that after hearing the praise his son was getting, he became Lawrence's biggest fan, pushing him relentlessly to enter competitions and make connections.

"I love to hear you sing, too," Chaney said.

"Yeah?"

"I told you how good you are."

"I'm good at other things, too—look at you. Don't be embarrassed, I'm just making noise."

Chaney wished she didn't blush so easily sometimes—and for what, especially this time? she thought. It's not like I can't hold my own in the bedroom.

"So you sing other things?" she asked, running her fingers through her hair and smiling to herself as she pictured, for a moment, the possibilities.

"Yes."

"I mean, besides classical music."

"Yes." He observed her, amused. "You don't believe me, do you?"

"Sure I do." She couldn't imagine it sounding good, though. She couldn't imagine it sounding anything but ridiculous.

"Distant lover . . ." he began, in full voice. Chaney looked around. People were staring. She wished she could leave, but to get up would look too conspicuous.

"Heaven knows that I long for you . . ." Lawrence narrowed his eyes as he sang this, and Chaney looked away, embarrassed. Suddenly, she thought about the words, and Taurique was back—just for a moment, because Lawrence's voice gave her chills. He sounded completely different, not even slightly op-

eratic. He stopped. A smattering of applause broke out around the restaurant. He was smiling—actually, he was glowing. It was the first time Chaney realized how much of a high he got from performing.

"I'm sorry," he said. "I shouldn't have done that. You're so *shy!*"

"You're very good," Chaney said sincerely.

"Thank you. You liked that better than that other stuff, huh?"

"Well . . ."

"I know. People think classical music is boring, but it's not. It can take you to places you never knew existed, just like Marvin Gaye. I'll show you."

The waitress came with the check.

"Back into the cold, cruel world," said Lawrence.

"Do we have to?"

"Nah, we can sleep out in the kitchen until spring."

Chaney smiled.

"Did you have a good time?" Lawrence asked.

"Yes."

"I'm glad." He looked relieved.

"You're a lot of fun."

"Really?"

"Yes."

"So—we can go out again, then?"

"Yes." Her answer came out without hesitation, and she smiled again.

"Thank God!" He stood up and glanced at his watch. "We missed the movie," he announced.

"Another time."

"Another time." Chaney rose and got ready to go back outside. She caught Lawrence looking at her.

"What?"

He grinned. "Nothing."

"That's not fair. You're looking at me funny—what?"

"You really want to know?"

"Yes." She was beginning to wonder if there was food on

her face. She began to subtly brush her fingers against the skin around her mouth.

"No, not that. I was thinking how much I'd like to see you taking off layers instead of putting them on. There, I told you."

She smiled. Me, too, she thought, and somehow, she wasn't embarrassed this time.

Lawrence put the money on the table and began to walk, gesturing with his head for Chaney to follow, then putting an arm around her when she caught up to him. She flinched.

"I'm sorry," he said, pulling away.

"It's okay."

"Just trying to keep warm," he said, and then he smiled.

"Right."

He opened the door and a gust of frigid air nearly moved them back a step. "Told you," he said, and they smiled at each other and stepped out into the night.

The phone was ringing and Nicole jumped up to answer it.

"It's Mrs. Watson," she announced, sitting back down and picking up her fork again.

Chaney sighed and rose to her feet.

"Hi, Pam," she said.

"Hi, Chaney. How've you been?"

"Oh, I can't complain."

"Good. I haven't been able to catch up with you in a while, I just wanted to check up on you."

"I'm fine, really."

"How's your husband?"

"He's fine."

"He's not here, is he?"

"No, he's in Italy."

"Really? Carl flew over to London today. Is Lawrence performing there soon?"

"No. Not this trip."

"That's too bad. You know Carl's a big fan of Lawrence's."

Yes, you say that every call, Chaney thought, bored.

"Well, Lawrence is a big fan of Carl's," she said without thinking, and Pam laughed.

"That's funny."

"No, really. Not everyone can fly a jumbo jet, Pam."

"I guess you're right." Pam laughed again. "Lawrence Rivers, a fan of my husband's."

Chaney winked at Ronnie, who was pretending to fall asleep. I'm really obvious, she thought.

"Pam, I appreciate your call, but you know what? I just sat down to eat dinner. Maybe I can call you some other time?"

"Oh . . . I'm sorry. Of course."

"Goodnight, Pam. Say hi to Carl for me, okay? And Nicole says hi to Tracey."

"Nicki says hi, Trace," Pam was saying, and in the background a little girl's voice screamed, "Hi, Nicole!"

"Okay, then, Pam, take care," said Chaney.

" 'Bye." Chaney hung up.

"Mommy?" Ronnie was asking, shoving a forkful of lasagna into his mouth.

"Yes, honey?"

"Do you like Mrs. Watson?"

"Don't talk with your mouth full, honey. Yes, of course I do."

"Oh."

"Mommy," Nicole said, "who is your friend?"

"Mrs. Watson."

"You had lunch with Mrs. Watson?"

"You're nosy, aren't you?"

"You had fun, though," Ronnie chimed in.

Chaney sat down. "Why do you say that?"

"Because you're in a good mood today."

"Are you saying I'm grouchy other days?" Chaney demanded, then she had to smile. "See, I'm grouchy every day," she said, picking up her fork.

"That's okay, I miss Daddy, too," said Nicole, and Chaney stopped in midair.

"He'll be back soon," she managed finally, wondering why this trip was still especially hard despite his surprise visit and resolving to put up a better front.

I need to talk to Perry, she decided. I *need* to talk to Lawrence—but I know who can put me in a good mood again . . .

Chaney began to eat faster. Perry. She was going to call Perry as soon as the kids were in bed, and they were going to talk about nothing special for at least an hour.

Six

October 22

Taurique had two brothers and two sisters, all older than he was. He didn't like to talk about his brothers—Chaney always assumed they didn't get along, or that the age difference was such that they couldn't relate, or something. They'd been together for over a year before Taurique had told her the truth—that one was in jail and the other couldn't hold a job because of his drug problem, and Taurique was ashamed to admit he was related to them. His sisters were twins, though not identical. This was a blessing, because Yvonne and Yvette were very different, and at least Yvette could avoid being blamed for the activities of her sister.

Yvonne was bad. Taurique was a bit wild, but Yvonne was just plain bad. She hung around with every lowlife on the block, and whatever experience Taurique had had with drugs she'd gotten rolling. When he was about ten, she'd thought it was funny to smoke reefer and blow it in his face. She was sixteen then and had already had two abortions. Taurique's mother suspected that Yvonne was the one who'd caused Taurique's father to drink so much. Taurique always thought his dad drank so much because he was an alcoholic, and that Yvonne was bad for the same reason.

Chaney always got along with Yvonne, though. She found her fascinating. She had a personality vaguely like that of

Chaney's first real best friend, Gloria Gordon, a little girl who lived down the street and took off all her clothes in the middle of school. That was the end of the friendship. After that, Chaney's father decided Gloria was an unhealthy influence on his six-year-old daughter and they were forbidden to associate. Chaney missed her. At Gloria's place, she could play cops and robbers, and Gloria taught her how to swear, a skill Chaney never used much (except sometimes in bed with Taurique), and Gloria was rough and tough and did absolutely everything Chaney's father and brothers tried to drum out of her. After the Gloria incident, Chaney's father was very afraid of letting her come under the influence of the neighborhood women. She had no relatives in New York—her aunts and uncles were either in Jamaica or in Canada. But at Gloria's house, there was always lots of family around, and Mrs. Gordon sat with her legs apart, if she felt like it, and Chaney and Gloria made lots of noise. The whole relationship lasted only a little while; not long after Gloria's exhibitionistic display, she moved.

Chaney's father was so afraid she would turn out somehow less than feminine because she didn't have a mother that he went overboard. Chaney's room was ultrapink, her clothes were ultrafrilly, and she wasn't allowed to play any sports except at school, not until the miraculous intervention of her phys ed teacher.

The only extracurricular activity Chaney was allowed in elementary school was studying the piano. She was made to continue lessons for two years before Perry convinced her father that she was not going to come around and start enjoying it. She was glad Perry had stepped in; her father never listened to anyone much, especially not her, but Perry could influence him most of the time, because he not only got excellent grades, he spoke his mind. Zac spoke his mind, but he was an average student. Chaney and Jimmy were excellent students, but neither was forceful enough to command Mr. Davis's respect, and Chaney had the additional handicap of being female.

Outsiders had even less influence on Chaney's father than

she did, with one exception—Ms. Gardner. She was Chaney's high school phys ed teacher, and the coach of the girls' volleyball, track, basketball, and soccer teams. She was also the object of many a pubescent fantasy: she was barely out of college, five-ten, and looked like the model Tyra Banks. She was legendary not only for her looks, but for the fact that she wouldn't take any crap from anybody, from the principal on down. During her first week on the job, she embarrassed a senior four inches taller and sixty pounds heavier than she was by demonstrating her command of jujitsu in the hallway after he'd grabbed her behind. After that, no one tried her. In fact, everybody was in awe of her, and she knew it, strolling the hallways with a quiet self-confidence that verged on, but never quite crossed over into, arrogance.

Ms. Gardner called Mr. Davis into her office early in the fall of Chaney's sophomore year. Did he realize how gifted his daughter was? Yes, he knew how intelligent she was; her grades demonstrated that fact. No, athletically. Chaney was a natural athlete. Mr. Davis shifted in his seat, and Chaney kept staring at her hands. He'd never let her play. *Never.*

"I want her on the volleyball team," said Ms. Gardner. "Actually, I want her on the basketball team and the track team, too—but she's informed me that you don't like her participating in sports any more than is required, so I'm picking just one. I'm not greedy."

Ms. Gardner waited, gazing steadily at Chaney's father. Chaney waited, praying he wouldn't embarrass her with his standard speech—there are too many women in this world, he would say, and not enough ladies. My little girl is going to be a lady, and if you don't like that, fine.

There was a silence. Finally, Chaney got up enough nerve to look at her father. When she did, her eyes widened. He was gazing at Ms. Gardner with a goofy grin on his face.

"Ms. Gardner . . ."

"Call me Tonya."

Chaney looked at her suddenly, and Ms. Gardner shot her

a little grin. She's playing him like a violin, thought Chaney, and despite the fact that it was her father who was being made to look foolish, she couldn't help but be impressed. I wish I could do that. Why can't I do that? Chaney was painfully aware of how attractive she was, but somehow, using lust as a weapon was beyond her. She knew boys would do things for her, like letting her cut into line, or buying her lunch, or helping her carry things without her asking for assistance, or just being nice for no particular reason. However, she had no grasp of truly controlling people, and since it was wrong anyway, she was never going to learn.

Still, it was fun to watch this woman at work, especially since she wasn't really *doing* anything. Her sex appeal was so effortless, all she had to do was smile, tilt her head a certain way, look at Mr. Davis directly, and ask him to call her by her first name.

"T-Tonya," said Mr. Davis—he was actually flustered. Chaney had never seen him like this in her life. "I have some reservations," he finished.

"I promise her grades won't suffer, Mr. Davis." Ms. Gardner's voice was dripping with honey. "If they do, I'll cut her."

"Oh, I know her grades won't suffer," Mr. Davis said quickly. "That's not the problem."

Tonya Gardner shook her head gently, her eyes never wavering for an instant. "I don't understand," she said, her forehead creasing ever so slightly.

"Well . . ." Mr. Davis hesitated.

Not the speech, Chaney prayed. *Anything* but the speech.

"You know my daughter has no mother."

She stared at her father in amazement, then back at Ms. Gardner, who was sitting on the edge of her desk, nodding sympathetically. If only there was a big rock somewhere, Chaney thought, I'd be under it in a second . . .

"I'm doing the best I can, Ms.—Tonya, but . . . I worry sometimes. She has three brothers, and no aunts or anything around here. I'm just—I'm trying to teach her how to be a lady, and . . ."

Ms. Gardner smiled warmly. "I see," she said. "You watch the way some athletic girls walk and it's kind of—masculine, and you don't want your daughter to be like that." She nodded, clasping her hands. "You have a difficult job, Mr. Davis, but based on what I've seen, you're doing very well with Chaney."

Mr. Davis tried not to grin. This is *too* funny, Chaney thought, disgusted that her father was so easily wrapped around this woman's fingers, and annoyed at her teacher for being so unabashedly manipulative, even though Chaney hoped Ms. Gardner would be successful.

"I can only say," Ms. Gardner went on, "that I've been an athlete all my life, and I don't think you have to choose between being involved in sports and being ladylike. Of course, it's your decision, Mr. Davis."

Tonya smiled again. Please, Lord, Chaney thought, let this be over before I lose all respect for these people.

"Well," said Mr. Davis, with a slightly glazed expression, "I suppose I could let her try it."

Ms. Gardner stood. "I'm sure you won't regret this," she said, taking his right hand and clasping it in both of hers. She turned to Chaney. "I'll see you at practice," she said, searching her face for approval or at least understanding.

"Let's go, Dad," Chaney said, taking his arm. He was standing, holding Ms. Gardner's hands as if hypnotized. As Chaney dragged him away, she found herself marveling at the woman's power and wishing, for a moment, that she had the personality to pull off that kind of display. She never felt completely comfortable around Ms. Gardner after that day, but she couldn't help but be intrigued by her. She also couldn't help but be more rebellious, internally, against her father and his rules.

Sometimes she thought it was her father who caused her to cry so much, because her tears were often the result of frustration, not sadness, and under his rule she was very often frustrated. Still, she found it hard to resent him, especially after she'd had children of her own, because he always made it clear that he loved her and was trying to protect her from living the kind of life that someone like Taurique's sister Yvonne had chosen. And as interesting as Chaney found Yvonne, she certainly wouldn't have traded places with her, not really.

Yvonne liked to tease Chaney. She called her Cinderella, because she said Chaney was like a little white princess. This wasn't very nice, but she made up for it by telling Chaney all about her sexual experiences, and Chaney found the stories incredibly enticing. This made her feel guilty, because she tried to imagine doing to Taurique all the things his sister had described. She couldn't *quite* imagine it; she had never seen a nude man. She didn't actually spend that much time alone with Yvonne, or she'd have at least seen pictures or videos—Yvonne was an enthusiastic collector of soft-core pornography. She said it gave her inspiration, since it was often more creative than the stuff some of her boyfriends came up with.

Chaney was innocent and she wasn't. She knew she'd never last until marriage; she found men just too exciting. So she set one standard: that she and the guy she slept with would have to love each other. She heard some of the stuff her brothers said about girls, and she was determined not to be somebody's conquest. Still, as much as she was looking forward to sex, she was afraid. What terrified her most was taking off her clothes in front of someone. Taking off her underwear. Being touched by someone, touched down there, between her legs. She had received so many lectures about respectable and unrespectable girls that she was afraid that if she did it once, everyone would look down on her. But how would they know? That's why he would have to love her, love her completely—so he wouldn't tell. So he wouldn't stop talking to her afterward.

It was so dirty. Which was why she didn't dare, because if any of her brothers found out . . . or worse, if her father found out . . . he would cry. She knew this because he'd told her so. When she was thirteen, he told her about sex. Actually, he didn't tell her anything; he told her a man and a woman were very different, and . . . well, did she have any questions? She was afraid to speak. So he said, don't listen to what men try to tell you. Until a girl is married, a man sleeps with her only to satisfy his own sinful desires. And there's plenty of time for you to think about marriage, so until then, just don't give in.

She summoned up her courage and asked him, what would you do if you found out . . . She couldn't finish the sentence. He thought about it, then he thought some more, and he said, I think I would cry. That was the worst. She couldn't imagine her father crying. From then on, she felt deeply guilty whenever she even felt attracted to a boy. The problem was that she was constantly aware of them, and they of her, and they were always at the house, and she talked to them, and became friends with them, and was tempted . . .

But she was too afraid of the consequences. She was never allowed to go anywhere with a boy anyway, so the whole thing was kind of hypothetical.

At 15, she asked permission. It was Perry's idea. He said, you and Rico have to get this out in the open, there's nothing wrong with you having a boyfriend. He didn't try anything, did he? No, he really hadn't. They were at school one time, and he asked her if could walk her home, and halfway there, he stopped walking and asked her if he could kiss her. She was embarrassed. She wasn't sure she'd know what to do.

"No—I don't know," she said, staring at the ground.

"Chaney," Taurique said after a while, in the gentlest of voices, and he held her hand, waiting. She finally looked at him again.

"Have you ever kissed a guy before?"

She hesitated, then shook her head. She was about to look away, but there was something so soft in his eyes that she didn't have to; there was no need.

"There's nothing wrong with that," Taurique said, with a little smile, and she relaxed. He started to walk again, still holding her hand. "Are you in a hurry to get home?"

"Not really." Her father wouldn't be in for a few hours, and she didn't have to start dinner right away.

"Do you want to sit in the park?"

"Okay."

They walked past the guard. Chaney glanced at the suggested contribution sign, but Taurique didn't slow down and didn't seem to care about that, so she followed along.

They walked around the huge lawn just past the gates. Chaney had always imagined having a wedding there, or something. They looked at the Japanese garden, they looked at the herbs, the rock garden, and the roses, which were still colorful enough to be stunning, even though they were obviously past their prime.

Taurique found a bench. "Let's sit down," he suggested.

"Okay."

They sat. He lifted her hand to his lips and kissed it and the inside of her wrist. She blushed, her heart racing. He gazed down the pathway, and then, after a while, at her.

"Do you trust me?" he asked.

"I guess so."

He laughed. "You *guess* so? Okay, that's fair. Let me ask you another question—do you trust me enough to let me kiss you now?"

Her eyes were very wide. She'd been waiting for this moment, but she was terrified. She nodded.

He smiled, then put his arms around her, pulling her close to him and kissing her gently on the cheek. He pulled back.

"Not so terrible, was it?" he asked.

She shook her head. She hoped that wasn't all.

"Now, you tell me," he said, leaning slowly closer to her again, "if I'm doing anything that makes you uncomfortable."

When he finished speaking, his voice was almost a whisper, and he was very close to her ear. He kissed her just below the lobe, on her neck, and she shivered involuntarily—she had never felt this good. He kissed her neck again, lower, and then her throat, and she closed her eyes. She felt like she was swimming, floating just underwater.

He finally found her lips. There's nothing to this, Chaney thought, completely relaxed, and she scarcely realized it when she felt his tongue. It was a strange sensation, but not an unpleasant one. The whole thing was very leisurely and gentle, and when he moved away from her, finally, she wasn't ready for it to be over.

"You should go home, huh?" Taurique said.

Chaney glanced at her watch, and her eyes were wide again.

"I'm gonna be late," she said, startled.

He smiled. "You're okay. *Are* you okay?"

"Yes."

"That was nice," he said.

Chaney blushed.

"Can I walk you home?"

"No, that's okay."

"I want to, Chaney."

"I do too, but . . . well . . ."

"Your dad doesn't know we're seeing each other."

It hit her: *I'm seeing somebody. And we kissed each other.* It was no longer imagination.

"How did you know?"

"Your brother told me about the situation."

"I'm not a baby, it's just, Perry's the only person at my house who seems to know that."

"Why don't you tell your dad about me? I mean, it's not like he hasn't met me or anything, I'm at the house all the time anyway."

"I should. I just don't know what he'd say."

"I want everyone to know you're my girl. I don't want it to be a big secret."

I'm his girl. He could have picked anybody, and he chose me, Chaney thought, and her heart leaped up into her throat and her insides flooded with warmth.

"Neither do I," she replied, with a smile.

"Do you want me to talk to him?"

"No. No, I'll deal with it." She wasn't sure quite what she meant by this, but the idea of her father and Taurique discussing her readiness to have a boyfriend—especially Taurique, who looked no more innocent than a nickname like "Technique" would suggest—well, sitting down with her father, just the two of them, was far less frightening.

"Okay," Taurique said. "So does that mean I can't even take you home?"

"Not yet."

"Okay." He smiled again. His smile was the sexiest thing she had ever seen, suddenly; something was happening inside her. She couldn't wait to kiss him again.

Taurique stood up. "Will I get shot at if I walk you to your block?" he asked.

Chaney laughed. "No, that should be safe."

"We'll hurry. Don't worry, I'll get you there on time."

"Okay."

So at fifteen, she'd asked permission to date, and it had been granted. She later found out that Perry had already talked to their father about it, so all she had to do was mention it. She thanked Perry for that one. Of course, he didn't know he was paving the way for her first sexual experience. Or maybe he did.

"Good morning, baby," Lawrence said, as Chaney picked up the phone. She yawned.

"Good morning, Lawrence."

"I woke you up."

"You woke me up. But that's okay. I can't think of a better way to start my day."

"I'm smiling."

"Mmm—I wish I could see you. I miss your smiles the most."

"Jump on a plane, I'll meet you at the airport in eight hours."

Chaney laughed. "Sure, I'll leave a note for Nicole and Ronnie."

"I think they could survive without you for a few days, Chaney. I think they're old enough."

"Yeah, but could I survive ten hours in an airplane?"

"Jack Daniels, baby. One or two would do it for you."

"You're a bad influence."

"Me? I couldn't be a bad influence if I tried. It's not in the Rivers blood—well, you know about the long line of outstanding citizens I came from."

"Yes, your dad gave me the speech."

"At least you only had to hear it a hundred times."

"Nothing wrong with being proud of a family that produces pillars of the African American community."

"Yeah, whatever. So you're not coming."

"I'd just get in your way."

"You know that's not true, so I guess I'm getting nowhere, so I guess I should change the subject. How are the kids?"

Chaney sat up and stretched. What would be so awful about flying to Europe, all by myself? she wondered. I can't, she thought. Maybe when the children are older, when they wouldn't feel as if I were abandoning them. I would never put them through that . . .

"Chaney?"

"Yes, baby?"

"You were thinking about it, weren't you?"

She smiled. "You read my mind. Anyway, I have no major complaints about Ronnie and Nicole."

"Minor?"

"No."

"Diminished?"

Musician humor—well, at least he didn't have to explain it anymore; she knew that in music, diminished was smaller than minor. At first, it had made her feel ignorant to listen to his telephone conversations with his Juilliard friends, and it was even worse when she and Lawrence got together with them, because they would gather around the piano and sing classical songs she had never heard of, and discuss the relative merits of Brahms and Beethoven. Even though she tended to be quiet at parties, she felt like if she had gone to the store and never come back, no one would have known the difference. It took months for Lawrence to notice how miserable she was. When he did catch on, he stopped socializing with his friends for a while, which made *him* miserable. Chaney soon felt guilty enough to decide to ask him to teach her a few musical terms, some of which she vaguely remembered from elementary school, so that they could start going to parties again, every once in a while, and having people over, even more infrequently. Which meant that even though she still rarely opened her mouth when the inevitable comparison of old opera singers came up, at least she could understand what was being discussed. Not that she *cared* that much, or anything. As much as she loved seeing Lawrence so happy, she could never quite share his passion for talking about classical music. After a while, she could understand why he loved to listen to it, and she never had a problem comprehending why the sound of his own voice gave him so much joy. But the *talking* about it . . . maybe that's why I haven't jumped on a plane to Europe, she thought. It's hard enough being surrounded by his opera friends right here in my own home.

"No," she said with a smile, "not even diminished."

"You seem much happier today. What's new?"

"Every day that goes by brings you closer to coming back."

"I'm smiling again."

"Good. How are the rehearsals going?"

"Should be a good production."

"How's Kathleen Battle?"

"We always get along."

"Hmm—not *too* well, I hope."

"Chaney, I'm surprised."

"Sometimes it's hard being married to a gorgeous man."

"I understand. Look, I can't help it if women follow me all day long. I tell them to go away, though. You know me, I get embarrassed."

Chaney smiled, picturing what he'd described and feeling an unexpected twinge of jealousy. "You're kidding," she responded, not quite casually enough.

Lawrence laughed. "Damn, Chaney, is everything all right?" he asked in an amused voice. "You almost sound like you think I'm serious."

"Nah." She yawned again, surprised at herself, because she had trusted Lawrence completely for years.

"How's Perry?" Lawrence asked.

"Great." Chaney was glad he'd changed the subject. "I spoke to him last night. He thinks he might be getting promoted again."

"Congratulate him for me."

"Okay."

"Tell me something new—what about Pam? You hung out with her lately?"

"We never hang out, Lawrence, you know that. She called me yesterday, though. The kids still play there sometimes anyway, just like when you're here."

"I'll never understand why you never go to lunch with her or something. I mean, both of you have husbands who travel a lot, you live next door, she's really a nice person . . ."

"This is all beginning to sound very familiar, or is that my imagination?" Chaney interrupted, irritated.

"Baby, you just don't like people, do you?"

"I love the kids, I love my brothers, and I adore you. I don't have a lot of affection left over after that."

"Chaney."

Her heartbeat suddenly quickened as she remembered Taurique. She debated telling Lawrence—she never kept things from him, but . . .

"Honey, I worry about you," he went on. "What if something happens to me?"

"Lawrence, I don't want you to think about that."

"Baby, I'm always traveling, something could happen to me. I'm realistic. You can't shut yourself off from everyone."

"What do you want me to do, take an embroidery class so I can meet some nice ladies my own age? Look, you knew I was a loner when you married me. You're my best friend. After that, there's Perry, Zac, and Jimmy. Some people just don't need a lot of friends."

"But you're not really a loner, Chaney. You need people. I know you do, or you wouldn't miss me like you do."

She was silent, hesitating. "Actually . . ." Her heart was pounding. "Um—I ran into . . ." She felt frozen. Her brain finished the sentence a hundred times, but somehow her mouth could not quite speak the words.

"You ran into . . . not the car, Chaney. Woman, you didn't scratch my *Jag,* did you?"

She laughed nervously, and he laughed, too.

"Why is this so hard?" he asked. "Who?"

"An old friend." I'm making this sound too suspicious, she thought, and I'm not doing anything wrong.

"Carrie?"

"Carrie who?"

"That white girl you went to school with."

"Carrie's not white."

"High yellow, whatever."

"She's half Puerto Rican, half black."

"Okay, Hispanic. She was at the wedding, anyway. She was so happy for you."

"Carrie moved to Miami. She was one of Perry's friends, mainly. We knew each other through him."

"Whatever, Chaney."

"No, it wasn't her." Chaney wondered briefly what had happened to Carrie. She was one of the few girls who didn't find it highly amusing that I was having a shotgun wedding, who didn't think I was stuck-up and a slut because I always hung out with men. Maybe I'll ask Perry, she thought.

"Who? I can't think of anyone."

"Um—Taurique."

"Taurique?"

"Yes."

There was a silence.

"Lawrence, what? Tell me what you're thinking."

"How did you run into him?" he asked, straining to sound indifferent.

"Just on the street."

"When was this?"

"About—oh, a few days ago."

"You didn't mention it."

"It wasn't really important."

He sighed. "How is he?"

"He's doing okay."

"Is he married?"

"Divorced, but he's seeing somebody."

"Uh-huh." He sounded unimpressed.

"Actually . . ." Her throat was dry, but she had to say this casually. I'm not doing anything wrong, she said to herself firmly. "We had lunch today."

"You did." There was a long silence.

"Lawrence, what are you thinking?"

There was another pause.

"I don't know," he finally said.

"Lawrence, there's nothing going on. He's just a friend."

"You're *friends* again, then. Just like that."

"You wanted me to have more adult friends." She closed her eyes, waiting.

"I didn't really have your ex-lover in mind, Chaney," he finally said, and his voice had taken on an edge. It was a relief, because his silences were frightening. Chaney had no way of knowing how deeply hurt or angry he was. As unnerving as his few explosions were, at least she knew where she stood then. That was one thing about Taurique—when he was annoyed, you always knew how much, and why.

"Lawrence, do you love me?" Chaney asked, trying to calm her nerves by taking a deep breath.

He paused again. "You know I do."

"Do you believe that I love you?"

He sighed. "Yes," he answered quietly. "I also know that this guy hurt you very badly just before we met and that there are probably unresolved feelings there and that I'm thousands of miles away."

Chaney felt her pulse quicken a bit. He's right, she thought, but it doesn't matter, because Taurique doesn't affect me like he used to anymore.

"Lawrence, do you trust me?" she asked.

"It's not you I don't trust."

"You've never even *met* Taurique."

"From what I hear, he's very attractive."

"So are you." She had hoped to ease the tension a bit, but his voice didn't relax.

"Chaney, you are my whole world. Please . . ."

"Lawrence, I love you, you said you believed that. There's no one on this earth who can take your place. I would not be married for nine years to a man I didn't want to be with. You're making this a really big deal, and it just isn't. But if you really trust me that little, if you're really that insecure about my commitment to you, I don't need to talk to Taurique again. Although it would be a little bit stupid for me to tell you about this if I was fooling around. I'd never cheat, Lawrence, I'd at least tell you it was over first. You know that, we've talked about it. But say the word, I don't need to be friends with him."

She held her breath, praying that he wouldn't take her friend away from her, not yet, remembering how her father had made similar decisions for her, and resenting, just slightly, the fact that she had felt it necessary to give her husband that power.

"What's his girlfriend's name?" he asked testily.

"Charmaine."

Clever, thought Chaney. That was one of the many things she had always loved about Lawrence—his intelligence. Yes, he did talk about his girlfriend, she exists, Chaney thought.

There was another long silence.

"I have no right," Lawrence said slowly, "to tell you who your friends can be. And I have no control over what you do, anyway."

"Lawrence . . ." It was exactly the answer she wanted from him, and yet it made her feel guilty.

"Let me finish, please?" There was another pause. "I have to trust you. I *do* trust you. But Chaney? If something happens, please—I want to know. Please."

"Lawrence . . ."

"And just let me say," he interrupted, "that I don't want you to see him. I don't want you to go near him. It makes me extremely uncomfortable that you had lunch."

"Can I say something?"

"Okay."

"You're overreacting by about 2,000 percent."

"Then why didn't you tell me before this that you saw him?"

"It wasn't that important, Lawrence."

"Be real for a minute, okay? How could it not be important?"

"I was also kind of afraid of your reaction and I didn't think I'd ever see him again, and quite frankly, it didn't matter all that much if I did or not."

Lawrence sighed. "Look, I have to go," he said flatly.

"Please, can we not leave it like this?"

"What do you want me to say?"

"Say you love me."

"Chaney, of course I love you, I told you that already. If I didn't love you, I wouldn't care."

"Well, I love you, too, Lawrence. And I miss you and only you. Just like always."

He paused. "I won't be able to call you tomorrow," he finally said, "because I perform the next day."

"I didn't want to upset you."

"I'm okay."

"Really?"

"Yeah, yeah, I'm okay. I have to go. Say hi to the kids for me, please."

"Okay."

"Chaney?"

"Yes."

"I love you. With my whole heart."

"I know," she replied, swallowing the lump that was trying to form in her throat.

"Goodbye, Chaney."

"Goodbye."

She hung up slowly, feeling very guilty. For what? she thought. For nothing. I did the right thing, telling him. I knew he wasn't going to take it very well, but just because he doesn't like it doesn't mean it's wrong for me to talk to Taurique. But she decided not to call Taurique and not to see him, definitely, until she could introduce him to Lawrence first. Better, she thought, that's a much better idea. I can't control his calling me, but I won't call him.

She climbed out of bed. Time to get the kids up for school.

As Chaney came in from dropping off the children, she was cornered by Pam, who was out on her front steps just enjoying the mildness of the weather.

"Chaney," she called out with a gap-toothed smile, waving.

"Hi," Chaney responded, smiling seraphically while trying to hurry into the house. I had to pick today to shop for food, she thought.

"Let me help you," Pam said, rising and walking across her lawn.

"Oh, that's sweet of you," Chaney said, "but you really don't have to."

"I'm not doing anything else," Pam said, taking the bags out of Chaney's hands. "There, now you can handle your keys."

Chaney opened the front door and held it open as Pam walked through to the kitchen. She was surprised such a little woman could lift so much weight—Pam was about five-two and she looked like she weighed a hundred pounds at most. There were only two things big about Pam: the shapeless mass of unprocessed hair on top of her head, and her eyes, which were wonderfully large and expressive, but which, in combination with the rest of her, made her look a bit like a troll.

"Any more?" Pam asked, setting the bags on the table.

"A couple, out in the car, but have a seat and I'll get them." Chaney sighed, going back outside. I'll give her tea, we'll talk briefly, and then I'll get rid of her, she thought. She was half-way up the walkway when she decided to try, just this once, to give her a chance. Even if she was a starstruck idiot who practically worshipped Lawrence, and who only came over so she could have access to him when he came home. It's just like when those girls used to use me to get to my brothers, she thought.

Chaney reentered the house, Pam holding the door for her.

"Thanks a lot, Pam," Chaney said, "but please, this isn't necessary. Why don't you have a seat in the living room?"

"Okay."

She's going to get on my nerves really quickly, I can feel it, Chaney thought, turning on the fire under the kettle and beginning to put away groceries.

"Would you like some tea?" she called out.

"Thank you," came the reply.

I'm not moving from this kitchen, thought Chaney, until the tea is ready.

"Why don't you watch TV while I'm making the tea?" she called out.

Footsteps. "Really, I can sit in the kitchen, Chaney. You don't have to wait on me." Pam appeared in the doorway.

"Oh—okay, whatever you prefer."

Pam seated herself. "So, have you heard from Lawrence?" she asked.

"He called this morning."

"How is he?"

"Fine. Tell me, when is Carl coming home?"

"A few days."

"I envy you."

"Don't, it still gets lonely sometimes. But I keep busy, I do volunteer work. You should consider that, Chaney, since you have a lot of free time."

"I don't know, Pam, I've seen people get so involved in that stuff that it takes over their lives. But I'll think about it." Chaney smiled.

"You must really enjoy your free time."

"I do."

"I'd miss my husband terribly if he was always gone as long as yours. Especially Lawrence, he's such a special guy."

"Carl's pretty special, too."

"Of course, I just meant . . . you know." Pam looked embarrassed.

That you'd swap in ten seconds, given half the chance, Chaney finished. The phone rang and the kettle whistled at the same time.

"I'll get it," said Pam, reaching for the phone.

"That's okay," Chaney protested, but Pam was already speaking.

"Hello?" she said.

That's *another* reason I don't like her, thought Chaney, she always makes herself a bit too much at home. She poured hot water into two teacups.

"It's for you, Chaney," Pam announced.

Really? I thought it would be for you, thought Chaney.

"Who is it?" she asked.

"A man."

"Maybe it's my brother."

Chaney put a teabag in each cup and placed Pam's in front of her. She picked up the phone.

"Hey, Shay-shay, how you be?" Taurique said.

"Fine." Chaney smiled, suddenly became aware of Pam's presence, and turned her back.

"Who was that?"

"I have company."

"Who?"

"No one you know, a neighbor."

"You're being neighborly now, ain't that nice? I bet she broke down the door."

Chaney laughed. "In a way."

"Well, I won't keep you, then."

"No, please do."

"You're being sociable for once, who am I to interrupt? I'll call you later, okay?"

"Okay."

"Later, Chaney."

"Later, Taurique."

She hung up, realizing that she had made a mistake, but deciding to play it off

"Who was that?" Pam asked, frowning slightly.

"A friend of mine."

"Taurique. That's an unusual name."

"He's an unusual person."

"Good friend?"

"Does it matter?" Chaney snapped. She had come to the end of her patience with this visit, especially if Pam was planning to continue to interrogate her.

"No." Pam looked away.

"Good." Chaney's voice became more pleasant. "How's your tea? Oh—I didn't offer you cream and sugar."

"I like it plain, thanks."

"Me, too." Chaney glanced at the clock. "Look, *The Young*

and the Restless is on. Would you like to join me in the living room?"

"Okay." Pam was looking at her strangely.

"What?" Chaney demanded.

"Your husband is a very special man," she said.

"Who are you telling? I married him."

"I thought about cheating on Carl once," Pam said hurriedly.

Chaney was trying not to get angry. She sipped her tea slowly. "I hope you didn't," she said, looking at her steadily. "I would hope you'd have a long talk with your husband and try to resolve whatever problems made you look elsewhere first. That would be the best thing to do."

"Oh, I agree," said Pam. She glanced at her watch, then sipped her tea. "You know, I forgot I told my mother to call me this afternoon, I'd better go soon."

"Well, at least finish your tea," said Chaney, thinking, the joke's on her, Lawrence already knows everything.

"Of course." Pam took another sip.

"Is Tracey still in gymnastics?"

"Yes, she is, and she enjoys it very much."

"Nicole's been asking me about it, I was just wondering."

"Oh, I think it's a great idea."

She's looking at me, thought Chaney, like I just handed state secrets to a hostile government.

"Is something wrong, Pam?" Chaney asked, trying to contain her annoyance.

Pam was taking another sip of tea—the cup was emptying at record speed.

"No, of course not."

"Because you've got a strange look on your face."

"I do?" Pam smiled slightly.

"You assumed I was cheating on my husband, just because I was talking in a very friendly way to another man. Right?"

"No."

"You couldn't be further off base."

"I never said . . ."

"You didn't have to. But that's okay, Lawrence knows what the situation is. I guess that's all that's important."

Pam was silent for a moment. She gazed out the window, then she turned her huge eyes back to Chaney.

"Look," she said, "I know it's hard, having your husband away so much. It has to be. I know pilots' wives, I know people in general. I would just hate to see you mess up your marriage because you're a bit lonely now. Okay, it's none of my business, I know." Pam put her teacup down on the table and rose. "I've got to go now," she said.

Chaney stood. *For once Pam knows when to make an exit,* she thought.

"Thanks for helping with the groceries," she said.

"No problem." Pam smiled a bit. "Goodbye, Chaney."

And she was gone. Chaney locked the door behind her and sat down. Suddenly, she was replaying in her mind the first time she had kissed Lawrence. It was their second date, and they went to a movie, and when they arrived at her door, they were talking, talking, and then suddenly they were kissing each other . . .

How many times had she kissed him? And in how many different ways—to celebrate his first major role, as a ritual every morning and evening when they were together, passionately when they made love, desperately when she saw him cry for the first and only time . . .

We've been through a lot together, she thought. *Tough, tough times, and he was always a rock. Not like Taurique.*

I'm thinking about him again, she realized. *Every time I think about Lawrence these days, I think about Taurique. Maybe I* need *to think about him. Maybe I need to get our past out of my system before Lawrence gets back.*

It flashed through her mind, uncontrollably, Taurique making love to her, kissing her neck . . .

She was nearly sixteen when she'd lost her virginity. She'd immediately regretted it, because somehow Taurique had seen fit to have a one-night stand with some woman he'd met at a party, as if to prove to himself that one female body was no different than another. Chaney had never told Perry—she'd assumed he never knew, because she was sure he and Taurique would have had at least a huge argument, if not a fistfight. Of course, it was reasonable that Perry didn't know—it almost seemed like she and Taurique and the woman were the only ones who knew. The girls at school hated her even more since she had started seeing Taurique, and it would have been big news.

When Taurique told her, he had tears in his eyes. Chaney listened with an emotion she couldn't explain—it was shock, disappointment, emptiness, humiliation, and fascination. Fascination, because Taurique had always seemed too cool to have tears in his eyes over something like this. He was drunk, but that didn't make it okay. He was garbage, and he didn't deserve her. He kept saying that there was no excuse, he kept apologizing, he wouldn't blame her for ending it, but he was asking her not to, because the way he was feeling right now confirmed that she wasn't like anybody else, and he didn't know what he would do if he lost her.

Chaney had never felt so profoundly alone. She was too embarrassed to talk to Perry, but she wasn't sure if this very charming, very attractive boy was telling the truth or feeding her a line, just like she'd seen her brothers do to various girls. And if she did forgive him, would he do it again? She was totally confused.

She gazed at him, trying to read his face. He promised not to go to another party without her. He begged her to forgive him, his eyes full of anguish. Then, he stopped talking. He wanted her to talk to him. He wanted to know what she was feeling, no matter how negative it was.

Things were all right by the time he left. Chaney knew, after that, that they would be together always, because he listened to her. He always listened to her, he always asked how she felt. I don't know, she would say time and time again, how do *you* feel? What do *you* want to do? Because it didn't really matter, she could go along with most things. She knew he'd never ask her to do anything that would be harmful to her.

I've always been lucky that way, Chaney thought. She was only four when her mother left—to this day she didn't know why—and her father and brothers became her mother. She sat on the couch, folding her legs beneath her, and smiled. Yes, they were strict, she thought, but it had turned out okay, especially since Perry was always there to balance things. She knew she'd disappointed everybody by not going to college, but that was a worthwhile sacrifice. A part of her always wanted a college education, a part of her just wanted to raise a family. Properly, not the way her mother had. She was always there for Nicole and Ronnie, and it would always be that way.

Chaney picked up the teacups and took them to the sink. There was her coat, where she'd left it that morning after the weather report had made her decide against wearing it. She picked it up and took it to the bedroom, was hanging it up when she remembered . . .

She reached into the pocket and took out Taurique's number. The writing was a mess, as usual. She smiled, wondering why he'd called. Just to talk, it seemed. It wasn't really wrong to call him just to talk, was it? *She* knew her intentions, even if Lawrence didn't. Besides, he had overreacted so much. That was one thing about Lawrence—he was almost always in control, but when he lost it, he really lost it. Sometimes, he was so passionate it frightened her—making love, getting angry. The anger was pretty rare, thank God. And he didn't really get mad about this, she thought, so chances were he'd be able to accept it.

Besides, what else am I doing? Not a damn thing, Chaney thought, dialing his work number.

"Taurique Williams, please."

"May I ask who's calling?"

"Perry's sister." Chaney grinned and waited.

"Perry's sister!" Taurique laughed. "What's up, Perry's sister? I'd better speak to that woman, putting through Perry's sister, she should screen people better than that."

"What, you're too important to talk to Perry's sister?"

"So you got rid of her, huh?"

"Actually, she left on her own."

"You were that friendly." Taurique laughed again. "I can imagine it."

"Anyway . . . why did you call me?"

"I had a free moment, that's all. What are you doing?"

"I was watching *The Young and the Restless*."

"And I thought *I* was doing something important."

"Ha, ha." She grinned.

"When was the last time you saw a Broadway show?"

"A while ago."

"Get a babysitter and come out with me."

"Come out and see a play?" Her voice was skeptical.

"Why not?"

"What about your girlfriend? What will she think?"

"She doesn't try to control who I talk to. Besides, she's a model. Right now, she's in Paris."

"A model!"

"I always had a weakness for beautiful women."

"What does she look like?"

"Almost as good as you."

Chaney rolled her eyes, smiling in spite of herself. "Blonde, brunette, redhead . . ."

"Actually, she has a short afro, she's five-eleven, and she's twice as dark as you are."

"I'm impressed."

"That's why she's in Europe so much—she does better over there."

"Of course. So does Lawrence."

"So I'm alone these days, and so are you. What do you want to see?"

"I can't, Taurique."

"C'mon—anything you want, Shay. You name it."

"Taurique, I can't."

"Call your neighbor—thanks, Donna, I'll be right there— call your neighbor and ask her if she'll look after your kids."

"No, Taurique, I really shouldn't."

"Shay—look, I'll call you later, please don't keep saying no."

"I *have* to, Taurique. Look, take Donna."

He laughed. "Yeah, right. She'd jump my ass before we got into the car. No, I don't think so. One last chance, Chaney."

"I'm sorry."

He sighed an exaggerated sigh. "Okay. Rejection, I can handle it."

Chaney smiled.

"Can we have lunch again tomorrow? I still don't feel caught up."

Chaney thought for a second. An evening out was one thing, but what was the big deal about lunch? "Okay," she finally said.

"Great. I'll call you to confirm. Gotta go, talk to you later, Shay."

"Goodbye, T."

She hung up. T. I called him T.—it's been a while since I did that. She smiled again. Maybe I do need friends, she thought. She'd thought she'd always love him, once upon a time. Well, like, anyway, she decided, going back into the living room to watch TV.

Seven

October 23

Same old story, Chaney thought, waiting for the light to change as she made her way home. I spill my guts and forget half the things I was going to ask him.

"Mommy, can we stop at Wendy's?" Nicole was asking.

"No, Nicole."

"Why not?" came in chorus from the back seat.

"Because that stuff is not good for you, and you know it."

"Please!"

Chaney glanced back, sighing. They were holding their breath, practically, because her hesitation meant there was a chance she might change her mind. She smiled.

"How about pizza?" she suggested.

"Yay!" came the screams from the back. Chaney laughed.

"Quiet, quiet, that's enough," she said, turning up the radio.

Where was I? she thought. Lunch with T. She had promised to answer him if he would answer her, then she'd talked so much that time had run out. It wasn't all that surprising, really—Taurique had a way of asking her questions that made her think, and he was always the world's greatest listener, when he wanted to be. Maybe I really needed to talk to somebody besides Perry about my situation, she thought. She certainly felt better afterward. Still, she wished she had shut up much sooner.

She started off okay. T. asked how she met Lawrence, and

she told him her husband was a Christmas present from God. Then Taurique asked what Lawrence was like—well, what is Lawrence like? She always had trouble describing people. Oh, he's tall, and very handsome—let me show you a picture. T. looked at it and smiled, admitted to her that Lawrence was his equal. But that wasn't what he meant. He wanted to know how and why she'd fallen in love with him.

Chaney hesitated. The question seemed so personal, coming from him. Then again, he was probably still hoping that it was mainly rebounding. So she explained again why it wasn't—Lawrence was talented, responsible, intelligent, and witty, and he loved her very much. And he knows what you need, Taurique added. Yes. But not as well as you used to, thought Chaney. So you would have probably ended up married, even without the baby, T. asked. Yes, she said.

She looked at him as he gazed down, caught herself studying his lips, and turned away.

She ended up telling him how unsure she'd been about marriage, how she felt she had become a mother too soon, how difficult it would have been if Lawrence's career hadn't taken off. She told him she wished she had continued school sometimes, but she stopped before she told him she was bored. She could barely admit it to herself. Actually, I'm only bored sometimes, she thought. Besides, she'd made a promise to herself to focus her energy on being there for her children. Why did she forget that, talking to T? And why did I end up telling him about my marriage again? she wondered. Well, it's too late now.

"Mommy, can we go to Pizza Hut?" Ronnie was asking, and Chaney snapped back to the present.

"Uh—I tell you what, we'll order it when we get home," she said, "and you can pay the delivery man."

"*I* wanna pay the delivery man," Nicole protested.

"Ronnie can pay him, and you can take the change, okay?" Nicole considered. "Okay," she said.

"Mommy, can we go see Uncle Perry today?" Ronnie asked.

"I don't know, why don't you call him?"

"Can I go play with Kenny and Calvin?"

"I don't know, honey, call your uncle and find out."

"Will you take me there?"

"I tell you what," said Chaney, turning onto her street, "why don't you invite Uncle Perry, Aunt Valerie, and the twins over for pizza?"

"Okay."

"It'll be like a party, right, Mommy?" Nicole asked.

"Well, not really," said Chaney, thinking, do we really have people over that rarely? Just because I'm antisocial doesn't mean they have to be. She resolved to be sure her kids spent more time with their friends. "More like a family get-together," she added.

"Except Daddy's not here."

Of course, Chaney thought, as she pulled into the driveway and turned off the ignition.

"Right," she replied.

"Can we call him?" Ronnie asked.

"Not today, baby," Chaney said, opening her door and climbing. The kids followed suit.

"Why not?"

"Because he has to rest his voice," Nicole said. "Right, Mommy?"

"Right." She opened the door and watched as the children ran in ahead of her.

"Can I call Uncle Perry?" Ronnie asked.

"Okay, then let me talk to him. And put your schoolbag away first."

Ronnie and Nicole started up the stairs, and Chaney locked the door. What a great idea, inviting Perry and Val over, she thought. Why don't I do this more often?

"Mommy! Uncle Perry's on the phone."

"Okay, Ronnie." Chaney picked up the receiver in the kitchen. "Hey, Mr. Davis, qué pasa?"

"What's this about us coming over?"

"Well, Ronnie and I came up with the idea."

"I knew you weren't working alone."

"What's that supposed to mean?"

"Just kidding, Shay. So you're making pizza?"

"Get real, Perry."

"You're ordering pizza."

"But I'll make salad."

"Don't hurt yourself."

"Ha, ha. *Now* I know why I don't do this more often."

"You know I only say things like that because you're a fabulous cook. Anyway, what are the adults going to do?"

"Talk. Some problem with that?"

"It's okay. Listen, we can start a tradition—maybe we can do this every week; that way your nephews might recognize you."

Chaney sighed. "Am I really that bad?"

"Uh-huh. But look, I love you anyway. We're coming over, but I'm bringing some cards, 'cause we're gonna play spades."

"Spades?"

"Oh, c'mon, we played spades all the time when we were kids. You and me against Jimmy and Zac."

"I'm not sure I even remember how, I haven't played in years. Besides, we only have three people."

"You can play with three. Or we could ask Pam to join us."

"No way. I'm not in the mood."

"Well, we'll deal with it. Val's great at poker."

"Whatever."

"Or I could find a fourth person."

"Like who?"

"I'll think of somebody."

"No strangers, Perry. It's got to be somebody I know, or nobody at all."

Perry laughed. "That narrows it down to about—oh—two or three."

"I mean it. I want to have fun, I don't want to have some person I've got to spend the whole evening trying to get used to."

"Okay, okay. Someone Chaney knows."

"So—what kind of pizza do you want?"

"Mushrooms and green peppers."

"You'd better ask Val."

"She'll go along with it, she's my woman, you know what time it is."

"Yeah, I know what time it is, put her on the phone."

Perry laughed. "No, really, mushrooms and green peppers. That's vegetarian. Val's—um—stopped eating meat."

Chaney laughed. "Mr. Head of the House. See you."

"I'll be over soon." He hung up.

In the middle of dinner, the doorbell rang.

"I'll get it," Ronnie screamed, narrowly beating Nicole out of her seat in the rush toward the door.

"Ronnie!" Chaney yelled. "Nicole! Stop that noise and walk like two civilized human beings."

"The mystery guest has arrived," said Perry with a smile, and Chaney looked at him, surprised—she'd assumed he hadn't been able to find anyone.

"Mommy, someone's here to see you," Nicole called.

It was Taurique. Chaney stared at him, then at Perry, then at Valerie, then back at Taurique.

"Hi, Chaney," he said. "Perry, Val. Ken, Calvin." He looked down at Chaney's children. "I would say hello to these gorgeous kids, but I don't think I've been introduced."

"Nicole, Ronnie, this is Mr. Williams."

"Hi, Mr. Williams," came in unison from the children, who were staring at Taurique wide-eyed.

"He's a friend of mine," Chaney explained quickly. "Taurique, have a seat—there's still some pizza and salad, if you want it. Perry, can I speak to you for a minute?"

"Sure." Nicole and Ronnie were still staring. Taurique looked a bit uncomfortable, but only for a moment. Chaney took Perry's arm and led him toward her bedroom, closing the door when they were both inside.

"What's up?" Perry asked, sitting in a chair by the bed.

"How *dare* you," Chaney snapped, glaring at him.

He blinked. "Huh?" he responded in disbelief.

"You heard me."

"You said I could bring a fourth person. You said it had to be someone you knew. Didn't you just have lunch with Taurique twice?"

"Yes, but there's a big difference between having lunch in a restaurant and having someone in your home, and you know that."

Perry folded his arms, paused, and asked, "Do you still have feelings for Taurique?"

Chaney took a deep breath, caught off guard. "I like him," she replied, cursing the note of uncertainty in her voice.

"I'm talking about sexual feelings, Chaney. Do you have *sexual* feelings for him?"

Perry was looking through her. She cleared her throat, determined to sound more assured.

"No," she said firmly.

Perry shook his head. "You're still attracted to him," he said as if it were a revelation. "Damn. Okay, let me ask you something else—can you handle it? I mean, I have friendships where the mutual attraction is part of the fun, because we both know that ain't nothin' going on. I mean, there's some of that in most male/female friendships. Anyway, if you can't handle that with Taurique . . . damn, Chaney, is it really all that? After all this time?"

She looked down, humiliated by her anger. It wasn't all that, after all. After the initial shock of running into him, she hadn't felt any lightning bolts, or anything. There was a strong current of awareness, but no explosion of lust. Except in her daydreams . . .

"Do you still have flashbacks," she asked slowly, "about some of the things you did with your old girlfriends?"

She looked into Perry's eyes, watching him smile slightly.

"Yeah," he said. "Every once in a while, I'll be in a place

or see somebody or something that reminds me of an old experience. Nothing serious. Look, I don't think this is such a big deal. I think you're just not used to having these—flashbacks, and they're bothering you more than they need to."

"You're probably right." She relaxed completely.

"But I'm sorry I invited Taurique without asking. I really thought it would be okay with you."

She smiled at him—it *is* okay, she thought. There's no reason for it not to be. After all, he's right, it's been a long time, too long for me to be worried about the old chemistry. Besides, I feel completely at ease around him; that's what friendship should be about.

"No big deal," she replied, tapping his outstretched fist with hers, and laughing.

Perry rose. "Look," he said, "see how you feel. If you're really uncomfortable, you'll know there's a problem. I honestly can't imagine why there *would* be a problem, but you know how you feel."

"Okay, okay." She was beginning to feel like an idiot for even wondering about herself, and she wanted the conversation to be over now. "Let's go back," she said, opening the door.

They left the room together, and as they entered the kitchen, Valerie and Taurique abruptly stopped speaking.

"Hey, don't stop on my account," Perry remarked. "What, were you asking my wife out, or something?"

Taurique grinned. "Our secret's out, Val," he said.

"Does this mean we're not going to Aruba?" Valerie asked, and the three of them laughed. Taurique glanced at Chaney, who smiled, and he looked relieved.

"Can you play Spades?" Chaney asked him.

"Not really."

"Girls against the boys!" Valerie exclaimed.

"Where are the kids?" Chaney asked.

"In Ronnie's room," Valerie replied.

"More important, where's the beer?" Perry asked, and everyone laughed.

"Have I *ever* been known to drink beer?" Chaney retorted.

"Kool-Aid, whatever."

"Yeah, Kool-Aid sounds good," Taurique remarked. "I'm gonna have to be really sober not to make a fool of myself."

"Anybody want to put money on this?" Chaney asked, grinning.

"I'm in," Valerie said.

"Okay," Perry agreed, "but you and Chaney have to drink three shots of bourbon first. Each."

"Let's play just for *fun,* okay?" Taurique suggested. "This is gonna be fun, ain't it, Davis?"

"This game," Perry said in mock reverence, "is a game of skill, a game of shrewd strategy, a game that only those of the highest intellect can master."

Taurique glanced at his watch. "Time for me to go now," he said, and everyone laughed again.

"You can play chess, can't you?" Perry said. "Listen, if you can beat me at chess even once, you can play this game. Come with me, I'll explain everything."

"Hey, wait a second," Valerie protested. "I don't see any reason we can't all hear this explanation."

"Are you saying . . ." Perry began.

"You cheat, Perry," Chaney interrupted, and Valerie chuckled.

"Now, *that* I can do," Taurique said, and seeing Chaney stop smiling, he added, "I mean . . ."

"We know," Perry said. "Okay, we all explain. Mrs. Davis— the cards, please."

They sat down at the kitchen table and Valerie began to shuffle. Taurique sought Chaney's eyes, but she avoided his gaze until it occurred to her that Perry was looking. I will not react to anything Taurique does or says any differently than if anyone else had said or done it, she decided. She smiled briefly in Taurique's direction. This could be a very long evening, she thought.

* * *

The ladies' team won, but Chaney was impressed with how quickly Taurique picked up the game. He was always a quick learner, she reminded herself. Now she and Valerie were sitting in the kitchen while Perry and Taurique were going through Chaney's CD collection in the living room, looking for something else to play.

"This is a change of pace," Valerie remarked, as strains of Gounod began to drift into the room.

"Yeah." Chaney wandered into the living room.

"Gone for the culture, Perry?" she asked. "Or the European version, anyway?"

"Nah, I insisted," Taurique said. "I wanted to hear your husband sing."

"You like opera?"

"I'm more into Peabo, actually," he said, glancing at Chaney with a little smile. She blushed—another flashback, and this time he had brought it up deliberately. She wondered if all ex-lovers who became friends did this, or if it was out of line. Well, she certainly wasn't going to embarrass herself by asking Perry about it. It was a pleasant memory, one way or the other.

"So was Chaney until recently," Perry was saying.

"Shh," Taurique said, listening intently, and Chaney glared at Perry, wishing that she'd never told him she'd ever been bored at the opera. Actually, she'd never been bored when Lawrence was singing, and now she kind of enjoyed opera. At first, though, it had seemed interminable and overblown, with acting that verged on ludicrous and plots almost as bad. She had told Perry all about the fact that she went only out of a sense of duty. And now he was bringing it up in front of Taurique. She would have to speak to him again.

How could she have fallen asleep in the middle of such beautiful music? She listened to Lawrence singing *Avant de quitter ces lieux,* from Faust, and glanced at Taurique, who was still concentrating. You can't do that, she thought. Lawrence's voice gave her chills, even now.

"*Sing,*" Valerie said, and Chaney smiled at her. The children appeared at the top of the stairs.

"That's Daddy," Ronnie said, sitting on the floor and leaning against the wall. There was no more talking until the aria was over.

"You know," Chaney said, "I think I fell in love with that man just hearing his voice."

Taurique smiled. "He's incredible," he said.

Kenny let out a loud yawn.

"I know what *that* means," Valerie said. "Time to get the coats and hit the road."

"Mommy!" Calvin protested. "I'm not sleepy."

"*I* am," Valerie said. "Did you hear what I said?"

"Yes, Mommy," the twins said, coming down the stairs.

"She gets results," Taurique remarked.

"Listen, man," Perry said, "my kids misbehave and I say I'm gonna tell their mother, and it's *over.*"

Valerie smiled. "I don't take no mess from no four-year-old," she said, helping Kenny into his coat.

Taurique and Perry were laughing, but Chaney found herself wondering, as she watched everyone get ready to go home, if putting up with four-year-olds was what had made her mother leave.

"Well, thanks for a lovely evening," Perry said, kissing his sister on the cheek.

"Yeah, Chaney," Valerie said, "next time over at our place, okay? Oh, I have a better idea—we're planning to go upstate soon, you guys can come with us."

"Okay." Valerie kissed her cheek, but Chaney didn't kiss back—she never did. It wasn't that she didn't like Valerie; she just never grew up kissing women. She hugged Valerie, though, and planted a quick kiss on each of her nephew's foreheads. "Get home safe," Chaney called after them as they headed down the front walk, and they all waved before getting into their car.

"Well, Chaney," Taurique said, coming up behind her and startling her by placing his hand on her shoulder, "thanks a lot.

I know I kind of surprised you. I hope I didn't cause too much trouble."

Chaney smiled. "No, it was fun," she said, feeling glad, after all, that he had come.

"I'll see you."

"Okay."

" 'Bye, Nicole. 'Bye Ronnie," he said, waving.

" 'Bye, Mr. Williams," they said, watching him.

"Mr. Williams." Taurique laughed. "Can't they call me something else?"

"Like what? Uncle Rico?"

Taurique smiled at his old nickname. "Mr. Taurique, maybe," he said. "Anyway, gotta go, babe." He hesitated, then turned and walked out the door, and Chaney was glad he hadn't kissed her. He glanced back and she waved to him, then closed the inner door and bolted it. She turned to face the children, waiting for questions.

"Do we have to go to bed now?" Ronnie asked, and Nicole slapped him.

"You dummy," she said. "Why'd you have to bring that up?"

"She hit me," Ronnie exclaimed, pointing. "You saw her."

"Yes, I saw her. Nicole, you crazy or something?"

Nicole looked down. "No, Mommy."

"Apologize."

"Sorry," she said, without looking at her brother.

"Better. And by the way, it's almost 9:30, you know it's time for bed, both of you. So go and brush your teeth."

"Mommy," Nicole asked, "who's Mr. Williams?"

Just when it seemed I wasn't going to have to answer any questions, Chaney thought. "He's a friend of mine and Uncle Perry's, from when we were teenagers."

"That was a *long* time ago," Nicole said, teasing.

"Not so long as you seem to think," Chaney replied, smiling. "It's bedtime, by the way."

"Okay, okay," said Nicole grudgingly, and Ronnie raced ahead of her up the stairs.

Eight

October 24

Chaney yawned, glancing at the TV as she completed her post-workout stretch. She had been used to getting up early for a while, but she had gotten out of the habit of going to sleep much later than 10 P.M. The night before she was in bed by 11, but she woke up in the middle of the night and was almost afraid to fall asleep again, afraid of what she had dreamed.

It started in the usual way—she was in the ship again, and no one was steering, and she was wandering around helplessly. She sat down in the hallway—she was doomed. She had her head in her hands and was crying, and then she felt two strong arms around her, holding her, and she relaxed, and suddenly she was kissing him, more and more passionately, and she lay back against the soft carpet and he was caressing her, undressing her, making love to her. Then she looked into his eyes and saw him smiling at her . . .

She woke up, and Taurique's face melted away. She turned on the light and sat up slowly. It doesn't necessarily mean I want to sleep with him, she thought, trying not to remember how good it had felt to imagine having him close to her again. It means I want to be close to him *emotionally*. This stuff isn't always literal.

She wondered if she was kidding herself. Maybe Perry was wrong; maybe her sudden memories weren't so meaningless.

Maybe it was more than a little sexual tension. Maybe she was still in love with him.

Chaney sighed, suddenly feeling like crying. "Why did you leave me?" She was surprised to hear herself speak it rather than just think it.

This is really stupid. It was just a dream. She switched legs, holding her left ankle and bringing her forehead to within an inch of her knee. It occurred to her that Lawrence was performing today—he'd call later this afternoon. That idea lasted about a second; Lawrence disappeared from her thoughts just as quickly as he'd appeared. She was wondering how Taurique had forgotten about her so quickly; she was wondering if he thought he had made a mistake. She was wondering how her life would have been if they'd stayed together.

I'm not thinking about this, Chaney decided. She stood and gazed out the window, tried to focus on the view. Times sure have changed, she thought. It seemed like it was so long ago, now, when the scenery was concrete, not grass. There were times when she felt a deep, bittersweet fondness for inner-city neighborhoods, when they brought back memories, not all of them happy, but memories nonetheless. Where were the boys who hung out on the corner so much they were part of the landscape? Not that she missed them that much, they were always up to no good, she thought. Or just socializing, maybe. Learning all the wrong things about how to treat a woman. Trying to be cool. Just like T . . .

And not like Lawrence. Lawrence hadn't been raised in the street. He had some street smarts, he hadn't always been an angel, he'd had his posse in high school, just as Taurique had. But all of Lawrence's friends knew they were going to college; their parents were all professionals. Taurique's dad was blue-collar, and he drank way too much, and Taurique was always on the verge of trouble. So what was the loss? Lawrence was the person girls like her should try to marry. Lawrence was someone *anyone* would be happy to marry.

But he didn't have that air of roguishness. And good girls

always like bad boys, thought Chaney. Even though they can't handle them for very long, because their values are so different. Except T. and I went out for years—what does that mean? It means I was very young. Or he wasn't really so bad.

Chaney sighed, turning away from the window and heading for the bathroom. One dream, one stupid dream, and suddenly she wasn't sure about her marriage for the first time since before Nicki was born. How idiotic am I? she wondered, running her fingers through her hair. And this time I can't talk to Perry, because he probably won't take me any more seriously than he did before. Besides, she'd had too many conversations with him about her problems with Lawrence. She recalled telling her brother that her husband was going to be in Milan on their anniversary.

"That's wrong, Chaney," Perry said disgustedly.

"You don't understand," Chaney replied. She was close to tears when she called, but now she was determined not to give in to them. "La Scala is one of the most prestigious opera houses in the world."

"Yeah? Well, if they wanted him to come and he said he was booked at the Met, do you think they'd ask him to come another time? I bet they would."

"But he's not booked at the Met."

"You understand my point."

Chaney's throat tightened, and she knew her voice was going to betray her, so she didn't respond, trying, in vain, to swallow.

"Look," Perry went on, "I understand that Lawrence is a performer. What I don't get is why his family has to come second all the time."

"I told you . . ."

"Yeah, I know, I know. You can't turn things down, all that mess. Maybe that's true. The thing is, while he's looking after his career, who's looking after you?"

Tears were rolling down Chaney's cheeks now, and she wiped her dripping nose with the back of her hand. "He looks after me," she said defensively.

"I don't mean does he send you things. I mean, is he there like you need him to be there?"

Chaney couldn't answer him; it was all she could do to keep herself from sobbing.

"Baby," Perry said gently, "you deserve better."

"Lawrence is a wonderful guy," she managed, sniffling.

"I'm not saying he isn't. I'm just saying maybe he's not giving you what you need."

Chaney took a deep breath, collecting herself a bit. "And what's that, Perry?"

"Companionship."

She laughed a bit, wiping her eyes. "You know I don't need that, Perry," she returned. "I've been a loner all my life."

"I wish I didn't live on Long Island."

"Look, I'm fine," Chaney insisted, her voice a bit stronger. "I'm just feeling sorry for myself."

"Let me take you out to dinner on your anniversary, or something."

Chaney smiled. "Thanks, Perry, but I promised I'd spend the evening with my children, doing something they want to do. I'll be fine."

There was a silence. "I don't like to see you unhappy," Perry said quietly.

"Thanks, but I'm okay now. I love you."

"Love you too, princess."

"Goodbye."

After that conversation, she vowed to stop complaining to him so much, because Perry and Lawrence, although far from hostile, never really connected on more than a superficial level, and Perry's reserves of goodwill were obviously running low.

It's not like I don't have any other family, Chaney thought, walking slowly to the bathroom to take a shower. After all, Perry's just one brother. I have two others I can call.

She turned on the tap, adjusting it until the water was this side of unbearably hot. I need a bath, she thought, stopping up the drain. A long one. She dropped two rose-scented bath beads into the water and pulled off her bike shorts, T-shirt, and underwear. She admired herself for a moment—breasts virtually unchanged by nursing, stomach still nearly flat after two children, long, muscular legs and curvy hips and thighs—you go, girl, she thought, slipping into the water and closing her eyes.

There are probably unresolved feelings and I'm thousands of miles away . . . Lawrence's words came back to her, and she suddenly imagined him lying beside her, saw herself gazing at his handsome face as he slept, as she loved to do—Lawrence snuggling against her in his sleep, dreaming peacefully as she stroked his hair.

Good girls like bad boys because they do all those exciting, forbidden things good girls could never do themselves but wish they had done at least once. But weren't there times, thought Chaney, when I looked at Taurique and felt very distant, when he talked about all the drugs he had experimented with or some of the things he and his friends had done? But I mellowed him, she thought. Or being with me made him want to mellow, more accurately. And it wasn't like he had no one to make sure he did his homework, no one to be a role model, no one to suggest there were other forms of entertainment than shoplifting; his mother was a schoolteacher, and even though his father was an alcoholic, he had always held a job.

I made him feel guilty, somehow. He was pretty close to a model citizen by the time he left for California. And then he forgot about me, and besides, he started dealing drugs. Why?

There are probably unresolved feelings . . . but should I resolve them? How? Can we talk about all this stuff in a public place? And can I let him know that I still think about something that happened so long ago, can I give him the satisfaction? And what about talking about it in a private place? What would happen if he told me he'd never stopped loving me?

Chaney reached for the soap, lathered her washcloth, and began smoothing away the effects of the workout. She closed her eyes, imagining the sensation of Taurique's touch and picturing the end of the dream as she stroked herself . . .

What would happen if we made love one last time? Could we still be friends, or would that have to be goodbye? Maybe it would be better to say goodbye right now, before anything happens, and to submerge all this stuff. I held it in this long, and I was okay.

It's too late. He's already back in my life. Screwing up my head, she thought bitterly, sitting up.

What would happen, she wondered, splashing herself with water to remove the remaining soap, if I *did* talk to Pam? She seems like she's had some temptation and fought it off. Chaney smiled. You're losing it, she thought. Lawrence is her main temptation; she'd be flat on her back in a minute if he gave her *any* encouragement. I'll call Jimmy. Jimmy always liked Lawrence, and he always had reservations about Taurique. This doesn't make him exactly neutral, but at least he's an antidote to Perry.

Jimmy, she thought, standing and opening the drain. He's the quiet one, he won't tell Zac or Perry—God knows I don't need Zac to start lecturing me.

Chaney got out of the bathtub and wrapped herself in a towel, walking into the bedroom. What a beautiful house, she thought suddenly, looking at her plush surroundings. What a lovely yard, what a wonderful neighborhood. All courtesy of her husband.

I'm an idiot, thought Chaney, pulling on the underwear, sweatshirt, and jeans she had laid out on the bed. Jimmy doesn't need to tell me. I know the deal. But maybe I'll call him anyway, just to see how he's doing . . .

"Dow Chemicals."

"James Davis, please."

"Thank you." There was a short pause.

"Hello, James Davis speaking."

"Jimmy."

There was a brief silence. "Chaney? Nah."

"Yes, it's me."

Jimmy laughed. "Chaney, how've you been? What's up?"

"Are you busy?"

"Yes. But that's okay. Wait a second—you write me letters, you never call me, except on my birthday and Christmas. Something is wrong, right, except—where's Perry?"

"Is Perry my only brother?"

"Kind of. No offense, or anything."

There was no resentment in his voice, but Chaney felt something tighten in her throat.

"I'm sorry," she said.

"Hey, don't be. I mean, you guys are close in age, you both live in New York, you were always really close. I'm not trying to make you feel bad, Chaney. Tell me you're not gonna feel bad."

Chaney sighed. "No," she said.

"Okay. Now—what's the matter?"

"I never said anything was wrong."

"But it is, right? And I know what the problem is."

"You do?"

"His name is Taurique."

Chaney was taken aback. "Perry told you?"

"Uh-huh. Look, don't be upset. Actually, he only told me that you had started talking to him again. I just figured that if there was trouble, he was the cause. So what did he do?"

"Nothing." Chaney was trying not to sound defensive, but she suddenly felt like she had to stick up for Taurique.

"He's not harassing you."

"No."

"So—what, then?"

"Nothing, really. I'm just feeling a little . . ."

"Vulnerable."

"Kind of."

"How vulnerable?"

"Well . . . Perry brought him by the house."

"He did? Why?"

"It's a long story, and it's not really the issue."

"Then what? He made a move, and you almost accepted?"

"No, he didn't try anything. I just dreamed he did."

Jimmy laughed. "Is that it?"

"Jimmy, he was making love to me!" Chaney's face was hot—maybe I'm just completely ridiculous, she thought, hurt. Her brother gradually stopped laughing.

"Chaney," he said, "just because you dreamed about him doesn't mean you're gonna have a real sexual encounter. Look, I'm sorry I laughed. I just expected to hear something more serious."

"But I think about him all the time! More than I think about Lawrence!"

"Uh-huh." Jimmy paused. "So what are you gonna do?"

"I don't know."

"Okay, I'll put it this way. There's only one thing *to* do."

"What?"

"Resolve this thing, once and for all."

"Really?"

"Yes, really. That's my advice. Resolve it, end that part of your life, and go back to dreaming about your husband."

"Just like that."

"You remember that vow you made?"

Chaney hesitated. "Of course."

"Well, you ain't dead yet, and neither is your husband. And he's a great guy."

"When he's around."

"So jump on a plane."

"Jimmy, be serious."

"Look, Perry lives there, I bet he and Valerie would look after the kids, take them to school, all that stuff, or you could leave Nicole and Ronnie with them on some long weekend—I mean, there must be a holiday coming up soon."

"I can't, Jimmy."

"Why not? Charge it."

"I don't want to dump my kids somewhere. You know that, I'm never going to just forget my responsibilities."

"Don't be dumb, Chaney. I didn't say to throw them in the

ocean—oh, just a second . . ." He covered the receiver. There were muffled voices, then, "Duty calls, sweetheart. I've got to go. Listen, you can call me whenever, okay? It was good to hear your voice. Take care, Chaney, and let me know what happens."

"Okay, Jimmy. And don't discuss this with Perry, please."

"Sure."

"Thanks, Jimmy."

"Don't mention it. See you."

She hung up, wondering why she picked Perry to be her sole confidant. Because Jimmy was always the baby, and Zac had a tendency to be dogmatic.

The breakfast dishes were in the sink—Chaney had been running late all morning. Could I leave all this behind? she wondered with a sarcastic grin, gazing around the kitchen. What would be so wrong with leaving the kids with Perry and Valerie and flying to Italy and getting caught up in Lawrence's arms as I stepped off the plane?

And suppose I liked it too much and I didn't come back to New York for a month? Suppose I never came back, suppose life was so exciting in Europe that I forgot about my children, like maybe my mother did, and I only came back when Lawrence did, which is at least a bit *more* than my mother did?

Maybe she got bored with being a housewife, maybe she took off and started all over as an independent woman. Bored to death with just the housework and picking up after four kids and making dinner and having an identity all tied up in either her kids or her husband. Mrs. William Davis, half of Mr. and Mrs. William Davis—she had lost even her first name; she was now an appendage to someone else.

Just like I am. I'm Ronnie and Nicole's mother, Perry's sister, and Mrs. Lawrence Rivers. And it's my fault, really, she thought. I could have stayed in school, except I got pregnant. I could do something with my days—like what? What do I like to do? More important, what could I do that wouldn't take up so much of my energy and interest that I would stop putting my children first? I can't risk it. My children have to be sure that they are much more important to me than anything else in the world. Period.

Besides, I don't know what I would do if I wasn't married to Lawrence. Where would I be living? The whole idea was mind-boggling—she couldn't begin to conceive of it. Yes, I'm just an old-fashioned girl, thought Chaney. That's why I lost my virginity before I hit sixteen, and was pregnant at my wedding. Maybe that was the real Chaney. Maybe all her sweetness and goodness was a charade. It felt like a straitjacket sometimes, this trying to do the right thing.

What's the matter with me? Chaney demanded, feeling her temples begin to throb. She ran hot water into the sink, squeezing in dishwashing liquid. I should start reading, there are so many books I haven't read . . .

No, I need people. I need a good friend, an adult, someone I feel comfortable with, someone who cares but doesn't feel like he has to guide me all the time, someone who can just listen. Someone like . . .

Chaney turned off the water. If only I could just be comfortable with Taurique, if only I could talk to him, and spend time with him without worrying what anyone else thinks, including him. Including me. Why shouldn't he be my friend now? Why should I feel like I'm doing something wrong by having him at my house? We didn't have an affair, he was a bona fide boyfriend, and it was nearly ten years ago. And so what if he's attractive. I'm not exactly going to jump on any attractive man I see. I had lots of attractive male friends while I was going out with Taurique. Yes, he was always around, but I'm a grown woman, I'm not some little girl who'll be at the mercy of any good-looking guy with a smooth line.

Chaney smiled bitterly. Who am I fooling? she thought. I can't be anything to him until I know why he forgot about me so quickly. And God only knows why it matters now, but it does. I *have* to know. A part of her wanted him back, she had to admit to herself. A part of her wanted his touch again, if only so that she could be the one to dump him this time.

No. That's not true. But what is? The throbbing in her temples continued, slowly, rhythmically. She tried concentrating on the dishes, but found that she couldn't. *What should I do?* She didn't know, she wished somehow it could be decided for her.

But it won't be, she thought, not this time. Chaney sighed and felt the full weight of how very alone she was in the house. *Jimmy said I should resolve it,* she recalled. She smiled, a lump forming in her throat. *Well, maybe Jimmy knows best.*

Lawrence called just as Chaney was serving dinner. As usual, Ronnie and Nicole raced to the phone and pushed each other out of the way trying to be the first to answer it. This time, Nicole won.

"Daddy!" she was practically screaming, as Ronnie gave up and headed for the other phone.

Chaney let them chatter excitedly until she finished serving their plates, and then called them away from the phone and picked it up in the bedroom.

"Chaney, it's good to hear your voice," Lawrence said, almost before she could say hello.

"Hi, baby."

"Hi." He laughed a bit.

"Well, how was it?"

"You really want to know?"

"Lawrence, don't be silly," she replied impatiently.

"Okay, it's just—I'm in such a good mood, and I don't want to *brag,* or nothin'."

"It went well?"

"Well. Ha—well? Is that the best word you can come up with? Try—incredibly. Or—phenomenally. Or—incomparably. Or—indubitably."

"Indubitably?"

"Just kidding."

"You'd better be, you and your grammar-correcting self, a man who corrected my grammar the first time I met him."

"You could take it."

"Indubitably."

"Ha, ha—that's my wife. Always a woman of wit."

"Anyway . . ." she answered with an easy smile.

"Anyway . . ."

"You really sang well?"

"I have to admit it. The curtain calls, baby. The shouting—man, I feel so high, I don't know *when* I'll come down. 'Cause these people aren't easy to please, you know. They'll actually throw rotten fruit if they don't like you and . . . they *loved* me."

"I'm so proud of you, Lawrence."

"Thank you. And you know what the best part is? Three more performances here, a few in France, a record date in England, and I come home to unwrap my present. Mmm—I can hardly wait."

Chaney smiled. "Me, too," she said, trying to picture his face and finding, for an alarming moment, that she could not.

"So, how are my babies doing?"

"Great. They still can't get over the way you dropped in from Milan."

"And I didn't get caught, either. I admit, I was a little nervous on the flight back, but as I said, it was worth it. Listen, kiss Nicki and Ronnie for me."

"Of course."

"How about you? Anything new happening there?" He sounded perfectly nonchalant. Chaney swallowed and tried, almost successfully, to match him.

"Same old thing," she said.

"You're sure? It doesn't have to be something important."

He was trying, but somehow his tone was a bit sarcastic. Enough of the games, thought Chaney.

"You mean Taurique?" she asked, sighing.

"Whatever."

"Trust me, okay?" she retorted, instantly regretting her tone of voice.

"I didn't say I didn't."

"You didn't have to."

"I think I have a right to ask questions about that situation, don't you?"

His voice was all reason and calm, and Chaney felt her palms start sweating. This is stupid; I haven't done anything, she thought, deciding she wasn't up to an argument.

"Of course, Lawrence."

"Did you have lunch with him again?"

"As a matter of fact, I did." Just a touch defiantly—what's wrong with you, she wondered, I thought you didn't want a fight . . .

"Oh? I thought nothing new was happening."

Chaney sighed. "Please, can we stop this?" she pleaded.

There was a silence. "All right, Chaney," Lawrence said, and Chaney filled in the rest in her mind—all right, Chaney, just don't give me any surprises when I come home. All right, Chaney, I don't want to hear about your tawdry affair anyway. All right, Chaney, I don't want to be hurt today. All right, Chaney, I can't do anything about it anyway. All right, Chaney, I knew I couldn't trust you, obviously you'd tell me all about it, if it was all so innocent . . .

"Maybe I'd better go," Lawrence said.

"No!" Chaney replied, louder than she'd planned, snapping out of her reverie. "Please don't, not yet."

"But we're not saying anything."

"Sweetheart, I was thinking, that's all."

"About what?"

"About how I don't want to argue with you, but how anything I say about the subject seems to upset you, and how I feel guilty even though I haven't done anything, just because of your reaction, so I'd rather not even start."

There was another long silence. "I'm sorry," he said finally.

"Lawrence, I understand why you're acting this way. I don't

blame you, you don't have to apologize, I just wish you'd believe me."

"I do. I just—I'm just . . . forget it."

"What?"

"Nothing. I . . ."

"Please?" she implored him.

"Okay." He took a deep breath. "Chaney, would you tell me . . ."

She forced herself to answer immediately—"Yes"—although every cell in her body was screaming, *"No."*

"Chaney?"

"Yes?"

"I don't want to have any doubts—I'm just—I'm just . . ."

"Lawrence . . ."

"I don't want to lose you. Maybe I'm being irrational, but . . ."

"Lawrence, baby, don't, *please?* I told you you have to trust me. You *have* to, after all this time." Slow down, she thought, listening to herself and realizing how unreassuring she sounded.

"Yeah—it was just easier when you weren't speaking to anybody, you know? That sounds awful, I know, but it's true."

Chaney sighed. "What happened to, 'I'm in such a good mood?' Can we go back to that part? Because I don't know what to say about any of the other stuff that hasn't already been covered."

"You're right," said Lawrence, after another long pause. "I love you, Chaney."

"I love you, too, Lawrence. And I'm very, very proud of you."

"Thank you." He sounded depressed.

"Goodnight."

"Goodnight. I'll be dreaming about you."

Chaney suddenly remembered what she had dreamed the night before. Her reply almost caught in her throat, but she was able to get it out—"Me, too."

"Goodbye."

"Goodbye."

She hung up, noticing that her hands were shaking. Thank God, she thought, he didn't call me closer to bedtime; I would be awake all night. I'll probably be awake all night anyway.

Chaney walked slowly out of the bedroom, switching off the light as she reached the door. I lied to him, she thought, about two very important things. It's come to that. I thought I would never get to this point, but I have.

So I guess I have to clear all this stuff up now, she decided, her heart pounding. I'll call Taurique tomorrow.

"What's the matter, Mommy?" Nicole was asking.

Chaney turned toward her daughter—she hadn't heard her approaching. Chaney tried to smile, but instead she just drew the child close to her.

"Nothing's wrong," she said. "I'm just a bit tired today."

"Oh." Nicole was silent for a while, then she said, "Mommy, did you and Daddy have a fight?"

Chaney pulled away, surprised. "No, baby. Why do you ask?"

The little girl shrugged.

"Honey, your father didn't upset me. I told you, I'm just tired, that's all. Don't worry."

"Okay." Nicole hugged Chaney. "I love you, Mommy," she said.

"I love you, too." Chaney blinked furiously, determined not to break down. "Did you—um . . ." Her voice was unsteady, and she cleared her throat. "Did you eat?" she managed.

"Uh-huh."

"You put your dishes away?"

"Uh-huh."

"Where's your brother?"

"He's watching TV."

"Okay—um, I'm gonna do the dishes."

"Do you want me to help you?"

Chaney smiled. "That's okay. You go watch TV with your brother. But thanks, honey."

Nicole smiled, then ran into the living room. Chaney watched her go, catching her breath—she really wanted to cry, but she didn't want Nicole to see her. I lied to her, too, after all, Chaney suddenly realized. She blinked and then swallowed very hard. Well, she thought, this will all be resolved very soon.

Chaney had tried to casually slip in the announcement that she was expecting another baby without hesitation, the memory of her first announcement still vivid in her mind. He was not going to belittle her for being timid, not again, so she summoned up her courage, waited until after dinner, and told him flat out, "I'm pregnant, Lawrence."

He was eating ice cream, and he stopped.

"You are?" he said simply, gazing at her.

She lost her nerve immediately, afraid of what he was going to do, what he would destroy. She waited.

"How long?" he finally asked.

"A month and a half."

Then he lowered his head. At first, Chaney wasn't sure what was happening—was he laughing, like last time? His shoulders were shaking. He sniffled quietly.

"Lawrence?"

She came toward him, put her hand on his arm. He recoiled slightly.

"Don't," he said, and he cleared his throat, coughing a few times.

"Don't what? Touch you? Why not?"

"I'm okay."

"No, you're not."

He wouldn't look at her.

There was nothing so unnerving, to Chaney, as seeing her husband cry. She hadn't seen it before, not even on that nightmarish day when she'd told him she was expecting Nicole, not even when he'd told his father it was his intention to marry her, and his father had told him he had his blessing, but since

Lawrence was a man now, he was on his own, financially, and too bad you'll have to forget about the vocal career. She saw him struggle to hold something way down inside many times, and she was familiar with the times he went running, just to release whatever anxiety or anger he was feeling. But she had never seen him cry. She hadn't even seen his eyes wet before.

"I'm sorry," she said, tears rolling down her cheeks, putting her arms around him. He held on tight.

"Don't be." He was fighting very hard, trying to regain control and losing.

"I should have been more careful. I'm sorry, Lawrence, I'm so sorry."

"What happened?"

"I guess sometimes if you take certain kinds of medications with the pill—I think that's what happened."

"Really?" There was no edge to his voice. He merely sounded miserable.

"I—I'm sorry. I should have asked the pharmacist."

"What am I gonna do?" He looked at her. "I can't afford this, Chaney. We're just making it now."

She gazed at him, speechless.

"I'm supposed to be a man," he continued, wiping his eyes ferociously.

"You *are.*"

"Yeah, I'm a great man. I can't even look after my family."

"What do you mean? You *always* look after us."

He looked into her eyes earnestly. "Chaney," he said, "I don't want to be . . . I don't want to be a church singer forever. I have to do more. I *need* to, you understand? I need to. But I still need to study right now, I don't feel ready to really start a career yet, and I can't afford lessons, really, at the moment, it's really hard, and now . . . don't get me wrong, I was glad to take responsibility for you and Nicole, I wouldn't trade the two of you for the world, and I think it's important for you to be at home, I don't want you to go out and work, but . . ."

He broke down again, and she kissed him—his face was salty, and he couldn't stop himself; he was sobbing.

"I'm sorry," Chaney said, crying again. "I'll do whatever you want."

"You don't have to do anything. It's me, not you."

"What do you mean?"

"He knew—he knew I couldn't handle this."

"Who?"

"I can't. He's right."

"Your father?"

He looked away. He was slowly regaining control.

"Your father?" Chaney repeated incredulously. "You're doing this to yourself because of your *father?* Lawrence, you're more man than he'll—I mean, how can you possibly feel bad? You are single-handedly taking care of a wife and a baby, plus finding time to work on your singing—you're *doing* it, whatever it is, doing it and working every day on top of that. You know what? Your dad has this twisted idea of what a man is because he doesn't want you to turn out like your uncle. You know what else? I love your uncle. He knows you're human. Your dad has set standards so high, there's no room for error, and that's not fair. No one can live up to that."

Lawrence was calm now. "It's not just that, Chaney. It's your family, too. I think Jimmy's the only one who likes me. Your father was so shocked that I got his little girl pregnant . . . I know he'll resent that for the rest of his life. And I know they think you made a mistake, ending up with a musician."

"But how does that make you less of a man?"

"I should be able to provide for my family."

"You do! I said that before."

"But we shouldn't be living so close to the edge that something that should be good news causes a big crisis."

Chaney sighed. "I don't know how I could have been so careless, especially after . . . it's not you. You're doing absolutely everything you can."

"It's not enough." He looked despondent.

"Lawrence, there's nothing wrong with asking for help."

He laughed. "Good idea," he said. "You got any suggestions? Not my father."

"Your mother."

"He rules that roost, baby; she doesn't have much of her own."

"Your uncle."

He paused. "Uncle Willie?" he asked.

"You've only got one uncle who'd do that for us."

He thought. "I can't," he said.

"Not because you'd feel less of a man."

He was silent.

"Lawrence, this is cutting off your nose to spite your face. You don't have to prove anything to anybody."

He stared at the table. "We can just use him as a last resort," Chaney said.

There was another long silence. She waited. She wanted to massage his shoulders, he looked so tense, but she was afraid to.

He looked up at her. "I'm gonna start entering some competitions," he said, "I need to find out if I'm gonna make it as a singer. I need to know if I'm wasting my time, if I should be trying to work my way up the ladder at my job. I'll call Uncle Willie if I have to, and I'll pay him back anything I owe him, with interest."

"Okay."

He relaxed slightly, then reached for her hand, pulling her gently down into his lap.

Chaney kissed him. "We'll be okay," she said, and they began to kiss each other, gently, then more desperately, and then they were crying again. It was the last time Chaney saw Lawrence cry.

Nine

October 28

Chaney's throat was completely dry, even though she had finished her second glass of water. She glanced at her watch, then glanced at the door. He's late, as usual, she thought, except this time she wasn't sure she could stand it. This meeting was already three days later than she'd planned, and every minute added to her nervousness.

It hadn't occurred to her that Taurique wouldn't be free for lunch on Friday. That meant three agonizing days, three nights of fitful sleep—she didn't want to meet him over the weekend, didn't want the children to find out. She debated dropping them off with Perry and Val on Saturday, but she didn't want Perry to know, either. She swore Taurique to secrecy—she debated that, too, but it was the only way. She knew she couldn't deal with Perry's questions about her feelings, not this time.

Maybe he won't show, she thought. After all, she had made the whole meeting seem like something very heavy. Maybe he decided he couldn't deal with it, maybe it was okay to have her in his life as long as everything was light and friendly and on his terms. Well, this time it wouldn't work that way—and he'd better *be* here, thought Chaney angrily, because I answered all his damned questions, the least he can do is answer mine. And if he doesn't come . . .

But he had arrived, just walked through the door, looking

suitably flustered as he scanned the restaurant, searching for Chaney's face, and suitably apologetic as he hurried to her table.

"I'm sorry, Chaney," said Taurique, in a voice dripping with brown sugar. "I got held up with a client."

"Oh, that's okay." She sounded exactly as uptight as she felt.

"You're the most understanding person I know," Taurique said, sitting down. "The thing is, I really tried, because I figured that it must have been important. I'm sorry."

"It's okay, Taurique." It wasn't really, but at least he had come. And it wasn't *really* his fault—lighten up, she thought.

"Thanks, baby, won't happen again." He smiled and picked up a menu. "What are you having?"

"The soup and salad."

"What a woman—that sounds so *healthy*. Makes me almost feel guilty for being in the mood for a bacon cheeseburger."

"Grease, Taurique, pure grease."

"Yeah, but real men like me *thrive* on red meat."

Chaney smiled. "Real men like that have heart attacks at 45. But hey, don't let me stand in the way of your macho destiny."

Taurique laughed. "I've missed you," he said. "Okay, I'll have the chicken fingers. Is that all right?"

"Yes, Taurique. It's fried, but it'll do."

"Good." The waitress approached them, and they ordered. As soon as she left, Taurique said, "So, what was so serious?"

"Well . . ." Chaney was tongue-tied. She looked away.

"You want to talk to me about . . ."

Chaney laughed nervously, realizing that as much as she felt she had to finally ask the questions she had been suppressing for years, she didn't really want to know the answers.

A waitress arrived with their drinks.

"Thanks," said Taurique, smiling—his every move, thought Chaney, is an act of flirtation. He can't do *anything* innocently, can't even smile a thank-you without being sexy. No wonder I lost my virginity to him.

"Shay," he was saying, "look, maybe we should get together later. I can see this conversation will need some time."

"No!" Chaney realized she had spoken far too loudly—people were staring at her. "Um—I really want to talk to you now," she mumbled.

"Okay." Taurique looked bewildered. "So—what is it, Chaney?"

"Well . . ." She was beginning to disgust herself—now! I'm saying it *now*. "It's about what happened ten years ago."

"Oh." Taurique sipped his drink, frowning slightly. "What do you need to know?"

"Well . . ." Why did you leave me? She couldn't get it out now. She took a deep breath and forced herself to speak.

"I want to know about California."

"Okay." Taurique gazed around, collecting his thoughts. "It's been a long time since that," he said finally.

"You said you'd tell me about Christine if I asked you really nicely."

He smiled. "Did I?"

"Uh-huh." Chaney watched him. She felt deeply relieved that the question was finally out, and somehow, Taurique's discomfort was reassuring.

"I probably did."

"Besides, I've been telling you the story of *my* life."

"What's fair is fair, right? Okay, okay. Where should I start?"

"You left New York . . ."

"The beginning. All right." He sipped his drink again, and took a deep breath. "Well—I left New York, went to California, it was like nothing I had seen before, I mean, it was totally different from where *I* grew up, which was kind of the whole point of leaving in the first place. Anyway, I liked it. I don't think I could have spent the rest of my life there, but I really had a good time. I was young, and I was willing to experience whatever was out there . . ."

"You mean, the women," Chaney interrupted, trying to sound like she really didn't care, but feeling a pain in her stomach.

"Women, the beaches, Hollywood—whatever, Chaney. The women weren't the main thing."

"But you made sure we weren't committed anymore before you left."

"That's because I didn't think it was practical. I mean, we were both so young at the time, I was all the way across the country . . ."

"I could have waited. I didn't date anybody else for months, I was looking forward to seeing you at Christmas. I could have waited until the summer, too."

Be cool, she reminded herself, feeling all the old hurt coming dangerously near the surface. She took a deep breath, looking away. When she focused on him again, he was watching her pensively.

"I always knew you were very special, Chaney," he said softly.

"You didn't think it'd last," she said, more matter-of-factly.

Taurique looked down. "I wasn't sure," he said.

"You didn't really love me, then." Damn it, she thought. The voice had held, but her ears were burning, and the rest of her face was beginning to flush.

"It wasn't that, Chaney. I loved you very much." He was gazing directly at her. "I just met you too soon."

"You *met* me too soon," she repeated, rolling her eyes.

"I really couldn't handle what had happened between us," he continued. "I tried to lie to myself for a while, but deep down, I knew I had a lot of living to do before I was sure who the hell I really was, and I knew the only way to get my head together was to get away from New York and be by myself for a while. I wasn't ready to be in love with you yet, it just happened."

"So once it happened, you decided to run from it," Chaney responded pointedly.

"Maybe." Taurique looked away. "Look, I knew I wasn't the kind of guy you deserved to be with, I just wanted to be with you so much that I convinced myself I could make it work out. I kept wondering how long it would take for me to screw up, like every guy in my family always does. And to tell the truth, when we first got together, I really thought that you were going to be my girlfriend, like girlfriends I'd had before. I mean, I knew it would be different, because you were different, but I wasn't ready for a serious relationship, not then."

"So you don't believe in that childhood sweetheart stuff."

"I was very young, Chaney. Look, what did you want me to do, marry you and take you with me? Be realistic, Chaney. I couldn't even take care of *myself* properly yet."

"You never wanted to marry me?" The question wasn't nearly as indifferent as she would have liked.

"Of course I did. *Eventually.* I just wasn't sure when, that's all. Not out of high school." He was gazing at her fondly, and she had to look away for a moment.

"I didn't expect that," she responded quietly. "I just thought you'd come home at Christmas, I thought you'd still care at least that long." I sound childish and ridiculous, she thought, but it's too late.

"To tell you the truth, Chaney," Taurique replied patiently, "my not coming home had more to do with the fact that I was finally away from my dad's drinking problem than with Christine."

She looked down. This explanation had never occurred to her. She felt embarrassed.

"I did care about you, Chaney. Look, I didn't think my relationship with Christine would last very long, necessarily. I mean, I liked her, I cared about her, we had a lot of fun, but I never forgot about you. I just felt like I needed to experience things. I wanted to see what it was like to date a white girl . . ."

"Oh please, Taurique." She rolled her eyes, instantly steaming.

"I'm being honest, Chaney."

"So you picked Christine to represent her whole race. That is such bull. Unless all those girls are the same. Did you date me because you wanted to know what black girls are like? Or maybe black *virgins?*"

"You have a serious chip on your shoulder, Chaney . . ."

"I don't have a chip on my shoulder, I just don't respect dating people because they are a category, especially one that doesn't reflect who *you* are. I'd have more respect if you told me, 'I liked her, I dated her, I didn't care if she was white or black.' But no, you just wanted some white pu . . ."

"Chaney!" His eyes were wide with amazement.

She stopped. She didn't usually use language like that, and she certainly hadn't planned to lose her temper or her self-control. She felt suddenly very embarrassed.

"I'm sorry, T," she finally said, unable to look at him for a long time. When she did, he was watching her again.

"What are you thinking?"

"I've never heard you say how you felt so—definitely before."

"I'm sorry, I said I was sorry."

"No, don't apologize." Taurique looked at her thoughtfully. "Go on, okay?" he said.

"Really?"

"I don't necessarily agree with what you're saying, but at least you're being honest with me. I've waited a long time to hear you really speak your mind without being pushed."

She frowned. "What does *that* mean?" she asked.

"I'll tell you later, I promise. Anyway, you were telling me all about myself."

He was smiling just slightly, and she had to smile back—she had lost her train of thought now, the bitterness had dissipated a bit, but she was going to go on.

"I just think," she said in a calmer voice, "that one person can't represent their whole race, so it's stup—it doesn't make sense to say you want to find out what dating a white girl is like, because there are Italians and Greeks and Jews and Germans and on and on and on, and besides, if you're not just doing it to do it, you have to assume that everyone is a bit different, and if you *are* doing it just to do it—well, I can't respect that, Taurique."

"Uh-huh." The waitress arrived with their food.

"Saved by the bell," Taurique remarked, and Chaney smiled a bit, still feeling dissatisfied.

"Then again," Taurique went on, "maybe I'm not off the hook yet."

Chaney had to laugh. "That obvious?" she asked.

"Uh-huh."

"Oh."

Taurique bit into a chicken finger. "This is good," he said. "Want some?" He held out the end he hadn't bitten. Chaney hesitated, then took a mouthful of chicken, her lips grazing his fingertips as she did.

"Sorry," she said, startled.

"Don't apologize," Taurique replied with a little smile, and he put what was left in his mouth, or rather, on his tongue, where he paused a split second before bringing his lips together.

Always with the flirtation, she thought, feeling her heart speed up slightly in spite of herself.

"So—what else?" Taurique asked.

Chaney chewed her salad, swallowed, and said, "How long were you with her?"

"About six months."

"What happened?"

Taurique shrugged. "Like I said, it wasn't supposed to last forever. I always liked her, it just kind of cooled off."

Chaney looked up suddenly—she had just seen a picture, inside her mind, that had made her chest tighten. "Meaning it was hot there for a while, huh, Taurique?" she blurted out, her eyes narrowed.

He rolled his eyes. "Come on, Shay."

"Was she good?"

Taurique bit off half of his third chicken finger. "You're out of line," he said calmly.

"Sorry." The apology was anything but sincere—it was a spontaneous question, and she knew it was rude, but having asked it, Chaney realized it was kind of important to know. She looked up from taking a mouthful of soup to see Taurique scrutinizing her. "What?" she asked. "Look, I said I was sorry."

"But you didn't mean it."

"I'm sorry, Taurique." She was unable to be genuine, somehow. She picked up her spoon again.

"Is your husband good?"

She stopped in midair. "Okay, you've made your point," she shot back.

"No, really." He was gazing at her unflinchingly, and she knew this was going to be a fight.

"Can we drop this?" she said.

"I bet you want it real bad about now. I bet you can barely stand it. That is, if he knows how to do all the freaky things it takes to make you hot."

Chaney wanted to stare him down but couldn't because all of a sudden she felt tears springing into her eyes, and she looked down, her ears burning. She felt two fingers under her chin and shook her head, glaring at him—a tear escaped, and she chased it fiercely, and then he was kneeling beside her chair, right there in the restaurant, with his hand on her arm, trying to look into her eyes.

"I'm sorry, Shay," he was saying over and over. "C'mon, look at me—I'm sorry," and the more he apologized, the more tears escaped, and suddenly she realized that he was holding her, and she was mortified.

"Stop it," she was whispering. "Just stop."

He pulled away, and she found herself gazing into his eyes. There it was, that same penitent expression from so long ago.

"I hurt you. I'm sorry, babe. That was really cruel. I'm sorry. I was mad at you."

"Taurique, sit down, please?"

"No, not till you feel better."

"I'll feel better if you sit down."

"I'm sorry. That was . . . inexcusable."

"Please, Taurique? You're embarrassing me."

"Okay." He got up and went back to his seat.

Chaney ate some more salad in silence. Her ears were still hot—she truly wished she could disappear; she wondered what everyone in the restaurant was thinking. She became aware that Taurique was still looking at her.

"Your food will get cold," she said curtly.

"I'm not hungry anymore."

"Suit yourself." She took a mouthful of soup.

"Talk to me, Chaney. Come on . . . look, I said I was sorry, I just thought you asked a very rude question, especially since I know you have an attitude about the girl, and I thought that if you weren't going to treat me with respect . . . I know I said I was glad you were speaking your mind, but . . . don't you think you were out of line, too?"

Chaney swallowed, then gazed at him, and the hurt melted away, somehow. "Yes," she admitted. "And I'm sorry. I mean it."

"Accepted," Taurique said quietly, with a hint of smile. There was silence, and then Taurique asked, "Would it really matter to you to know?"

Chaney was embarrassed again. "You don't have to . . ."

"I'm serious. Would you deal better with the whole thing if you knew?"

"T . . ."

"Yeah, she was pretty good, but she was nothing compared to you. That's what you wanted to know, right?"

She coughed, wishing she had never decided to resolve

things. She wished she could go back to before that stupid question—what was the point of it, anyway? What she really needed to know was that she never left his memory, not that she was the best screw he ever had.

"What now?" Taurique was saying. "I'm—look, I made a mess of this, right? It wasn't . . . I didn't want it to be this way. God, I'm really an idiot sometimes."

"No, T." She took a deep breath. "You're not an idiot. I was the one who brought it up."

He looked very sad. "I'm sorry, I have to go soon—I just don't want it to end this way. Can I take you out to dinner sometime? Please? Because—then we won't have a deadline, we can relax and have our fight and then have time to really be friends again."

He smiled, and Chaney laughed a bit.

"Sure," she said. He took her hand and squeezed it, with an irresistibly boyish expression on his face that made her suddenly want to hug him.

"Thanks," he said, and then he started to eat with lightning speed, and she laughed again.

How did I do without this for so long? she was thinking. God, I've missed you, Taurique, she heard herself saying.

He paused, surprised. "You have?" he asked, and Chaney wished, once again, she had kept her mouth shut. But it was too late.

"I guess so," she said.

He wiped his mouth with his napkin. "You know what?" he said. "I've missed you, too. I wish I hadn't taken so long to see you again. But maybe it was better this way."

"Because we can really be friends now."

"Right." They were gazing at each other again, and Chaney felt uncomfortable. She was afraid she was looking at him the way he was looking at her.

"I'm sorry, babe," he said, rising. "I really have to go now."

"I understand." He reached for his wallet.

"No way, my treat," Chaney said. Lawrence's treat, actually, it occurred to her.

"Okay." He hesitated, then bent over and kissed her cheek. "Can I call you about dinner?"

"Sure."

"Goodbye, Shay."

"Goodbye, T."

He took three steps back, then turned and hurried out of the restaurant.

Ten

October 29

Tuesday was not a good day. Lawrence called—Chaney had forgotten that he had a performance the night before, and didn't ask him how it went, which made him upset, which made him suspicious, which made her feel bad, which made her try to play it off, with eventual success, but not before he said that he was going to stop calling home, because worrying about her being unfaithful was the last thing he needed when he was trying to prepare for a performance, all said in a cold tone of voice that she hadn't heard in a long time.

Chaney hadn't slept very much that night—she kept seeing the way Taurique had looked at her just before he'd left her in the restaurant, and thinking about what he had said: "I bet you want it real bad about now . . ." She tried, fought with all her power, to re-create making love to Lawrence, but all she saw were Taurique's lips, and his tongue, slowly retreating into his mouth, and she felt that warmth—not heat, but warmth—that made her blurt out that she missed him.

My God, she thought, running the vacuum over the living room carpet, how can I possibly have dinner with him? What could I possibly do to explain to my children where I was going? Just me, and a man who isn't their father, out for the evening?

"I'm so stupid," she said, and the fear began to creep from

the pit of her stomach toward her throat. She felt weak—like in the dream, she thought, completely helpless. Perry was no help, of course—he would just convince her what she was feeling was silly. And she knew what Jimmy would say—she'd resolved it; why was she going out to dinner with him? Or that if she still had questions, why ask them in such an intimate setting?

But how is dinner worse than lunch? Because things are changing . . . no. I'm attracted to him of course; he's very attractive. But it was *warmth*, not heat. If I love him, it's a different kind of love. I've been away from my husband enough times to know how to handle temptation.

But nothing like this. She turned off the vacuum, took up a broom to sweep the front step—a car was pulling up next door. Carl was back. She could make out Pam's face—she looked almost radiant. A knot formed in Chaney's throat. She swallowed, but it wasn't quite gone when Carl called out a greeting to her, so she just smiled and waved.

"How've you been?" he said, retrieving his luggage and slamming the trunk of his car.

"Okay."

"When is Lawrence due back?"

"A few weeks. How long are you here now?"

"Week and a half"

"Good to see you."

"Same. Well, I'd better take my stuff inside."

"Okay Carl. Pam."

"Chaney."

She watched them go inside. You're not so friendly now, are you? she thought. Pam barely looked at me since Carl is back. My dear friend, obviously she's using me. At least I have the decency not to pretend I want to be around her just so I can amuse myself.

Chaney walked into the house. Pam's probably just too happy to think about me right now, it occurred to her. Like she should be . . .

I am so tired of thinking about this, Chaney realized. The phone rang, and she jumped. Who could that be? Her heart was pounding. Of course, T making dinner arrangements . . .

"Hello," she said tentatively.

"Hi, Shay-shay."

She relaxed. "Perry."

"Of course. Who else?"

"Nobody. So, what's up?"

"Val and I are taking Ken and Calvin to see Val's sister upstate this weekend, and we want to take you, Nicole, and Ronnie with us."

"Sounds like fun," she replied, her mind suddenly full of possibilities, "but Lawrence will be worried if he can't reach me."

"So call him and leave the number. I'll give it to you. Don't say no, Chaney, you know you could use a change of scenery."

Chaney sighed, sitting down. "Perry, can I ask you something?" she said.

"Anything. What's wrong?"

"Taurique asked me to have dinner with him."

There was a short silence. "Oh?" Perry responded finally. "When?"

"This weekend."

"I *see.*" Perry let out a low whistle.

"No, it's not like that, Perry," Chaney said quickly. "It's all really innocent. I just—I just don't know how to explain it to the kids. I mean, they're not exactly used to me hanging out."

"Uh-huh. So you want me to take them, and leave you in New York."

"No . . . well, yeah. If it's okay with . . ."

"You know what, Chaney?" Perry interrupted. "I think I was wrong about you and Taurique. Maybe it *is* all that, after all this time. Not because you're having dinner, because of the way you sound right now."

"You're wrong," she protested, but her heart was pounding and she could hear how defensive her voice was.

"Look, you're a big girl, and I know you're not exactly feeling fulfilled by your marriage . . ."

"I'm *not* having an affair, Perry!" Chaney was surprised at how loudly she had just screamed at him. She took a deep breath, calming down. "Look, I'm sorry," she said. "It's just that everyone keeps jumping to conclusions about things, and they don't even know what's going on."

"What's going on?"

"Nothing!"

"Honestly? Look, this is *me*, Chaney. It's Perry. I'm not gonna judge you, remember? And to tell the truth, I don't care about Lawrence or Taurique half as much as I care about you, so whatever you do with either of them is fine with me if it makes you happy. A divorce can be a really painful experience. Everybody I've known who's had one says so, but then again, you don't get a medal for spending thirty or forty years being ignored . . ."

"Who said anything about a divorce?" Chaney was yelling again, infuriated by his half-baked deductions.

"Then you're talking about an affair."

Chaney closed her eyes, swearing silently. "I'm talking about dinner," she said evenly. "And I'm sorry I even mentioned it."

There was a pause. Then Perry said, "I'd be happy to take Nicki and Ronnie upstate. Look, I'm glad you're having a completely innocent dinner with Taurique. And even if it's not so innocent, it's pretty clear you don't want to discuss it, so I guess that's all there is to say, right?"

Chaney sighed—he sounded very offended. Still, there was no point telling him anything more, because he couldn't really understand, and even if he could, she didn't feel like explaining. No, this was one time she was going to have to sort things out all by herself.

"Right," she said. "Thanks, Perry. Look—I've got to go. I'll talk to you soon."

"Goodbye, Chaney."

She hung up, feeling very tired. Maybe Perry was right. Maybe it wasn't just dinner . . . I want to do the right thing, she thought, but—I have to see Taurique again, because being around him makes me feel good, even though we have our disagreements. And what's wrong with dinner? It's like a date. But not really, because . . .

She accidentally glanced at the clock.

"Whoops . . ." Time to pick up the kids from school. If they're excited about the trip, I'll send them, and if they ask a lot of questions about it, I'll go, too.

She smiled wearily, her head beginning to hurt. I can handle this, she decided, as she headed out the door, repeating the thought over and over in an effort to convince herself.

Eleven

November 1

Chaney glanced at herself in the rearview mirror for the umpteenth time. This is really, really ridiculous, she thought. But I look fantastic . . .

She hadn't gone to the hairdresser, because she wasn't making a big deal out of this dinner, but what she had done with herself, all by herself, was stunning, if she did say so herself. She had gone for simple elegance—a little red dress with a square neckline under a red swing coat, with gold slingback shoes and gold hoop earrings, subtle, gold-kissed makeup with the exception of her crimson lips, and her hair shiny and loosely curled.

It had almost been too easy arranging the dinner—the kids wanted to go away, they thought it was an adventure to spend a couple of nights away from Mommy, so they didn't ask questions. Even Pam obliged by going away with Carl and Tracey for a week—the only problem was that Chaney had to feed their dog, and she didn't particularly like dogs. But that was okay; she had agreed immediately because that meant she could go out all dressed up and not worry about Pam's speculations.

It occurred to her that Taurique could have picked her up. Oh, well, it's better this way, she decided, at least I can leave if things get out of hand. Not that I don't trust him, or anything.

Of course, now I have to pay for parking. Her trip across 68th

Street had been fruitless, so she'd decided to give up and park in the garage near Lincoln Center. The attendant looked her up and down as she got out of the car—damn, I'm good, she thought, handing him the keys with a dazzling smile on her face, and heading up onto the street with her sexiest walk. She had to chuckle—truly ridiculous, she thought. This whole evening is the stupidest idea I've had in years. But somehow, the idea of doing something she probably shouldn't was so exhilarating that it was all she could do to keep from skipping down the street.

Sfuzzi—there was the banner, it was just as she remembered it. Another man was staring at her. It seemed like ages since she'd been looked at like that. Of course, because I'm never dressed to kill and unescorted at the same time. And when Chaney was escorted, she never looked around—it didn't seem right.

What a good girl you are, she thought, crossing the street. What's a nice girl like you doing in a place like this, meeting a man like Taurique? Just having fun, for a change. She was almost giddy; nothing was serious tonight. It's better that way, she decided, opening the door and marching up to the hostess's podium.

"I'm here to meet Mr. Taurique Williams," she announced. The woman smiled knowingly. "Right this way."

Chaney followed her up the steps to a table by the wall. Taurique rose when he saw her approaching, a huge grin on his face.

"Mr. Williams, I presume?" Chaney said.

"Baby, I'll be whoever you want me to be, as fine as you are."

Chaney laughed. "May I join you?"

"Just try to escape," Taurique said.

"Oh, I'd never do that." Chaney sat down, and the hostess handed her a menu. She glanced up to see Taurique still staring at her with a little smile on his face. "Oh, stop it," she said. "I ain't *that* fine."

"You're right," he responded, looking down.

"You could have argued."

He smiled. "Read your menu," he said.

A waiter arrived to take their drink order.

"A bottle of Dom Perignon," Taurique said, and Chaney looked at him questioningly.

"What's the occasion?" she asked.

"You like champagne, don't you?"

"Yes."

"That's enough for me. Now, pick something, woman, I'm hungry."

She glared at him, then smiled and searched the menu—no spaghetti, because spaghetti is hard to eat without looking like a slob—big deal, I've known this fool for ages . . .

Chicken with Romano cheese—that looked good. The orders were placed, the bread put on the table, and the champagne was poured . . . and poured . . .

"A toast to Chaney Rivers, the most beautiful woman in the world," Taurique was saying—he was on his third glass of champagne.

Chaney giggled. The serious expression on his face was too funny. She raised her glass—number one and a half, but already she was a little dizzy—this is completely insane, she thought, feeling profoundly contented.

"To Taurique Williams, the sexiest single man in the world," she said, raising her glass again—my God, I'm out of control, she thought, putting the champagne flute on the table, her smile fading. She looked around—saved by the bell, the food was arriving. She glanced at Taurique, who was swallowing more champagne. At least he didn't seem to be reacting to what had just come out of her mouth.

One bite, and she forgot herself again.

"This is *incredible!*" she exclaimed, smiling.

"Wait until dessert. *That's* incredible."

"Okay."

"More champagne?"

"No thanks."

"Oh, c'mon." He refilled her glass.

"T . . ."

"That's it—see?" He held up the nearly empty bottle. "No more—I promise."

"Okay, okay." She swallowed some more champagne and took another mouthful of food. I'm drunk, she thought. She hadn't been drunk in ages, not since Lawrence's first major role in a major house, when they'd bought a bottle of wine and she'd made him a beautiful dinner, and they drank to him, to her, to both of them, and most of all, to a budding career bursting into full flower.

Why am I drinking with someone other than my husband? Because I'm behaving badly. It suddenly struck her that they were practically across the street from the Met, any of Lawrence's opera friends could be here. The elation was finally beginning to wane. What if someone told Lawrence? Consequences, there are always consequences—Chaney was slipping, she could feel the euphoria giving way, being transformed into misery.

"What's the matter, Chaney?"

She snapped out of her reverie. "Nothing."

"Oh, come on, you can't lie to me."

Chaney stared out the window. "This is wrong," she said slowly.

"What?"

"This is wrong."

"Look at me and say that."

She turned. She was unable to read his face. "You heard me."

"Yes, but I don't understand."

"I've been acting completely—this is wrong, Taurique."

"What's wrong with it? We're just having dinner, a few drinks, that's all."

"I've had too much. This isn't . . ."

"Respectable? What? Lighten up, Shay-shay, you're not breaking any laws. Don't worry, I won't take advantage of you, or anything. I can't swear you won't take advantage of *me,* of course."

It wasn't funny anymore.

"Ooops—sorry, I'm drunk. Listen, you know what your problem is? You need more champagne."

"I should go."

Taurique was serious now. "Please don't," he implored her. "I'm sorry—here." He picked up her champagne glass and finished the contents. "Just have dessert, okay? Don't leave before dessert, Chaney." He paused. "Now what?"

"You just drank that champagne very fast, T. Are you driving home?"

"No. Are you?"

"Yes."

"No, you're not."

"Yes, I am. How else am I getting home?"

"In a cab."

"What about my car?"

"What about it?"

"I'll be okay by the time I have coffee."

He smiled. "You're staying?"

"I guess I have to, don't I?"

"Damned right." He raised his glass. "To Chaney, who is doing me the great honor of putting up with me until after dessert."

She shook her head, smiling. "You're crazy," she said.

"Nah, just a bit intoxicated. Finish your meal." He was pouring the rest of the champagne into his glass.

"No way, T, you've had enough," Chaney said, grabbing the glass and gulping down what little was in it. How stupid are you? she thought, putting the glass back down.

"You're *really* not driving," he said, looking amused. "Are you finished eating?"

"Except for dessert, I guess."

"Of course, dessert. You're not going home without it. In fact, if I had my way, you wouldn't be going home at all. Don't look at me like that, I mean I don't want you driving in your condition."

"I'll have coffee."

"That's bull, Chaney. Coffee don't make you sober, you're smarter than that."

"Leave me alone."

"Look, I'm not going to be responsible for you putting marks on that gorgeous face. I will personally put you in a cab."

"Taurique, I'm not picking up my car tomorrow," Chaney insisted. "It's too expensive to park overnight, and besides, it's a waste of my time to come back and get it."

"What else are you doing?"

She glared at him murderously.

"Look, I'll drive you home."

Chaney laughed, and Taurique had to join her.

"Not a good idea," he admitted. "Okay—here's the deal. We'll hang out for a while, a few hours, and then I'll let you drive, but I'll be saying a prayer the whole time, and you'll call me the minute you walk in the door. Got it?"

She considered. "Okay."

"Fabulous!" Taurique exclaimed, and they both laughed. "Now, if we can get the waiter over here—excuse me, sir."

Taurique was getting louder. Chaney glanced around—no one was staring yet.

"Dessert would be great right about now. Do you recommend something?"

"Well," the waiter began.

"Actually," Taurique interrupted, "the lady *loves* chocolate, and, well . . ." He glanced at Chaney wickedly, wetting his lips. "It's always been *my* favorite flavor. So how about some chocolate mousse, one for each of us? And I'll have a cappuccino—make that two. Thank you."

The waiter was leaving, and suddenly Taurique looked at Chaney. "Is that okay?" he asked. "I should have checked it with you first. I'm sorry."

"It's okay, T." She was puzzled. "What's the big deal?"

"I wasn't going to do that anymore."

"You know I like chocolate and cappuccino. I said I was having dessert and coffee. What's the problem?"

"Forget it." He considered. "I want some more champagne."

Chaney laughed. "What for?"

"I haven't been high in a long time, but it's wearing off a bit already."

"So?"

"So, I'm not ready yet. Don't worry, I'm in complete control. You know, we haven't talked about a damn thing all evening."

"It's better that way," said Chaney, "don't you think? I think I learned something from last time."

"Maybe." The mousse was arriving.

"Fabulous," Taurique exclaimed, a bit too loudly.

"Stop it," said Chaney under her breath, glancing around.

"Sorry—I forgot how easily you get embarrassed. *Relax,* Chaney. Okay, I'm sorry, Shay. No more, I promise."

He was waiting.

"What?" she asked testily.

"Forgive me, Shay?"

"Okay, forgiven," she snapped. "Can we eat now?"

"Great idea. I mean, fabulous idea—okay, I'm sorry, couldn't resist." He grabbed her spoon, and put some mousse on it, holding it to her lips. "Try some."

"Will you behave?" she demanded, rolling her eyes.

"After this, cross my heart."

"T . . ."

"C'mon. *Try* it."

He had a look of almost childlike anticipation on his face, and Chaney smiled in spite of herself, because he suddenly looked almost unbearably sexy. She opened her mouth.

"Mmm . . ."

"Almost like sex, isn't it?" Taurique said. "You remember sex . . . did it *again,* Shay. Sorry, I think I *am* out of control. Sorry, sweetheart. Look—don't take me seriously. Promise?"

"My spoon, please."

He handed it to her, scrutinizing her. "Are you having a good time?" he asked seriously.

Chaney had taken another mouthful of her dessert—it *is* like sex, she thought. Very good sex, and it felt like ages.

"Not the silent treatment. Anything but that."

Chaney cracked a smile.

"Does that mean you're enjoying yourself?" he asked.

"Eat your chocolate mousse."

"Yes, ma'am." He put some in his mouth, lingering a moment before withdrawing the spoon. "Mmm-*mmm*. I'm sorry, Chaney, but this is like having an orgasm. The truth is the truth, baby."

Chaney had to laugh. "You're insane, Taurique, have I mentioned that?"

"Constantly."

"Just making sure you're aware of it."

"You wouldn't love me if I weren't."

"Maybe not."

The coffee came, the bill was paid, and Taurique rose to leave. Now what? Chaney thought. She felt fine, but standing up made her realize that the champagne was still very much in her bloodstream. She must have looked a bit unsteady, because Taurique put his arm around her and whispered, "Stick with me, kid I'll get you out of here okay."

"I'm fine."

"Just trust me for once, okay?"

She gazed at him. He was being sincere, it seemed.

"All right," she said.

They walked slowly out of the restaurant, crossing the street and heading uptown on Columbus.

"Where are we going?" Chaney demanded.

"Trust me."

"Where have I heard that before from you?"

"Oh—starting on about our second or third date. But was I wrong?"

"Actually . . ."

"Okay, I messed up, I know I did, but I also treated you like a queen."

Chaney laughed. "A *queen?*"

"Admit it, Chaney. If you had it to do all over again, of all the guys you could have trusted with your virginity—admit it, Shay, I was the best choice by a whole lot."

"That's quite a statement, Taurique."

"Admit it."

She looked away. "You're embarrassing me," she said.

"Why? You're an adult, in case you forgot."

"That has nothing to do with it."

"You've had two kids, Chaney, and you can't talk about sex? You'd better learn, baby, there are a whole lot of sick people out there, and if you can't tell your kids about it, they could end up getting messed up by some crazy person."

Chaney looked at him. "This public service announcement has been brought to you by . . ."

"I'm very serious, Chaney."

"Yes, I know. You're right, of course." She took a deep breath. "So—tell me why I was right to trust you."

"You really don't think you were?"

Chaney rolled her eyes. "Okay, I was right."

"Why?"

She hit him.

"Okay, okay. Don't get violent. I don't think this topic has a whole lot of potential . . ."

"Thank you."

"But let me put it this way—a woman loses her virginity only once . . ."

"Unlike a *man,* of course."

He stopped walking, staring at her. "I've created a monster," he said. "Look, from now on, speak your mind only half the time, okay?"

"Sorry. *Please* continue, Dr. Ruth."

"Sarcasm? Chaney, I'm shocked."

"It's the champagne. Anyway, go on."

He started walking again. "All I was saying was—well, when a woman—okay, a person, but I don't care, I think especially when a woman—okay, when she loses her virginity, it should be very, very special. Especially when *she's* very special to begin with. And I started to say—I don't believe this, Chaney, I'm embarrassed now."

"You were saying that you treated me like a queen."

"Damn, I'm arrogant, sometimes."

She gazed at a point far in the distance, thinking. "It's true, though," she said, eventually. "I mean, my first time—it was really a beautiful thing. I know that sounds corny."

"I'm glad, though."

He had turned onto one of the tree-lined streets that branch off Columbus in the Seventies.

"Where are we going?" Chaney asked, this time casually.

"I wanted you to see where I live."

"Okay." Okay? Yes, okay. Warmth, not heat, is going on here. I've walked for blocks with his arm around me, and I feel safe, not excited, and he's flirted, but that's pretty standard, so why not?

He took out his keys, and they started up the steps of a brownstone. He opened the outer door, and then they continued up another flight, and he opened the door to his apartment. It was very dark, and as Chaney took off her coat, she shivered a bit— now that he wasn't holding her, she felt slightly chilly. Taurique turned on the torchière light, and the room was illuminated.

"Welcome to *chez Taurique*," he said, and Chaney slipped off her shoes, looking around.

"Nice," she said. The place was about what she would have expected—sleek, black, modern, with a large-screen TV and a leather couch and matching chair on an Oriental rug.

"Thanks. Can I offer you something?"

"No, thanks."

"I insist. How about some orange juice? That goes well with champagne."

"Okay, okay."

"How are you feeling?"

"Pretty sober."

"Great, you can leave in an hour. If you want."

"We'll see."

He smiled, loosening his tie. "Excuse me, I'm gonna take some clothes off. You can watch, if you want to."

"I'll pass."

"Don't say I didn't offer." He walked into his bedroom, unbuttoning his shirt as he went.

"You can turn on the TV or some music if you want," he called through the partially open door.

"Okay." She turned on the radio—the Quiet Storm was on, and By All Means's "I Surrender to Your Love" filled the room. Chaney was gazing out the window and humming along when she felt Taurique's arms encircling her from behind.

"You know, I traveled all around the world—and I'd give it all just to have you by my side . . ." Taurique was singing, moving her from side to side, and then grabbing her hand, spinning her around, and pulling her closer only to start waltzing wildly around the room.

"Taurique . . ." Chaney was saying, laughing uncontrollably, nearly losing her balance as he suddenly dipped her.

"What's the matter, can't keep up?" he said, standing her back up and moving away.

"Have I mentioned that you're crazy?"

The song changed. "No, I'm a fool," he said, grabbing her again. "A sentimental fool—sing it, Johnny—*'Put on your red dress' . . ."*

He was dancing slower now—"My, my, my" was too romantic to be made into a joke. It's been years, Chaney thought, since I've slow-danced with a man. Lawrence didn't like to slow dance, for reasons Chaney couldn't understand, because he certainly had the rhythm. Maybe it was just that it wouldn't occur to him to do something like that in his own living room for no reason except that there was a slow song on the radio.

One thing was certain—Chaney had missed the feeling of

moving in unison with someone, bodies against each other, feeling somehow sheltered by the music and her partner's arms. Her cheek was against Taurique's chest, and she could feel him breathing into her hair, and she closed her eyes, barely noticing that she had moved even closer to him, and her face was hot again, but it was okay this time, because she was losing herself in the warmth of his bare skin.

Her hair was being caressed, and then she felt his lips on the top of her head, and she opened her eyes, a sudden chill shooting up her spine. She had to stop now . . . he was so close to her . . . She turned her head, moving her face away from him in an effort to break the spell, and succeeded only in brushing her lips against him. He bent down to kiss her neck—it would be too late if he started doing that—but he was already doing it, his tongue and his lips and his breath on the skin of her neck were making her forget why she was supposed to stop—and then she wasn't going to stop; her mouth was seeking his, and she was kissing him passionately, hungrily, and she heard her own heavy breathing blending with the soft humming sound he was making, which was almost a moan, but not quite, and she felt him getting hotter, sweat trickling from his neck down his chest, and then the hardness against her . . .

He stopped, gazing at her, blinking several times in disbelief, then turning his back. "I'm sorry," he said.

Chaney opened her mouth, but couldn't conceive of what to say.

"I don't blame you for being angry, I was—"

"I'm not angry," she interrupted, and her heart was pounding when he faced her again.

"I'm glad, Chaney, but that doesn't excuse what I just did."

"What *we* just did, Taurique."

"What I started," he said firmly. "I hope you believe that I wasn't planning this when I brought you here. I know I've been saying a lot of crap, but I . . ." He sat down suddenly, put his face in his hands, then looked up.

"I've been on the edge from the beginning, I've been one

step away from messing this up every single time we've seen each other, and I don't know what I can do to keep myself from destroying our relationship completely. Obviously—I'm still very attracted to you. I think that's been clear all along. And you're—anyway, I know you're—I know you're married, and I don't want to take advantage of the fact that you miss your husband a whole lot right now . . ." He was staring at his hands. "I really wanted to be your friend. I suppose that's impossible now." He looked at her hopefully, then out the window. "Well, think about it, anyway. I mean, think about if we can still talk to each other now."

"T . . ."

"What?" he said quietly, his eyes on her again.

"I don't want to stop talking to you." Her heart was in her throat now.

"Thank you."

"And . . ." I'm glad we danced. I haven't felt like that in a while. Maybe if I felt like that more often, I wouldn't have almost . . .

"And?" Taurique asked.

"We won't slow-dance anymore."

He laughed, and she could see some of the tension leaving his shoulders. "Okay." He sighed, then glanced at her and smiled. "Okay." He stood up. "Coffee?"

"Sure."

"Coming right up."

He turned and walked into the kitchen, and Chaney didn't watch, because the whole time that he was apologizing she had noticed how cut his stomach still was and he had always been legendary for his perfectly shaped butt and she could still feel him, not just his arms and his chest and his lips and his breath, but also that part of him that had frightened her when she was younger, before she'd trusted him, before he'd soothed her apprehensions away and made love to her, just as they would have been making love if the stopping had been up to her.

Twelve

November 2

When the phone rang, Chaney was dreaming about walking through a forest where seven-foot snakes grew out of the ground like trees, all standing at attention, not quite upright, but stretched stiffly, at a slight angle, their heads pointing toward the sky, their bodies like young saplings, round and hard . . .

And then the phone rang. Doesn't take a genius to figure out *that* one, Chaney was thinking, as she reached for the receiver.

"Hello?"

"Hi, sweetheart. How are you?"

"Okay, I guess. Aren't you performing tomorrow?"

"You remembered!"

"Lawrence, can we please not . . ."

"Of course," he said lightly.

"I can't believe you're calling me the day before a performance."

"I miss you."

"You do?"

"Of course I do. Do you miss me?"

"Uh-huh."

"You do?"

"Very much." It wasn't a lie—she'd been dreaming about

snakes that looked like seven-foot erections; obviously, his presence would have been nice. Then again, that wasn't all she missed. She missed that sweet guy she had rushed into marrying, but whose wife she had always been glad to be, because he was responsible and his smile lit up a whole neighborhood and he had a sense of humor and a gorgeous voice that made her proud to leave concert halls on his arm. She missed the man who had convinced her that there is no one great love in a person's life. And she needed to be reminded of that . . .

"I'm sorry," Lawrence was saying.

"Why?"

"I mean—I'm glad you miss me, but . . . I'm sorry you *have* to miss me. I'm sorry I'm not around you as much as you want me to be."

"I understand."

"Do you?"

He wants to say something, Chaney thought; why can't he just *talk* to me?

"Lawrence?" she asked.

"Yes?"

"What is it?"

He laughed softly—it was a nervous sound. "Nothing."

"Really?"

"Really. Listen, I should go. I just wanted you to know how much I love you and miss you."

"I'm glad you called. I love you, too."

"Goodbye, Chaney."

"Goodbye, Lawrence. And, oh—*in boca lupo.*"

He laughed. *"Grazie. Ciao, bella."*

"Ciao—soave."

He laughed again. "Kiss the kids for me," he said wistfully.

"Okay."

He hung up.

Chaney slowly put the phone down, trying to imagine what he was thinking, but not really minding that she didn't know. This is terrible, she thought, trying her best to feel guilty, but feeling only a weird calm. What will he do now? she wondered. Probably feel better about his marriage, go out tomorrow and blow away the crowd, call me up for more adulation, tell me he loves me again, and then call me again and again and tell me the same thing—and mean it, of course. Then he'll come home, make passionate love to me, and then barely notice me until just before the next trip.

Chaney sat up, stretching. Of course, she knew she was being unfair. Lawrence did the best he could. He would never deliberately neglect her. And he needed to unwind when he was home. The performing took a lot of energy; it would be hard for him to come home and dote on her. And I know he loves me, he means that. He takes me a little for granted, but after this many years, that's probably normal. What do I want, anyway?

She remembered, suddenly, dancing with Taurique—the first time, the funny, ridiculous dance that could have laid waste to his carefully decorated apartment. Taurique loves me, too, she thought. He loves me still, after all these years, and he cares enough to put my feelings first. He does treat me like a queen. He wants me to be happy, and . . .

Idiot, Chaney rebuked herself. Anyone can indulge you for a few weeks. And when Charmaine comes back, then what? Maybe he's just killing time with me until she returns. And if I told him I wanted a relationship again, he'd probably take off like a scared rabbit. It's just the way he wants it. I'm married and out of reach. No commitment possible. He's obviously different in some ways, but he's the same old Taurique in many ways, too.

But he'd have married me, she thought. He *would* have, if I hadn't gotten pregnant and done what no one else seems to choose to do these days. And would he have divorced me two years later? Who knows? And things go as they do for a reason. Right? Of course.

Chaney clicked on the TV, stretching again. It had been a long time since she'd really been alone in the house so early in the day with no plans or commitments. It felt really good. What to do? Absolutely nothing. Maybe I'll watch some cartoons, or something. The phone rang again, and Chaney reached over casually to answer it.

"Chaney Rivers here," she said.

Taurique laughed. "Good morning, Chaney Rivers," he said.

"Hi, T." Her enthusiasm made her nervous. "Why are you up so early?"

"I wake up early sometimes," he retorted.

"You do?"

"Well, I'm talking to you now, ain't I?"

"That's true."

"You're up early, too. I didn't even wake you up."

"You were trying to wake me up? Gee, thanks, T."

"No . . ." His voice was softer. "I wanted to get you before you went out."

Chaney yawned. "Where would I be going? I'm here by myself."

"I don't know. Don't you ever do anything by yourself?"

"Yes, but not unless there's a reason."

"Like what? 'I feel like it' works for me."

She laughed a bit. "I mean, unless I have somewhere to go. I'm getting my hair done, or I have to pick up the kids, or go shopping, and I have none of that today, so I'm gonna do absolutely *nothing!*"

"You sound so happy about it."

"You know, I am. I'll probably feel guilty later, but . . ."

"Why?"

"Well, because I got rid of the kids for the weekend."

"Do you want to come out and play?"

Chaney laughed again. "What did you have in mind?"

"A movie, maybe. Or just a walk or something."

"When?"

"Well, I have to show some apartments, but if you're going to be in, why don't I call you?"

"Okay."

"Okay!" His enthusiasm made her nervous.

"T?" Chaney ventured. "Why are you up so early, T?"

"I told you."

"You know me better than that; you know I have no plans." Why not just leave it alone? she thought, her pulse quickening a bit. Because she needed to hear him say it . . .

Taurique sighed. "Why'd I ask," he said.

"You wanted to know what was on my mind."

"I did, didn't I?" There was a pause. "Okay, I'll be honest. Please don't—anyway—well, yeah, don't get the wrong idea, Shay-shay. I couldn't sleep too well last night. I was—well, I'll be honest with you. I'll be completely honest, and then you can tell me if you want to meet me this afternoon. I—first of all, I should have told you this a long time ago. Charmaine isn't—well, I do know someone named Charmaine, and we go out, and she's a model, but—she's not my lady, or anything. She really means nothing to me. She's fun, but not really my type, and—I'm sorry I lied. I just didn't want to scare you away. I'm really sorry. And also . . . ," he took a deep breath, "I couldn't sleep because I was freaking out about last night, and . . . kissing you like that. I still don't forgive myself. I was so wrong—I just . . ."

He swallowed. "I've gone this far, huh?" He laughed a little. "Me and my mouth. Um—Shay—I'm glad you're not upset. I waited as long as I could stand it to call you. To be honest, I couldn't sleep at all. I was afraid you'd think about what happened and not see me or talk to me again. And—I . . . well, I just didn't want that to happen again. That's all."

Chaney's heart was pounding. She had started imagining, halfway through the speech, his body, and him undressing her. She imagined him kissing her, but this time—she was terrified. Why don't you come over? she thought. She was trying to suppress it, but the thought was echoing so loudly through her brain that she was very relieved to discover that she hadn't screamed it.

"Chaney?"

"Yes?" Her voice wavered a bit, and she cleared her throat.

"I'm sorry. I'm really, really sorry, I wasn't gonna say any of this—well, I was going to tell you about Charmaine soon, but—damn it."

She was frozen.

He sighed again. "It's all screwed up now, for real, huh, Chaney? I—great, Taurique, you're a genius. I was trying . . . I knew I couldn't do this. I was being very honest—well, it's screwed up now, anyway." His voice had changed, hardened suddenly. "I'll tell you, the whole truth is, I don't think we can be friends. I really wanted it, but the problem is, I want *you*. I wanted you so badly last night, I was really scared. I was imagining a million things to do to you and with you and for you, and you wouldn't have had to do anything, it was getting me hot just *dancing* with you. And I wanted to make love to you so much, I didn't even want you to do anything to me. I just wanted to show you . . ."

He stopped. "I have to go." His voice was quiet again. "I'm sorry. Goodbye, Chaney." He hung up.

Please let this be part of a dream, she was thinking. But it wasn't. I want to go back, she was pleading. Please, can I go back? And then the guilt came. It was like smashing into a wall at a hundred miles an hour, and she was momentarily unable to breathe, and then the tears came. I was so irresponsible, she thought. I knew not to have lunch—why were you acting and thinking like such a slut? The one man who really, really knows me . . . maybe. She stared at the phone. What could she possibly say to him now? Could she ever speak to him again? I had to push him. I had to hear him admit he never got over me. Congratulations, Chaney—he never got over you. Happy?

I've never, ever been this miserable, she was thinking, and just admitting it to herself made her start sobbing uncontrollably. T was back, he was finally back in my life—and now he's gone. Five minutes ago, I would have been seeing him this afternoon. And now . . .

He's gone. He left me again.

She curled up under the covers, suddenly very cold, the tears spilling over onto her pillow. He left me again. Taurique's gone, again. Why?

But everyone leaves me, she thought. Everyone. Taurique. Zac and Jimmy—they moved to Atlanta, and when do they call me? Perry's still here, but when does he ever come and see me? And Daddy's gone. And Lawrence's whole *life* is leaving me behind. And the kids had no trouble being away for a weekend without me. Even Pam's gone.

She laughed for a second, a choked laugh. That's hysterical, she thought. "No, you're hysterical," she said out loud, and she was laughing again.

And Mother left, too, she left me a long time ago, and she could be alive or dead, and I wouldn't know it. She left her only little girl . . . The tears were coming faster as the anger began to boil inside her. Yeah, she left and she never looked back. And now T's gone again. He's running away from me again. He can't deal with his feelings for me, again. I hate you, she thought. I hate you. You didn't have to come into my life. I never asked you to chase after me. I also never told you to stop—why did you stop? Why did you have to stop, when I needed you so much I couldn't even explain it if I had tried to? Don't you know me well enough to feel when I need you? Couldn't you tell how desperately I wanted you? *Needed* you? How could you possibly walk away from me?

She remembered—he was trembling. He was so hot that sweat had started trickling down his bare chest. He was throbbing. Throbbing for me, she thought. He wanted me that much. He was afraid of his own thoughts. Because I'm married. He was making that sound, singing that sweet song he always sang when he got really passionate, that hum that started not really in his throat, but somewhere else, somewhere so deep it was hard to find it, somewhere she could touch, but only her—

that's what he'd told her. He'd told her he never felt the way he did when he was with her with anyone else. But that was so long ago—surely someone else had done that to him, made that melody come out, all by itself . . .

But I'm married. I'm married, I am *married* . . . She stared at her rings—the engagement ring Lawrence had bought her last year, to replace the other one, because it wasn't big enough, he said. And she looked at the beautiful stone and was glad, but really, she didn't need a bigger ring. All she needed—or wanted, maybe she just wanted it—was for him to stay. Just to stay, and to hold her and come home every night. But she pushed her selfish thoughts way down, until they were almost lost somewhere. Almost.

I'm married, she thought again and again. She looked at the phone. Why don't you call me, T? Please? Don't leave me. Not again . . .

Thirteen

November 4

"Come on, Ronnie," Chaney was yelling. "You're gonna make your sister late."

Ronnie appeared at the top of the stairs. Prince Charming. The costume that is the boy, thought Chaney.

"Hurry up, I've been telling you to hurry for the last half hour—what is taking you so long? How many times do you have to stare at yourself in the mirror?"

There was a silence, then Ronnie began to sniffle. Chaney saw, out of the corner of her eye, Nicole gazing at her with an expression she had never seen before.

"Come on, Ronnie," the little girl said. "We're not late."

Chaney looked at her, and Nicole's eyes met hers and held them. Chaney had to wonder at her, and despite her anger, she was proud of her daughter, in a way.

"It *is* late," Chaney said, "and don't you ever, *ever* contradict me again. You got that?"

Nicole nodded, but her eyes didn't change. "Yes, Mommy," she said.

Ronnie's sniffles were becoming little sobs.

"Come here," Chaney said finally, and he obeyed. She bent down and hugged him, then she hugged Nicole.

"I'm sorry," she said. "I didn't mean to get so upset. But

can you promise Mommy that you'll pay more attention to what she tells you?"

They both nodded. Nicole's eyes had finally melted a bit.

"Mommy, what's the matter?" she asked again. She had asked it twice last night, and she was not giving up yet. Can't you leave me alone? Chaney was thinking. She was also thinking that at least Nicole cared.

"It's not you guys," Chaney finally said—"nothing" obviously wouldn't work this time.

"What is it, then?"

"Do you ever have times when you like to play with your toys, or something, but you don't feel like sharing them with Tracey or even your brother, even though you love them both a lot?"

Nicole nodded—thank God, thought Chaney. She wasn't sure how else she could explain herself, and even that explanation had been pretty strange.

"Well, that's how Mommy is right now, sweetie," she said.

"Mommy?"

"Yes, Nicole?"

"Will it be better when Daddy comes back?"

"Uh-huh. Let's go, okay, kids?"

"Okay." Ronnie opened the door. This little girl, thought Chaney . . . and she couldn't finish it; all she was thinking was how much she loved her babies. She followed them out of the house, locking the door behind her.

Chaney drove around aimlessly for a while after she dropped off her children. What should I do? she was wondering, and it made her feel emptier that she could think of nothing. Shopping? The idea was almost embarrassing, it was so frivolous. So was the other suddenly ludicrous thing she always did to cheer herself—going to Elizabeth Arden. Stupid, stupid, stupid. My God, she was thinking, I have no life. She remembered, all at once, Taurique's question—didn't she ever do anything just because she felt like it? Here was an opportunity, like the other countless opportunities, and she could only think of going shopping or getting a facial, and that was it.

Or you could drop by T's office. I'm truly neurotic, she thought, because she had been driving, not entirely unconsciously, toward the place where they had first bumped into each other. I have time to find out the exact address of his office. I have the number. I could be waiting outside—I'd probably run into him . . .

Desperate and pathetic, and for what? For years he was a shadow, and you were fine. In a matter of less than a month, he's taken over your life and your mind to the point that you're doing insane things.

Except I don't want to hurt him, I just need to talk to him. And what would I say? I'm sorry. I shouldn't have pushed you. I'm sorry. I don't want things to go back to the way they were, I just want us to be friends. I'm sorry, I need you, I'm sorry you won't speak to me. I'm sorry, ad infinitum.

A horn blared, she slammed on the brakes, and there were squealing tires behind her. She blinked. What had happened? She looked around—the horn had been meant for a pedestrian up ahead, not her; she had slammed on the brakes unnecessarily; and suddenly she was wide awake and completely alert. That would solve everything, she thought; I could just have a fatal accident and forget all this.

And Taurique and Lawrence would be at the funeral, watching me get slowly lowered into the ground, and they could fight it out over me, right there in the middle of the cemetery.

She almost smiled. It would never happen, she thought, because Lawrence would walk away. Or maybe not. Maybe he would explode, pick up a tombstone, and knock Taurique senseless. Or maybe T. would be so upset he wouldn't be able to attend. Or maybe he would just stand there with his dark glasses on, behind the scenes, because it wasn't right for him to be up there with the family. Or maybe Lawrence's agent would call him the day before, and the funeral would have to be scheduled on the day after a performance, because crying is hard on the throat and at least then there would be time for him to recover before the next performance.

Not that Lawrence would cry, anyway. He'd be upset, but he wouldn't cry. Maybe when he got home, maybe when he had to go through her things . . .

Enough, she thought. This fantasy was way out of hand now, it was becoming unpleasant. Chaney sighed and turned on the radio, then increased the volume to what was very loud, for her. Where are you going, Chaney? she asked herself. There was the street corner, there was the hot dog stand—her stomach knotted. T wasn't there. She hadn't really expected him to be, and she was almost glad not to see him. Home . . . you're going home.

Chaney walked into her bedroom and saw that she had received a phone call while she was out. Her heart was pounding as she rewound the tape. It was Perry. She relaxed, disappointed. He wanted her to call his office.

What now? she wondered, dialing. He probably wants the details of my dinner with Taurique, and since I don't want to talk about it, this is gonna be a really short conversation.

"Perry Davis, please. Chaney Rivers calling."

She was on hold for a moment, then, "Chaney! Hi. Wow, that's service—I just called you."

"Just walked in. What can I do for you?"

"Nothing. I was just wondering how it went this weekend."

"Fine." That was too abrupt to be convincing, Chaney thought, resolving to be more conversational.

"No, it didn't."

"Oh, really?" Chaney retorted. "Then why ask me how it went in the first place?"

There was a pause. "What's wrong, Chaney?"

"You tell me," she snapped.

"Look, you're not yourself, and neither is Taurique. I just wanted to know . . ."

"I can't take this," she said, wishing, for a split second, that she *had* been in a fatal collision. She felt as if her mind were collapsing inward, like a house of cards, being leveled to a flatness, in complete disarray. She wanted to explode, that was the only thing she could think of that would make it better—a fire, destructive, consuming everyone and everything in its path, leaving smoldering ash and nothing else . . .

And she would rise, phoenix-like, out of it, and start over again. No, she would be burned beyond recognition, and no one would watch her get lowered into the ground, because there would be nothing left. They would sweep her up, and into the wastebasket she would go. Waste, a wasted life. Stop it . . .

"Chaney? Chaney?"

She tuned in again. "What?" Her voice surprised her. It was almost lifeless.

"What happened with you and Taurique?"

"It's none of your business, Perry," she said, her voice trembling a bit as she thought about T. never speaking to her again.

"I know," said Perry, "but I still think you should talk about it."

"How do you know something's wrong, anyway?" It was a ridiculous question, especially since she was obviously on the verge of breaking down.

"Because I called Taurique and he sounded like hell—I don't know what he was drinking, but he'd had a lot of it. Then I call you, and you sound all upset, and I don't know how I can help either of you."

"Maybe you can't, Perry." She was crying now—damn it! Why did she always have to cry at the worst possible times?

"Don't cry, Chaney. Look, we'll meet somewhere and talk about it."

"No, Perry." She sniffled, struggling to regain control.

"I don't understand," he said, exasperated. "Why won't you let me help you?"

"Because you help me too much already. I've got to handle this myself."

Perry sighed. "Okay," he said quietly.

"I love you, Perry."

"You know I love you, too."

"Yes."

"If you need anything . . ."

"I'll call you. Thanks for everything."

She hung up, realizing there was absolutely nobody in this world she could talk to about this. Not Jimmy, not Zac, not Perry—that exhausted her repertoire. Not Taurique. Certainly not Lawrence.

How did I get like this? she thought. Not a friend in the world. She wished she could like Pam, but it seemed like it would be such a lie. It would be forced, and she wanted the real thing. Where were all those men she used to know? They didn't want to know her anymore. All those instant buddies from high school—Perry's friends, Zac's friends, mainly, but she could talk to them and laugh with them so easily. Tell them things.

But nothing like this. I think I'm in love with someone besides my husband. What should I do?

It sounded like a topic for a talk show: *married women who are still in love with their old flames.* No . . . *when old flames come back into your life.* On the next *Oprah.*

And what would be Oprah's celebrity analyst's opinion? Stay away from him? No—that was too simplistic. That would be the two or three members of the audience who inevitably said exactly the same thing, usually very self-righteously. The psychiatrist would say, talk to him.

Or Chaney would say that, because that's what Chaney wants. But is that so terrible? she wondered. Suppose we had lunch one last time. Suppose we set it up so T. and I could take an extra-long time, so we wouldn't have to rush. Suppose we were very honest, and didn't run away from our feelings, like we usually do. Like we've done, for whatever reason, for ten years. And let the chips fall where they may. I sleep with him one more time, I tell Lawrence it's over. I sleep with him one more time, I get him out of my system. Whatever happens happens.

As long as I sleep with him. She wasn't even ashamed. As long as we make love one more time. If I can just do that, maybe it can really be over. She imagined lying next to Taurique, under him, being on top of him, her hair in wild disarray, gazing into his eyes as their bodies moved in rhythm, feeling his penis move in and out, in and out until she could stand it no longer, him touching her, caressing her, kissing her neck, his tongue flicking delicately against her nipples . . .

And she would scream, she would lose all control, as she had lost control the last time they were together . . . and it would feel *so* good.

She still wasn't ashamed. What's happening to me? she wondered, only mildly interested, picking up the phone. And how can I call him now? she asked herself, the fantasy still lingering in her mind. I could say anything. I was imagining my mouth on your . . .

"Hello—um—Taurique Williams, please."

The receptionist's voice had barely found its way through her imagination and into her consciousness.

"Who may I say is calling?"

"Chaney Rivers."

"Hold a moment, please."

The calm was gone. She had been holding a long time. Maybe he wasn't going to pick up the phone. Maybe Donna was helping him to concoct a story. Or maybe he was just telling her to get rid of Chaney any way she saw fit. Or maybe . . .

"Hello."

He didn't sound excited, or happy, or even slightly pleased.

Chaney marshaled all her strength to keep from hanging up without uttering a word. She cleared her throat instead.

"Hello, Taurique."

"I'm with a client."

"Oh." A stabbing pain shot through her stomach. I'm making a fool of myself she thought, feeling like a thirteen-year-old chasing after the object of her first crush.

"What can I do for you?"

Not unkind. Not kind, but slightly warmer.

"Um—can—can we . . ." She took a deep breath. "Can we talk? Not now, of course. I mean . . . I understand if you don't want to, I just need . . . I just think it would be better if we could talk one more time. Even if it's just one more time. Could you do that for me? I mean—have lunch with me one more time. Please?"

Pathetic. Her voice was breaking. I'm begging, she thought. The words had started rushing out, going straight from deep inside her brain onto the tip of her tongue without being screened.

A long pause. "Thursday?" His voice sounded choked. He cleared his throat, coughed once.

"When?" Chaney was sure she'd have a stroke soon—it felt like a battery of percussion, an entire drum choir, was pounding in her temples.

"Noon?"

"Okay."

"I'll . . ." He cleared his throat again. "Excuse me." She heard him gulp down some water, very loudly. Like there's something in his throat, she thought, but with no feelings of triumph whatsoever this time. A lump. Because of my bad judgment.

"I'll book off a few hours."

"Thanks."

"Where do you want to meet?"

"Wherever you want."

He paused to consider. "Sfuzzi?"

"Okay."

"I have to go now."

"Okay." She hung up, her hands shaking. Sfuzzi. The scene of the crime, almost. A short walk from his house. What does he have in mind?

How am I going to keep myself together until Thursday? Chaney wondered. She gazed at herself in the mirror and saw nothing. There was a reflection, of course, but it was like she wasn't there, somehow. Her features seemed meaningless, irrelevant.

How am I going to keep myself together on Thursday? Making love to him was the furthest thing from her mind now. She was shivering; she felt suddenly cold. I'm losing it, she thought, standing up. Time to start the housework—God, please don't let anyone else call me today, she prayed. Maybe if she cleaned hard enough, all this would go away. She knew better, but she had to get rid of this somehow. Get rid of what? Not a chance. Maybe on Thursday.

One evening, when they were dating, Taurique and Chaney went to a movie and they came back to his house, like they sometimes did. It was still early—about 9 P.M., so she wouldn't have to be home for a few hours.

Nobody was there. Taurique turned on the lights and they sat in the kitchen.

"You want something?" he asked.

"No—maybe a glass of juice."

"Okay—coming up." He took an ice tray out of the freezer, loosened a few cubes, dropped them in a glass, and filled it with apple juice.

"Thanks," she said, and took a long drink. It was warm—hot actually—outside, even though it was early November. It was one of those ridiculous days that have no business in that season, a holdover from August. The evening had cooled off a lot, so it felt very pleasant now, as she was sipping apple juice in Taurique's kitchen.

"Where is everybody?" Chaney asked.

"My parents are having dinner with Aaron's parents." Aaron was Yvette's boyfriend.

"What does that mean? Must be serious."

"Maybe. She was acting funny all day, took longer than usual to get dressed, which is really saying something."

"Maybe they're getting engaged."

"Maybe they're already married. Maybe she's pregnant."

"Yvette?"

"You think she's still a virgin at 23?"

"That's not possible?"

"Anything's possible." He studied her face.

"What?" she asked.

"Nothing." He smiled and sat down beside her. She suddenly felt nervous.

"Where's Yvonne?"

He shrugged. "Off doing the usual mess."

"So we're alone?"

He laughed. "We've been alone before," he said.

Never in your house, though, thought Chaney. But what difference does that make? And why am I so nervous?

"You want to watch TV?"

"Okay."

"Why are you so nervous?" He was looking at her wide-eyed.

"I don't know." She turned away from him and he gently touched her cheek so that she would face him again.

"I'm not gonna hurt you," he said softly. "You know that, right?"

She looked into his eyes, and saw that they were full of tenderness. "Yes," she said.

"So why are you afraid to be alone with me?"

"I'm not." She was relaxed now.

"I'm glad, Chaney. Can I call you Shay?"

"If you want."

"No—I mean, do you like that? I want to call you something special, besides your name. Your name is special, and all, but—do you mind?"

"No."

"Shay. Or Shay-shay. Can I call you Shay-shay?"

She laughed. "That's a bit babyish."

"You're my baby, though, right?" he said in a childlike voice.

She laughed again. "Yes, Taurique, I'm your baby."

"And I'm your baby, too. So you should think of a name for me."

"Taurique, you're silly."

"I'm hurt." He put on an expression of exaggerated sadness.

Chaney rolled her eyes and kissed him on the cheek. "Okay, baby, I'll think of a name for you."

He smiled. He looked so much like a little boy that she had to laugh again. Nicknames—she wasn't a nickname person. "Rico" had been used already. Maybe something unrelated— Muffin? He wasn't the muffin type. Adonis? A bit much. My little . . . the whole thing was dumb. He was waiting.

"How about . . . T?"

"Just—T?"

"T. Take it or leave it."

He considered. "I'll take it." He stood. "Shall we watch TV?"

"Yes, we shall. T."

They laughed, and went into the living room. There was a movie on—one of those TV movie-of-the-week things, a historical romance. Taurique looked at her, made a face, and she shook her head. He changed the channel—sports. She shook her head again. He was flipping rapidly through the channels when he stopped suddenly.

"I can't believe it," he exclaimed.

"What?"

The picture was in black and white.

"This is a classic. Have you seen *Casablanca?*"

"No."

"*No?* Well, that's what we're watching. It's just started, too." He sat down beside her, putting his arm around her.

"I don't like old movies," Chaney protested.

"You don't watch them, do you?"

"No," she admitted.

"That's why you don't like them."

He was right. When it was over, Chaney was fighting back tears.

"You liked it?" Taurique said.

"Yes. It was—great. It was sad, though."

"So's life, baby."

She smiled. "You're deep, Taurique."

"I know." He looked at her. "You're crying."

"No, I'm not."

"Your eyes are wet. Aww—it *was* sad, wasn't it?" He pulled her close to him, stroking her hair. "I'll make you feel better," he said, and he started kissing her.

Any excuse, thought Chaney, smiling.

"What's so funny?" Taurique asked.

"You. But that's okay. Go ahead and make me feel better."

"You feel better already? Okay, I'll stop." He moved away, and sat on the other end of the couch.

"Taurique." He wouldn't look at her. "T . . ."

He suddenly pounced, pinning her on her back. She screamed, then started laughing.

"She's thrown for a loss at the ten-yard line!" he exclaimed, and kissed her. She was laughing and kissing him, and then they were attacking each other, and before she knew it, his hands were all over her.

"Taurique," she whispered, suddenly frightened.

He stopped. "I'm sorry," he said, "am I going too fast?"

She didn't answer. She trusted him, but . . .

"Anybody could walk in," she said.

"You're right. I'm sorry." He stood and offered his hand to her, and she let him pull her to her feet. "Do you want to go home?" he asked.

She stared at him. No, she thought.

"Do you want to go somewhere more private?"

She was frozen. He hugged her.

"Baby," he said, "I'm gonna tell you something I've never told anyone before. I'll tell you the truth, I've never been this patient before. I've never really wanted to be. Or maybe I've never had to be, women don't tend to make me wait much—maybe that says more about them than about me. Whatever, what I'm trying to say is . . . I don't want to rush you or push you or talk you into anything. I can't say I don't want you, because I do; you don't know how much. And I promise you, whenever you're ready—this sounds corny, but, well, I'll take it slow. I've never met anybody like you, Shay-shay. I've never felt this way about anybody before. To tell you the truth . . . well, I really think . . . I really think I'm in love with you. In fact, I know I am. And it's a little bit scary, because I wasn't planning to be. I wasn't planning this at all."

He paused, then pulled away from her and looked into her eyes.

"Could you please stay?" he asked. His face was very hopeful. "You don't have to. I promise I won't do anything you don't want me to."

"Okay." Chaney felt the nerves dissipate slightly.

"Do you want to go in my room?"

She nodded. He smiled and then waited for her to move, following her and guiding her with his hands on her waist. Once they were in his room, he closed the door. He turned on the lamp by his bed and turned off the overhead light, thought a moment, then put the overhead light on again and removed the bedside lamp's bulb, replacing it with a blue one. When he turned off the overhead light this time, the room took on a cool glow.

"Is this okay?" he asked.

She nodded, smiling. Taurique's love nest, she thought, and she couldn't help but wonder how many others had been there before her.

He went to the stereo and put in a tape. It was Peabo Bryson. Chaney smiled again. Everything seemed so planned, and yet it was all wonderful, somehow. The room, the music, the familiar furniture—everything made her feel safe, and all she was experiencing now was anticipation.

Taurique sat beside her. "Peabo's one of my favorites," he said, leaning toward her. As soon as their lips touched, they were where they'd left off in the living room. Chaney realized she was leaning back. The whole thing had happened so naturally, she was a bit surprised to find that he was on top of her.

"Come on and feel the fire . . ." Peabo was exhorting, and Taurique was kissing her neck. He stayed there a long time, then he began to move down, undoing the buttons as he went.

"Are you okay?" he asked, stopping to look at her.

She nodded. Her heart was pounding, but with excitement, not fear. He kissed her stomach and traced a line, very lightly, with his tongue, up the center of her body. Her arms were at her sides, and he gently moved them over her head.

"You tell me if you're not okay," he whispered urgently, "and I promise I'll stop."

She nodded, smiling faintly, and he slipped his hand under her and unfastened her bra. She was suddenly aware that they had crossed a line; they were in uncharted territory, for her; and then she felt his mouth on her breast and she wasn't aware of anything anymore except a sensation unlike anything she had ever felt before.

"Are you okay?" he whispered, his fingers caressing her nipples, his lips grazing her earlobe.

"Uh-huh," was all she could manage. She wasn't sure what would happen next, but she didn't want him to stop. She felt him unfasten the waist of her jeans, slowly unzip them.

"Can I take these off?" he asked her.

She nodded. He slipped them off. It wasn't easy, but he did it without her help. He stood for a moment, dropping them on the floor, then pulled off his shirt. Chaney opened her eyes to see his sculptured body coming back toward her, and she felt a surge of something she couldn't define—desire, but also joy, joy that she was actually going to get next to *that.*

He was back on top of her, kissing her, and her hips started rocking almost involuntarily. That was when she heard the song for the first time, the sound that was like a moan, but sweeter, somehow.

"Yes, baby," he was saying, "that's it."

She would later find out that he was being unusually quiet. He told her, later, when they had explored almost every position known to man or woman, that he hadn't wanted to scare her. Which seemed hilarious by then, but at that moment the fact that she was doing something right was very exciting, and she rocked him harder, felt him growing and growing, and was exhilarated.

"Chaney," he said, their bodies still moving in rhythm.

"Uh-huh?"

"If you don't wanna go through with this, can we please stop now?"

She said nothing, only held him as tightly as she could.

"Are you sure?" he asked urgently, stopping and looking into her eyes.

She hesitated. "Yes," she said, and they smiled at each other, and he kissed her, then slid his hand underneath her again, to pull down her underwear. He kneeled above her for a moment, looking at her. She felt completely exposed, but still safe somehow.

"You are beautiful," he whispered, and he began to caress her gently. Then he slid out of his jeans, leaving his underwear on.

"I want you to undress me the rest of the way," he said,

standing in front of her. She hesitated. "Don't be afraid," he said, "I promise I won't hurt you."

She pulled his briefs down and looked at him. She had never seen anything like this before—she had seen sculptures and paintings, but never a live, fully erect penis. It was like a living thing, something separate from Taurique's body. Her eyes were wide.

"You can touch me," he urged her, and she realized that her hand was in midair. She stroked him then and felt the aliveness under her fingers. "Harder," he said, and she obeyed. Then he lay on top of her again, and with his hand he parted her legs, and he put one of his fingers inside her.

"You want me?" he asked, his voice a whisper.

"Yes."

"Are you sure?" Two fingers were moving in and out, exploring her slowly.

"Yes." It was a gasp.

It was as if he had read her mind. "Am I hurting you?" he asked, concerned.

"A little."

"I'm sorry—look, I think it always does the first time. Do you want me to stop?"

"No."

"Just try to relax, okay? It won't hurt so much if you relax. Do you trust me?"

"Yes."

He spread her legs a bit more, reaching with his other hand beside the bed. He placed something in her hand.

"Open it, okay?"

"Okay." It was a condom. She had seen them in Zac's room, and she was sure Perry had them, too. Her hands were trembling now. This was really it, the point of absolutely no return. His mouth was back on her breast. She was fumbling with the wrapper, afraid she would drop it—she had never felt like this before, nothing even vaguely similar. She arched her back, listening to herself making high-pitched noises, and the fact that she was making sounds like that made it even more exciting.

"You're so wet for me," Taurique whispered, the fingers moving faster—and then he was touching her somewhere else, and she was writhing, she wanted to scream. It was a feeling almost like pain, but not quite, and his tongue on her breast and his finger there made her completely lose all perspective and start moaning.

"Does that feel good?" Taurique was asking.

"Uh-huh." It was like a sob now. Her whole body was tingling, waves of sensation radiating throughout her body—it built and built and then dissipated.

"Do you want me inside you?"

"Yes."

He sighed, taking the open package from her. He removed the condom, kneeling over her, and slipped it on.

"I'm gonna go slow," he said softly, as she watched with fascination. He was really going to put all that inside her. She couldn't believe this was really happening. He lowered himself onto her, and then he spread her legs apart a bit further, and she stared upward as she felt him enter her, just barely.

"Is it okay?" he asked.

She shook her head, then he slid further in and she caught her breath. It hurt now.

"Relax, baby," he was soothing her. "Relax, okay?"

"Okay." She thought she was going to cry, but she bit her lip. It didn't feel like there was room for all of him—and then she realized he was all the way in, moving slowly in and out—it still hurt, but it also felt good, and she was relaxing now.

"I'm gonna push—a little harder. Tell me—if I'm hurting you." And he started to thrust deeper and faster, and she felt like he would burst through her, split her in two—but it also felt good, in a way. I'm lying here like I'm dead, she thought. She had felt like she was unable to move, but now she started rocking again.

"Yeah," Taurique responded. "Oh yeah, that feels good." So

she kept moving with him for what seemed like forever until he asked, "Can you squeeze me inside?"

She opened her eyes and looked at him. He was a million miles away, it seemed. She tightened her stomach.

"Just like that. Yes, Chaney. Oh yeah, Shay-shay."

Maybe he wasn't so far away—he was calling her name, not one of the others'. *He called my name.* It was thrilling, and she squeezed him harder, and found that it didn't hurt so much now.

"You're gonna make me scream," he gasped, and she squeezed as hard as she could. She wanted to make him scream like he had made her scream. Then he shifted his position and he was rubbing against that place again, and she could no longer think rationally.

"Taurique . . ." She tried not to be too loud, but she couldn't help it.

"Look at me, baby." She opened her eyes and saw him gazing at her tenderly, then grimacing, then looking at her tenderly again. "Look how good I feel." He started to move faster and faster, and she was smiling. She was amazed that she had the power to make him feel so good. He stopped suddenly.

"Relax!" he commanded, lowering himself onto her and trembling. Then he started to laugh; it was a sound of pure mirth. "Mmm—Chaney," he said, still laughing. Finally he was limp on top of her, his heart beating very fast. He put his face next to hers, kissing her cheek.

"Are you okay?" he asked gently, gazing lovingly into her eyes.

"Uh-huh."

"Did you feel good?"

"Oh yeah."

"Oh yeah." He imitated her, smiling. "You wanna do it again?"

"Oh yeah."

His smile faded. "I've created a monster," he said, collapsing, and she laughed.

They made love over and over, three times, and when they were both completely exhausted, Taurique held her hand and told her he loved her, again, and she told him she loved him, and they made love again. By then it was after midnight, and the house was full, and Chaney was completely embarrassed to emerge from Taurique's room with her makeup smeared and her hair a mess and to have to say goodbye to Taurique's parents like that, and besides, Yvonne was laughing at her, because she could barely walk. But as ashamed as she felt then, she soon learned that no one in Taurique's family seemed to like her any less, and so she and Taurique camouflaged their noise by blasting music by Peabo, or Luther, or Teddy, or any number of others, while they laughed and made love in the glow of the blue light, and afterward they talked and kissed and pledged their love. Chaney never felt so free, or even free at all, really, as when she was making love, and she found that she was almost insatiable, so Taurique kept coming up with new positions and approaches, or at least, he tried to.

After a while, though, she began to feel guilty, because she had always been taught that what she was doing was immoral. She didn't want it to stop—it was her one assertion of her independence, and besides, it *felt* right to express her feelings for Taurique that way. So she made it okay by reminding herself that he was never going to be with anybody else, and neither was she, so the excitement they felt was just a preview of what would happen after the wedding. Which was inevitable, of course . . .

Fourteen

November 7

Thursday. It took forever to get here, thought Chaney, and it's still too soon. The children were in school, and she was sitting on a bench just inside the entrance to Central Park, across from the Dakota. *"Strawberry Fields forever,"* she thought. Lennon's suffering and death at the hands of a madman. She watched little rosy-cheeked white toddlers with brown-skinned nannies. Rats lurking in the bushes. Good and evil, cheek by jowl.

Chaney exhaled, and a fine mist formed in the air. It was chilly, but not yet really cold. Still pleasant enough to sit in the park underneath the trees, which had all been recently denuded by the wind. Pleasant to sit in the park, trying not to be afraid of taking action, for once.

The last few days had been hell. Lawrence had called; she couldn't keep up her end of the conversation, so she claimed to have the flu. It wasn't far from the truth, really—she felt hot or cold all the time, and the night of the first of November she threw up twice after trying to force herself to consume a dinner that she knew she could not digest. The next morning she crawled out of bed and had to crawl back in. She could not take anybody anywhere today. Great, she thought. I know it's all psychological, and yet I can't get up. How will the children get to school?

She coughed. Her stomach was still churning, and she had
a dull headache. Think. *Think.* Then it hit her—Pam. For once,
the woman would serve some useful purpose. She dialed the
number.

"Hello."

"Hi, Pam."

"Who is this?"

"Chaney Rivers."

Pam genuinely sounded alarmed. "You sound terrible," she
said. "Are you okay?"

"I have a virus."

"Sounds that way. Have you been to the doctor?"

"No. Look, I'm all right. Can you do something for me,
though?"

"Anything."

"I need someone to take Nicole and Ronnie to school.
Would you?"

"Of course. Can you get them ready?"

"Yes."

"Okay, I'll pick them up in 45 minutes."

"Thank you, Pam. I really appreciate this."

"No problem."

Chaney was almost touched. Pam hadn't asked any questions, and she had been willing to do anything to help. I'm
awful, thought Chaney. But she couldn't deal with that now;
she had other things to wallow in right now . . .

She sat up again. She was still dizzy. She closed her eyes
and took slow, deep breaths. It was getting better. She stood.
Okay—one step at a time . . . ridiculous, she thought, making
her way to the door. This can't go on, she resolved.

Somehow, she got the children ready and supervised their
breakfast. As she lay on the couch listening to Pam's car pull
away, she wasn't sure how she had managed it. But now she
was alone. Alone with those thoughts again, the ones she had
been trying to avoid . . .

She was too exhausted to avoid them anymore. Taurique,

Lawrence, Perry, Jimmy—they all swirled in her mind in kaleidoscopic configurations. Underneath, though, was the question, "What am I going to do?"

The headache was sharper. Can aspirin relieve psychosomatic illnesses? she wondered. She sat up, then immediately decided against it. It sure *feels* real, she thought. But I should be able to make it go away.

Maybe if I make a decision, it will. Decide about what? Let's see. Taurique, or Lawrence?

Well, I can stay with Lawrence, and spend most of my time without a husband. Or I can leave him and risk spending most of my time without my children. It was the same dead end she had been running into for days. There has to be something I'm leaving out, she thought.

The silence was suddenly deafening. She rolled off the couch and crawled over to the stereo. She flipped through her CDs—no music to have a nervous breakdown by? *That* would be a million-seller, especially in New York City. Then, she saw the Faust recording that had been played at the card party. She put it on, finding the appropriate spot . . .

There was that voice again, that almost inhumanly beautiful sound. She sat cross-legged on the floor.

I could never ask him to choose between his gift and me, she realized. A talent like that has to be shared. So he's doing exactly what he needs to be doing.

And what the hell am *I* doing? Lawrence spends hours working on his craft. What do I do for fulfillment?

She was a natural athlete, but that was hardly the stuff of which to make a career at this point, since she wasn't exactly the aerobics instructor type. The truth was, she had never decided on a career in high school, and when she got married her only focus was being a good mother. People had often told her she had a knack for decorating. Maybe that has some potential, she thought.

Lawrence's aria finished, and the opera continued. Chaney didn't bother to turn off the CD, as she usually did . . .

It's beautiful, she thought. She had heard it before, but not recently. Just by doing something different, changing my routine, she thought, I added something to my life. Something small, but it goes to show how change can make things better.

So dump Lawrence, run off with T. *That* would be a change. She lay on her back. Her stomach was gurgling. Start over with T. It would be exciting, unpredictable . . .

Why? Because he would make it that way. She sat up then, slowly. Because he would make it that way. He would. He.

And what would *I* do? Suddenly, the dream made sense. Nothing, she realized. I'd do nothing. I'd just go along for the ride.

The music was swelling, but she wasn't aware of it. The headache was losing its grip. I love you, T, she thought. I love you, Lawrence. And my happiness or unhappiness with either of you isn't your fault. It's mine. My fault.

She smiled for the first time in days. It's my fault, she thought. It's all on me. It was terrifying, but liberating. It's up to me, and I don't need anyone's advice. Because I know what to do . . .

I have a life. I don't need a new one. I don't need to start over, and I can't, anyway. I have two children and a husband who loves me, and a lover would destroy that. Even if he *is* the best friend I've ever had.

The turmoil in her intestines had subsided a bit, but she still had a sick feeling in the pit of her stomach. I'm not ready to give you up, T, she thought. Not yet.

She remembered again dancing with him, laughing with him. It was different than with Lawrence. But that doesn't matter. Lawrence and I have our own thing. And more important, Lawrence is my husband, and I'm his wife, and that's all there is to it. Period.

It was this final thought that she repeated, almost like a mantra, for the rest of the day. It was the same thought she was focusing on in a vain attempt to calm her nerves, as she waited in Strawberry Fields for it to be time for her to go.

She gazed up at the gray November sky. Lord, she prayed, I haven't been good for much lately, and for that I'm sorry. I have no right to approach You at all, but in Your mercy, could You please help me to do what I know is the right thing today? Amen.

She glanced at her watch. It was time to meet Taurique.

When Chaney walked into Sfuzzi, Taurique was waiting. He was sipping a glass of wine and glancing at his watch, frowning. Chaney attempted to swallow, but her throat had gone dry, and it took two or three tries.

"Williams, party of two?" she said, and was pleased that her voice sounded recognizable. She followed the hostess to the same table they'd had before. Her palms were sweating.

Taurique smiled uncertainly. "You look great," he said.

"Thanks." The hostess pulled out her chair and she sat down, accepted a menu, and began to scan it.

"Look at me," Taurique said.

Chaney raised her eyes. He was staring at her. "You're a very beautiful woman, Chaney. I hope you realize how beautiful you are. I don't mean just the way you look. I mean, you, your personality."

Chaney didn't know what to say. "Thanks," she finally managed. She was afraid to turn away from him. He broke the spell by taking up his menu.

"Would you like something to drink before your meal?" the waiter was asking, startling Chaney.

"No."

He took their order and left, and she buried her head in the menu. She wasn't hungry. There's chicken salad, she thought, that's what I'll have. She closed her menu. Taurique was still gazing at her.

"Please stop," she said.

"Please don't make me. I might not see you again."

Chaney sighed, glancing away. "Are you hungry?" she asked.

"No. Are you?"

"No." She paused. "Do you want to stay here?" There was her heart, on cue.

"No. But I think we should stay here."

"I meant we could get hot dogs and sit in the park."

Taurique smiled. "That would be great," he said. "It would complete the circle."

Chaney rolled her eyes. "T, what are you talking about? I'm not going anywhere."

"This is reality," he snapped.

"Don't take that tone with me."

He was taken aback, and then he laughed.

"What are you laughing at?" Chaney was irritated.

"I'm sorry. I'm sorry. You sound like a mother."

"I've got two kids."

"I ain't one of them. But you're right. What are you having?"

"Chicken salad."

"I'll have the pasta of the day."

"Good."

"Excuse me . . ." Taurique summoned the waiter, and placed the order.

As soon as they were alone again, Taurique asked, "What are we going to talk about?"

"Everything."

"He smiled and sipped some more wine. "Everything?" He glanced at his watch. "Good thing I took off an extra hour."

"I can be specific."

"Good."

She wasn't nervous anymore. She wasn't sure why, but she was glad.

"What happened between us?"

Taurique laughed, shaking his head. "That's specific?" he responded. Chaney smiled a little, watching him sip some more wine. He's more nervous than I've ever seen him, she thought. And I've never been this calm. Maybe it was all that thinking the other day. I wonder if I can keep this up—damn, now she was getting nervous, just a little—I'm never calm in tough situations, so the one time I am, I sabotage it. Great . . .

"What happened?" he repeated, then he looked up. "I messed everything up. That's what happened."

"It wasn't your fault."

"Yes, it was. And the thing is, I really thought that I could finally do for you what you did for me."

Chaney frowned. "What do you mean?" she asked.

"I mean, I thought I could help you to want to do better."

Chaney shook her head, chuckling derisively.

"Don't be offended," he implored her.

She narrowed her eyes. "Why shouldn't I be?" she demanded.

"Because—I don't know, because I'm not saying it for any other reason than that I care."

"I see." She sat glaring at him, but she looked up suddenly as the waiter arrived with their appetizers.

"Thank you," Taurique said, sampling the calamari.

"You were saying?" Chaney prodded him.

Taurique took another bite, studying her face. "Nothing," he finally said.

Chaney rolled her eyes, glancing away for a moment. "No games, Taurique, okay? I thought the whole point of this was to be honest about everything."

"So you're really going to listen to what I have to say."

"Yes."

"Okay." He swallowed, all traces of nerves now vanished. "You know that Perry and I have been friends for a while— almost a year, actually. Anyway, every once in a while he likes to talk about you and what you're doing—well, sometimes I bring it up, I admit it. Over the last six months or so he's been really worried about you—told me you were all depressed and uptight because your husband was gone so much. Said you'd always gotten a little lonely, but now it was really obvious. So I asked him a few more questions about your life and how it was different, and it occurred to me that your youngest was in school, and I remembered how you used to tell me you'd never be the kind of lousy mother yours was, and suddenly the whole thing made sense."

Chaney opened her mouth to protest, and he held up his hand.

"I'm not finished," he said. "You know what your problem is? You like being a little girl. You've lived your whole life that way. Your dad looked after you. Your brothers looked after you. Hell, Perry *still* looks after you. I looked after you, too; I'm just as guilty. You . . ."

"I am the mother of two . . ."

"You're a mother, big deal. That doesn't mean you're a grownup. It just means you're taking responsibility for *some-body's* life. Certainly not yours."

"Just because I'm staying at home . . ."

"You're running away from life, Chaney! Not because you're a housewife. Because you don't *want* to be a housewife."

Chaney's face was hot. "There's nothing wrong . . ."

"You're right, if that's what you want, but you don't. You're *bored,* Chaney. And what for? What the hell are you proving? That you're a better woman than your mother? Maybe you are, maybe you're not. This isn't proving it one way or the other, and besides, maybe she had good reasons for leaving. Maybe your daddy treated her like she treated you. Maybe he tried to suck the life out of her, maybe he tried to convince her she couldn't think for herself and she decided she couldn't take it. You don't *know,* Chaney. You don't know what went on, sweetheart. There are two sides to everything. It's none of your business now, and you can't find out what happened, so forget about it."

"Like you forgot about me?"

He stared. "What does that have to do with anything?"

She was trembling, but she was determined not to start crying again in a restaurant. She ate some calamari without looking at him and could think of no legitimate reason for making her last comment—there *was* a reason. Oh, yes . . . she was now completely rattled . . .

"It has to do with it because some things you can't just forget, that's all," she said, still unable to look at him, searching for her composure.

"I see." There was a long silence. "Maybe I'm wrong," Taurique said finally. Chaney looked up.

"About?"

"About forgetting. You're right. Sometimes you can't. I certainly didn't forget about you. All you can do is deal with things the best you can, so they don't screw up your life too much." He smiled a bit. "That's something I picked up at an Adult Children of Alcoholics meeting," he remarked.

Chaney turned away, sighing. The World According to Taurique. Life 101. And the point was?

"What do you want?" she asked him.

"What do you mean?"

"From me? What do you want me to do?"

"What do *you* want to do?"

She sighed again.

"Be honest with me, Chaney. You said we might never see each other again, so . . ."

"You said that."

"You're right."

She focused on him. He was watching her. "I don't know what I want to do," she said. "Not yet." She took a deep breath. He had knocked her off balance, but she was okay now. The calm was coming back. I'm okay, she thought, no tears, or anything. She felt suddenly stronger than she could remember feeling in a long time.

"I've been thinking about it, though," she said. "I could have told you that myself, but you started attacking me, so I ended up just trying to defend myself."

"I'm sorry." He picked up his water glass and stared at it, swirling the contents around.

"Anyway, I've been thinking a lot these last few days. About you and Lawrence, but especially about me. I'll be honest, I wasn't sure what I was going to say to you today. I just really wanted to see you again. I needed to. I couldn't stand the idea of another ten years of unfinished business. You know? But I'll admit that wasn't what made me call you and embarrass myself, begging you to have lunch with me."

"You didn't embarrass yourself."

"Yes, I did."

"No, you didn't. You just beat me to the punch. I was suffering, Chaney."

"Really?"

"I didn't sound like I was suffering?"

"I wasn't sure."

"Trust me, I was. Anyway, you were thinking?"

"Obsessively. About how all alone I was in the world, not a soul to tell my troubles to, stuff like that."

"You and your shadow." He smiled.

"Anyway, it comes down to this. I've spent my whole life, practically, being afraid."

"Of what?"

"Too many things to talk about. Like, I was afraid that if I started working part-time or taking a class or something I would see that I wanted a job or an education more than I wanted my children, and maybe I'd leave."

"You really think you're like that?"

"No."

"Neither do I."

"I wasn't sure, though. But you know what? If I started feeling that way, I'd have to decide what to do about it. And you know what else? You were right. I don't make enough decisions. People decide for me. But only because I let them."

"I thought I could help you see that, Shay. And I thought I could help you see that you could do more with your time if you wanted to, that it was okay." His voice was very soft. "But I wasn't strong enough to be a real friend."

Chaney gazed at him. He was always beautiful when he let

his guard completely down. "T," she said, "it wasn't your job.
I have to tell you, I didn't always know what you were up to.
Actually, I didn't always know what *I* was up to, but I believe
you when you say you meant well."

She felt very close to him now. She wanted to touch him,
to touch his face or his hand, but she didn't.

The meal arrived.

"Great-looking salad," said Taurique.

"Great-looking pasta," Chaney replied. They smiled at each
other. I want to reach across the table and touch him, Chaney
was thinking, but she picked up her fork instead, took a mouthful of food.

"Thank you," she said suddenly.

"You're welcome." Tenderly, that's how he's looking at me,
she thought. That's what I'm feeling. Tenderness . . .

"Do you mind if I ask you about Lawrence again?" Taurique
said, after a while.

"No."

Taurique ate some more. Building up courage, Chaney
thought, wondering what he was going to say.

"Does he make you happy? I mean . . . do you think, sometimes, that you couldn't be with somebody better?"

He waited. His voice had been nonchalant, but he'd asked
the question a bit too fast to be convincing.

"Yes." Chaney watched him. She wasn't sure if she was
getting back at him, still, for not being there for years, or if
she was telling the truth. After all, Lawrence was far from
perfect; she knew that before she married him. But then again,
who's perfect? she thought. Taurique? Neither one of them is
any paragon. And Lawrence has so many positive qualities,
and he tries to be good to me; if I just talked to him more
about what upsets me . . . She knew, then, that it was the truth.

"Does he also make you unhappy?"

"Yes. Isn't that normal?"

"It doesn't have to be. You could tell him things to help
him understand you better."

She gazed out the window. "I guess it's just that . . ."

"What?" His voice was very quiet.

"I guess . . ." Chaney cleared her throat. "I guess I wish he'd *ask* me things."

"He probably doesn't know what to ask you."

"You always do." She realized, in mid-sentence, what she was saying. Their eyes met.

"I grew up with you. I know you very well." Taurique's gaze was unwavering.

"Lawrence has known me longer than you have. I've been with him longer than I was with you."

"That's true."

"Taurique . . ."

"Yes?" Had he blinked? It didn't seem so.

"Do you sometimes wonder . . ."

"Yes."

She laughed. He was smiling now, but he hadn't looked away. "You don't know what I was going to say," she protested.

"Yes, I do."

"What was I going to say, then?"

"Do I wonder what it would have been like if we had gotten married."

"Almost."

"Only almost?" He leaned back in his chair, surprised. "What, then?"

"I was going to ask if . . ." She hesitated.

"Don't stop, we've gone too far in this conversation to stop being honest now."

"You're right." She took a deep breath. "T, do you think we were really meant to be together all along? Do you think we still are?"

The question was dangerous. Chaney's heart was fluttering wildly—I don't need to know this, she rebuked herself because Lawrence is my present and my future. If only you'd learn to think before you speak . . .

Taurique looked away, licking his lips, frowning slightly.

Then he faced her again, and she could see that his eyes were moist. He blinked.

"Chaney . . ." He formed his words very carefully. "I think . . ."

He was struggling. He exhaled slowly. "I think we were meant . . . I think we should have been together. I think we could have been very happy, and I think that you're the best person in the world for me and that maybe I've finally grown up enough to be the best person in the world for you. But . . ." He started toying with his pasta, and his voice sounded very distant when he spoke again. "It's—it's too late now."

He looked up. Chaney gazed at him, feeling suddenly hollow. "I know," she said.

He smiled, laughed a bit, and then he started blinking again, very rapidly. He began to eat now without looking at her, and she began to eat, too, watching him and feeling profoundly sad.

"It's not your fault, T," she finally said.

He looked at her. "Really?" He sounded completely dejected.

"Really. It's not your fault and it's not my fault. It just happened this way. And I'm not . . . I can't help it, I *want* to be the only woman for you. That's not fair, and besides, I know it's not true, and . . . if I'm not always satisfied with my life, I can't just blame Lawrence, and . . . you know what I wish?"

"What?"

"I wish things had turned out the way you planned. I wish you had just gone away and we had just both learned more about ourselves and come back together."

"But things turned out this way for a reason, right?"

"I always said that, didn't I?"

"And you love your husband and your kids."

"Yes."

"So no regrets, then, right? Even though I always thought that was a dumb reason to get married."

"That's what Perry said."

"The one time you didn't listen."

"Yes."

"But then again, you were too happy."

She looked down, grinning. "Well, actually, I was terrified, but yes, I was happy, too."

"And you will be again. You'll both be very happy. You'll meet him at the airport, and you'll *both* be very happy. And if you'd had my kids, who knows, they might have turned out like me, and you know I was trouble."

Chaney laughed. "You were. Except, you're so—wise these days."

"Wise?" He cracked up.

"I mean it. You know so much now. You could have been a psychologist."

"Right."

They finished eating.

"Delicious," Taurique said.

"Delicious."

"Dessert?"

"No, thanks. I think it was the dessert that got us in trouble last time."

They smiled at each other.

"I'll have a cappuccino, though" Chaney said.

"Okay." Taurique summoned the waiter and ordered two cappuccinos, which were soon brought to the table. They drank in relative silence, and then the check came. Once that was paid, Taurique glanced at his watch.

"I suppose I should go back," he said.

"Thanks for lunch."

"You're welcome."

"I don't feel like going home. Maybe I'll go to a movie or something."

"Wish I could come."

"Some other time."

He gazed out the window. "I don't think so," he said.

"Why not?" It truly seemed safe, now that everything was out in the open and dealt with.

His eyes rested on her again. "Did you ever see *Camelot?*" he asked.

"There are a lot of old movies I've never seen."

"You always watched them with me."

"And I liked them, but they reminded me of you, so I stopped."

"Oh." He looked down. "Well," he said after a while, "you're missing something. You shouldn't miss out on things on my account."

"I won't."

"Okay."

"So anyway, what about *Camelot?*"

"There's a song in it—Lancelot sings it—you see, Guinevere's married to Arthur, but she is in love with Lancelot, who is a trusted friend, and . . ."

"Sounds like opera."

"It's a musical."

"Does somebody die?"

"Watch it yourself sometime."

She rolled her eyes. "Okay, okay. Anyway, the song . . ."

"It's called, 'Before I Gaze at You Again.' And he says, basically, that he needs to get over her, so he's got to stay away for a while."

"I see." Chaney looked down. "Not forever, though."

"I don't want that."

"I'm glad."

"So—I won't see you for a while, or talk to you."

"Okay." She sighed, looking at him again. "I'll miss you," she said, in as steady a voice as she could manage.

"You know I'll miss you." He smiled suddenly, and rose. She stood up as well. "You remember *Casablanca?* I know you must remember *Casablanca.*"

She smiled. "So I'm supposed to go get on my plane now."

"Something like that. Now, if I could just find someone to start a beautiful, friendship with."

Chaney glanced around. "No one here up to your standards," she decided.

"Actually, if you recall, the friendship was with a man."

"Obviously, the movie wasn't the Taurique Williams story."

He seemed very pleased with himself, and he was smiling as he began to walk out of the restaurant.

When they got to the street, the smile was gone. They stood, rather awkwardly, without looking at each other.

"I guess I should go," Taurique said eventually.

"You have to go now?"

"I should."

"Okay."

Neither of them moved.

"So this is goodbye," Taurique said.

"Goodbye, T. Thanks again for everything."

Neither of them moved.

"I hate goodbyes," said Taurique.

"I'm pretty good at them by now, but I'm not enjoying this a whole lot."

He laughed a bit. "So we should just say goodbye, since neither of us is having fun anymore."

"It's what's best, right?"

"We both agreed on that, didn't we?"

"Yes. And no. Look, I can't take much more of this." She was pleading, and she felt like she was going to start crying soon.

"I'm sorry," Taurique whispered.

"It's not your fault."

"Okay." He hesitated, then took her hands and squeezed them. "Goodbye, Chaney," he said, gazing into her eyes. Then, he moved toward her, kissed her gently on the cheek, kissed the inside of each of her wrists, slowly lowered her hands, and released them. He took a cautious step backward, still looking at her, then he turned quickly and soon disappeared from view.

Chaney caught her breath sharply, resisting the urge to run

after him as she watched him leaving. This time, she under-
stood why. It didn't make it easier, though. She began to walk,
slowly, then faster and faster, toward her car. She fumbled with
the key and had just slammed the door when the tears started.
She didn't try to stop them this time. She didn't care who was
looking at her. She just sat with her head against the steering
wheel, sobbing hysterically.

An hour later, her eyes were nearly swollen shut, but she
knew that it was really over. And that she would survive.

Epilogue

November 9

The phone was ringing—Chaney gradually became aware that the sound was not part of her dream. She rolled over, fumbling for the receiver.

"Hello."

"Hi."

"Lawrence," she said affectionately. "Baby, how are you?"

"I'm okay." He sounded strange.

"What's the matter?"

"Nothing."

"Don't do this, Lawrence, don't spare me, okay? It's too important that you talk to me. Please?"

He sighed. "You were so distant yesterday," he said, "I didn't know what to expect."

"I'm sorry. I had a lot on my mind."

"Oh."

"I'll tell you about it as soon as I see you, okay? It's nothing terrible, I just realized I can't keep doing things like I have been."

"Meaning what?"

"I promise I'll explain it to you, Lawrence. By the way, do you still want me to come to Europe?"

"Of course I do."

"Can I meet you in Paris?"

There was a silence. "Are you serious?" he asked hopefully.
"Yes."

He laughed. "What about Nicole and Ronnie?"

"I'll speak to Perry tonight." His happiness made her feel warm inside—I should have done this a long, long time ago, she thought.

"I knew you'd realize one day that they'll be okay without you for a little while," Lawrence was saying excitedly.

"You were right." For a second she almost wished she could explain how she had found this out.

"So you're really serious, then?" He still sounded a bit unsure.

"Yes."

"So you love me, then?"

She took a deep breath. I've been awful to him, she thought, or he wouldn't even have to ask. "I always did," she said tenderly.

"What happened?"

She considered. How much to say, how much to leave out? Leave out most of it, she decided.

"To tell the truth," she began—well, the half-truth, anyway—"being around Taurique again helped me see that I'm not living life as fully as I could be, and that I can love you and love the children and still take time out for me. He turned out to be a really good friend."

There was another silence. "I was a real jerk about all that, wasn't I?" Lawrence finally said.

"No. But I'm glad I didn't listen to you." She yawned. What did I just say, she suddenly thought. Lawrence was laughing, though.

"Boy, are you grouchy," he said.

"No, I'm not."

"I woke you up, didn't I?"

"That's not unusual, Lawrence."

"What were you dreaming about?"

"Funny you should ask that." She sat up, hugging her knees

to her chest. "Remember that dream I used to have, that nightmare about the ship?"

"Yes."

"It was different this time. This time, I ran into somebody in the hall who was just as lost as I was, so we both started wandering around and we found the crew. They were just on another deck."

"For real?"

"Would I lie?"

"I hope not, otherwise I'll look pretty stupid camping out at Charles DeGaulle."

She smiled. "Don't worry, I'll be there. I miss you."

"I miss you, too. And I love you." His voice was full of longing.

"I love you, too," she replied softly.

"Kiss the kids for me, okay?"

"Okay."

"And let me know when you're coming—you really meant that, Chaney?"

"Yes."

"I can't wait. So everything's okay?"

"It's okay. But we'll talk when I get there, all right?"

"Whatever you want. Goodbye, Chaney."

"Goodbye, Lawrence. I love you."

"I love you, too."

She hung up, then stretched. It's over, she thought. Even the dream is history—Taurique had still managed to sneak into her subconscious, but she had expected that. At least my days will belong to my family, she thought. She glanced at the clock, considered getting out of bed, then chose not to, not for another five minutes or so.

To my family, she thought, and to me.